About the Author

The author is Terry Easton. He has a loving blended family with four girls, aged two, seven, eight, and nine, and an amazing fiancée. He studied catering at college before changing his career and became a restaurant manager at a well-known steak house. When he was fifteen, he was involved in a hit and run and whilst he was recovering, he started to make plans for this book. However, when he was fully recovered, he no longer had the time to pursue it. He always dreamt of writing his own book so, in 2020, when the nation went into lockdown, he knew it was the perfect time to fully focus on completing it and here it is. He hopes that all will enjoy reading it as much as he enjoyed writing it. He would like to dedicate this book to his father, Paul Easton, whom he sadly lost in 2020. RIP Dad x

The Snitch in Bedmoor

Terry Easton

The Snitch in Bedmoor

Olympia Publishers
London

www.olympiapublishers.com

OLYMPIA PAPERBACK EDITION

A CIP catalogue record for this title is
available from the British Library.

ISBN: 978-1-80074-464-6

This is a work of fiction.
Names, characters, places and incidents originate from the writer's
imagination. Any resemblance to actual persons, living or dead, is
purely coincidental.

First Published in 2022

Olympia Publishers
Tallis House
2 Tallis Street
London
EC4Y 0AB

Printed in Great Britain

Acknowledgements

For my daughters, Rosie and Millie. Thank you to my fiancée, Connie, and her mum, Lisa, for encouraging me in completing my book.

Chapter 1

25th May 2018, HMP Barlinnie. Scotland

The office of the probation officer smelt of rotten wood, dirty windows with broken chips letting in a small draft of wind. On the desk were loads of files of prisoners and their names. There were two files in front of an empty chair; sitting on the chairs were two guys in grey jumpsuits. The oldest one looked in his late sixties, long grey hair, teeth missing or dark black. The second guy sitting next to him looking in his late forties, head was clean shaven, with dark yellow teeth. Standing behind them were two prison officers, both guards in their late thirties watching them closely. Both of them were waiting on the probation officer when the door opened on a middle-aged man wearing a smart blue suit and shiny black shoes. 'I am Ken Ratner, your probation officer. Donald McDonald, you have served twenty years with us for the murder of John Kilen, also attempted rape of Lucy Swell. Gary McDonald, you been with us for twenty years for accessory of murder on John Kilen, and rape of Lucy Swell. The judge sentenced you for twenty years without parole. It is time for both to be released. Any questions?' he asks, looking at them both.

'Well, thank you so much for letting us stay in this lovely place, the service has been perfect. I won't be back and you can trust me.' Donald smiled with a grin on his face.

The probation officer looked through his notes when he came across something. 'In your notes, you must not have contact with Sarah, or someone connected with Sarah. There is an injunction out on this, breaking this injunction, the police will be called and you will be brought straight back to prison.'

Gary stood up slowly leaning over to the probation officer. 'I will make sure I don't come back to this scummy place. The Scottish police system set us up, we may have a bad name in Glasgow but that was bang out of order. I don't trust anyone, you lot will do anything to put us back here. Mark my words, you will not see me again. Take me back to my cell.' Ken nodded towards the guards.

The door closed and Ken was left alone in his office, picking up the phone. 'Hi, it's Ken Ratner. Can we put Donald McDonald and Gary McDonald on daily sign-in at the probation office, for six months? Also, first week, can we have them on watch,' he said, closing both of their files.

Looking at his phone, while walking around his office, his phone rings. 'Hi Sarah. How you doing?'

'I am feeling the best I can, my mind is going mad about them being released. Do we have a date when they will be out of prison? I need to protect my family from them, trust is one word they hate and I don't trust them.'

Ken sat back down in his chair knowing how worried she was, 'They have been told about the injunction out on them. They know they can't get in contact with you or they will be breaking the rules and back inside immediately. We have put measures out so they can't leave Scotland, we will do anything to protect your family.'

'They are so sneaky on getting away with stuff, do they know my surname which I asked you to leave out?' Sarah sounded shaky on the phone.

'Yes, it says your maiden name before you got married. We got protection which they will not find out, only we know that kind of information. Once we have more information, I will ring you and let you know. Please enjoy your holiday and I will ring you in two weeks. Bye, Sarah.'

'Okay, thank you so much. Bye.'

As Ken got off the phone, walking over to his window, he watched the prisoners in the courtyard. Ken was thinking to himself how long before they'd be back. Most prisoners always came back somehow, it's just waiting for them to mess up.

31st May 2018

It was a typical day in Scotland, that rain clouds open up and not stopping. The HMP looked grey, old and rusty old bars on all windows. It was protected by big wooden doors with two guards outside. Ken arrived on time for work as normal, never been late in his career. 'Morning, Ken,' said the guard opening the door for him.

Ken went straight to his office, knowing he was about to release two prisoners into the public with a history of being ex-gangsters. The police and CID on the case, investigated if anyone was still alive, no one. Family members of them, none, his last child died ten years ago. Only one, Gary's father, but in his late nineties?

The place they lived was Bedmoor Estate where they committed their crimes, which was still there but with new members of gangs taken over. Their cell mates were searched, including their history outside the HMP. He was making himself a black coffee when the door knocked twice. 'Come in,' he said as Ken sat down waiting for the pair to enter with the prison guards.

The McDonalds sat themselves down while Ken was getting their release papers ready. The pair were out of the prison grey jumpsuit, and into a pair of knackered blue jeans, pop band of the eighties T-shirts and black bomber jackets. The pair were smiling as the day was coming, back into the world. 'Lads, we have some paperwork to be signed before you're released. First, every day for six months you will be required to sign the probation office register at twelve o'clock. Second, you will be housed in a hostel until you can find somewhere. Third, you are not to contact Sarah or anyone to do with her. If you break any of these probation rules, you will end up back in prison. Do we agree?'

The McDonalds looked at each other smiling 'Yes, Ken. We will follow the rules and after six months of signing the probation forms, what happens?'

'We will discuss that in six months' time; can you both sign the paperwork which you both agree on?'

Both of the McDonalds talked underneath their breath, a few seconds later, they both signed. The prison officer walked them through the cold, dark corridors of the prison to the front desk. The front desk officer gave them a bag of personal items, details of hostels and details of where the probation office was. As the guys stood in front of the big wooden doors, they waited a few minutes before they could see freedom, twenty years behind bars and now free. The McDonalds walked out of prison and towards the open road, lighting up a cigarette and shouting 'Freedom!'

'Wonder if the Old Recklands is still standing, I fancy a nice pint. Come on, Donald, we've been dreaming of this for twenty years. That silly bitch Sarah made our life hell, we need a drink.'

'No, Gary, we have plans and need to meet Frank. Time is not on our hands, she knows we are out and she has no idea what she did to my family. Your dad wanted this, our name is big and people are scared of us.' Donald was furious every time Gary said Sarah's name.

The guys kept walking down, when they reached their destination, the house was boarded up with broken roof tiles, when the door opened. 'This is the place, Gary, we go in then follow me. We are being followed by the filth, the blue Vauxhall I saw outside HMP. We need to be careful,' he said as the guys went inside the house.

Donald and Gary went inside, the walls were filthy with spray paint on. Massive holes in doors or broken off, floor boards missing when they went through the kitchen, back garden more like a jungle. 'Where are we going, Donald, I thought we were meeting in the house?'

'Don't be silly, we need to lose them. We are going through the back streets to where we'll be sleeping tonight, or do you want to sleep in a hostel, also avoid the filth?' he said as they kept walking for another ten minutes.

The guys arrived at the destination, with each street looking worse than the last one. Every other house they went by was boarded up, smashed windows or burnt-out cars. Standing at the door, the door handle was broken and the glass squares were smashed in. Knocking on the wood, a middle age man answered the door, 'Come this way guys,' letting them in the house.

Leading them up the stairs with empty bottles of whiskey, cigarette ends everywhere. Opening the door on the first floor to where two people were sitting on the sofa. A lady in her late forties smoking a cigarette, wearing a short red dress and long black jacket. Next to her was a young man in his twenties, bald with a leather jacket. 'Thank you, here is the money I promised you. Remember we were not here; do we have an agreement?'

'Yes, Mrs K, I promise you,' he said, shaking when grabbing the money.

Leaving the room with the three of them alone, Gary and Donald sat on the bed looking at her. 'Where is he, you promised me he would be here when I get out,' he said, looking at Mrs K.

'I am sorry if the boy is not here yet, we had to give him another passport. His last one is on the wanted list so got a bit delayed. Have you spoken to your dad yet?'

'No, after this I will contact him. Do you know where he is? How is his health doing?'

Mrs K stood up looking out the window. 'Your dad is fine. He stopped drinking about ten years ago, I will give you the details later. From our last conversation we had, we're still going ahead with the kidnap,' she said, putting out her cigarette on the floor.

'Yes, I am still in with the plan. How far are we along with the plan Mrs K?'

Passing them a file, the guys opened it with pictures of Sarah and her kids. 'This is looking good, so Sarah had four kids in total. So many to choose from, do we know which one we are taking?'

'Yes, we do know which one you're taking, but we got a

few problems on places. It will be sorted in time,' she said, lighting up another cigarette.

'We do not have time, Sarah needs to pay and I am not waiting,' Gary said, getting up kicking the empty bottle around the room.

'Sit down, Gary, now, unfortunately you're on probation for six months. So, you have no choice, John wants this done with no problems and I promised him. In the meantime, be a good boy, stay out of trouble and look nice. Don't contact the boy till I tell you, I got the two boys doing the work in London. They will contact me at all times, I know you want to see him but this will pay off. We will be rich at the end, we can leave the country and start a new life,' she said, throwing her cigarette.

'What rules do you want us to do Mrs K?'

'Good question, Donald. Here are your phones to use, only use these numbers until I can give you his number, you can visit your dad in the care home. The best one, you can have a drink in any pub.'

'What about visiting Bedmoor Estate?'

'Yes, you can visit your old stomping ground. One last rule, do not use our names on messages, or meetings, as we don't know if the police are listening. At the end of all this, one of her children will die. Revenge is coming to us.'

Chapter 2

26th February 2019, London.

Silence, peace and calmness in Nick's room, on the top floor of the house. The top floor was his room, own bathroom and spare room opposite. Silence didn't last till some little boy wearing his Power Rangers pyjamas jumped on Nick, in his bed. Nick was the oldest child in the household, nineteen, while Micky the little boy was six. Nick tried to fake sleep but with siblings that never works. 'What do you want, little boy?' Nick asked as he turned over to see his face staring at his.

'Time to get ready, we are going to football. My first game, come on Queens Park Rangers, Queens Park Rangers,' he said as Nick pushed Micky out of the bed.

'It's eight in the morning, nobody wakes up at this time on Saturday. I have told you to annoy your sisters, they love been woken up at this time. I am looking forward to taking you to your first game, it's a special moment for you. We have to wait for Katie, as her dad has the tickets for us.'

That moment Nick kicked Mickey out of the room, Nick fell back to sleep dreaming of Queens Park Rangers winning the match. One of his favourite hobbies was football, supporting them since he was little. Knowing their history of the first match until the last one, every manager, records of the players. The only problem was Queens Park Rangers not winning cups; they were a middle team club in the championship club, which meant falling too early or nothing at all. The best result was second in the first division back in 1975.

Nick's door opened. 'The next time you open that bloody door, Mickey, I will make sure you never attend football again. Do you understand?'

'Well, Nickolas, I take back the tickets and say to my uncle he can sell them on,' Katie said, standing over him.

Katie was his girlfriend since starting university eighteen months ago, Nick and Katie were in the same class, studying law. Their future was to be joint lawyers in a firm, husband and wife team. Both families got on really well, Katie's dad liked him and he seemed a genuinely good lad. 'Well, if you had an annoying little brother, you would understand. Unfortunately, you're lucky, Emily is always away doing her dancing competitions. Meaning quiet nights, no one bothering you. Come and join me in bed.' Nick winked at Katie and patted the bed.

Katie walked over to him, took her coat off and joined Nick. 'I am only guessing what's on your mind. There is more to life then sex, while we change the subject of sex. My uncle has given us VIP seats at the game, we will get a meal, and watch the game at executive boxes,' she said as both were cuddling under the covers.

'Well, I must say, you are the best girlfriend in the world only problem is, you're a Leeds fan. Might need to convert you into a Queens Park Rangers fan. We got time if you want.' Nick started kissing Katie on the neck and touching her body.

'I don't think so, Nick, I am not getting sex hair before

17

breakfast with your family.'

Katie jumped out of the bed, leaving the room before showing him her ass cheek, Nick followed her to join the rest of the family for breakfast.

Standing in the street smoking a cigarette, Nick was standing round the back from his house when his father appeared from out of nowhere. 'This is the first place I know you are when your mother is out of the house, I have ordered you a taxi. It will be here in ten minutes, give me a quick puff.' His father had a few puffs before spraying his mouth with mint.

'I know Mother hates it, why is Mother so stressed out lately? I know she is always stressed but last few months her mood swings have been more.' Nick put out the cigarette with his foot.

'It's nothing to worry about, Nick, me and your mother are sorting it. What do you think the score will be today? I am thinking two nil to Leeds, Queens Park Rangers are failing this season. Also, Leeds are fighting for promotion.'

'Nah, Father, Queens Park Rangers will fight, they may have lost their last two games but trust me. One day, Father, Queens Park Rangers will be playing your team Chelsea. The mighty blues will be scared of us,' Nick said as he showed his father his club badge while laughing.

Both of them went inside, when the two guys entered the living room, Nick's girlfriend was sitting in between Jade and Ellie. Jade and Ellie were Nick's twin sisters, both of them were fifteen years old. The twins looked the same but these two were different in personality, Jade was more girly into looking good and attracting boys. Ellie was more natural, was not into getting boyfriends. For Ellie, studies came first, day

18

and night. Ellie wanted to be crime investigation officer; Mother didn't agree.

'I can only guess what you are talking about, Jade.' Nick was looking at her make-up set.

'This is my future job, Nick, some of us want to look good even knowing it's a football match. Men would never understand how long it takes us women to look this good.' Jade placed a bit of powder onto Katie's cheeks.

'Katie, the taxi will be here soon. Katie looks good all the time with make-up and no make-up. You should take hints from Ellie, Ellie doesn't wear make-up. I am not saying make-up artist is not a good job but is it a good paid job? I am saying to live in Hammersmith, it's not cheap. I think you should think of a back-up job in case it doesn't work.'

Before Jade could speak back, there was a honk outside. 'Let's go, Katie.' Both of them left the house holding hands and kissing before getting in the taxi with Mickey.

The crowds of Loftus Road were mental, every Queens Park Rangers fan singing. All the fans holding their scarves, marching down shouting one nil to Queens Park Rangers. A few roads away, Nick was holding onto Katie's hand as the noise got less with Mickey walking in front of them. 'Well, what can I say. The mighty London club has beaten Leeds, a bet is a bet.' Nick placed his scarf over Katie.

'I love football, I love football. Best club in London.' Mickey was talking to himself saying football is the best.

'Two things, Nick and Mickey, Queens Park Rangers is not the mighty London club, maybe in the championship. Second if you want your bet, take that scarf off me. It was not a goal, it was handball then went into the goal. In the future,

VAR will be coming our way then that would have been a draw.' Nick removed his scarf off Katie.

'Well, it's still a goal, I love you,' Nick said as he grabbed Katie to kiss her.

Both of them passionately kissing, feeling the love between each other. 'You have no idea how much I love you. You turned my head so much, you are my best mate, soul mate and future husband,' Katie said as she kissed Nick.

'Yuck, why do you two have to kiss? I am never going to kiss girls.'

Katie kissed Mickey on the cheek before moving to stand next to his brother, as Nick laughed messing up his hair.

'Before I met you, my first love was Queens Park Rangers, now you're number one, and football, second. I can't wait for the future. People say we are young but I believe in us, my parents fell in love young and are still together,' Nick said as he pulled over a black cab.

'Folkestone Street, Hammersmith.' They left the area to go home.

The same evening, Nick was sitting in his bed, his parents had arranged a dinner date for the family. It was his parents' twenty years of marriage, still on the bed when his door opened. Jade walked in then shut the door. 'Our parents are talking privately again. There is something going on, Nick, the last few months. Mother has been getting more and more stressed,' Jade said as she looked at Nick.

Nick placed his phone to the side and sat up. 'I have seen it but not our problem. Mother and Father have busy lives, they have been married for twenty years. Mother is always scared when Father has new cases at work, remember when Father had that case but it got too close to home when he won the case. The other party wanted Father dead, it's probably another strong case.'

Nick cuddled Jade making her feel safe. 'I know, Nick. I hate it when they are like that, it seemed like they were talking about an old case when Dad was calming her down. Life is a lot easier with an easy job, you sure you want to be a lawyer like Father?'

'I want to be a lawyer, I have the passion to get innocent people off who have been framed or didn't commit the crime. Sometimes you may need to defend the wrong ones but only to get noticed, I might make you my assistant.' Nick raised his eyebrows at her.

'I don't think so, I'd be your personal slave. I can do your hair and make-up,' Jade said as she and Nick went downstairs to join the rest of the family laughing.

As Nick was walking past his parents' room, there was no shouting. When he heard crying, he wondered why his mother was crying. His mother was a strong person who never let anyone get to her, her personality made her strong so, no one walked over her. Only a few things really got to her, any one hurting her family and that they were financially safe. Their mother made sure all their university bills were paid by them, so when they got a full-time job, they could start building their career without thinking of their debt. She cared for them twenty-four-seven. When Nick was growing up, his mother said I want you all to have a great childhood, and have fun with friends. As Nick and Jade entered the living room, his brother Mickey, sister Ellie and girlfriend Katie were watching television. Nick sat next to Katie on the sofa kissing her. 'What are you after? You only kiss me like that when you want

21

something,' Katie asked as she kissed him back.

'I am giving my girlfriend a kiss because I love you, fancy a drink before we go? We got thirty minutes also we got to wait for Nan.'

'Make mine a lager, son.' Father walked in the living room.

'Jade, your mother wants to see you. Nick, beer please.' Jade went upstairs and the two guys went into the kitchen.

Sitting at the kitchen table, Nick opened two beers and a glass of white wine for Katie. 'So, Nick, how was the football? Mickey seems happy to have seen his first match, I was a bit scared in case anything kicked off,' he said, swooping a gulp from his beer.

'Nah, it was nothing to worry about, Father, I would never put Mickey at risk. I would do anything to protect him, I would rather get hurt so he was safe. Being the oldest child, my job is to look after them. Big brother is always there to look after them. Back to match, it was the best game I have seen for a while. At one moment I was thinking it was going to be a draw, they say a point is a point but winning is better.'

'Remember, what Grandad said. Being a middle team is boring, a win is like winning the championship. I like my team winning trophies. Six years since the last time in the top flight for Queens Park Rangers, even worse for Leeds. I think it's sixteen years and that's worse when…' Katie walked into the kitchen staring at James and Nick.

'I can only guess what you two guys are talking about, let me guess. Leeds United and last time we were in the top league. We like to keep it simple, you know, championship, few good years but one day we will return.' Katie drank some of her wine then continued, 'My dad believes in Leeds. We have a lot of passion. What restaurant are we going to tonight, James?'

'We are going to the "Bistro la steak" they serve the best steak; my mum loves it there. I remember my dad going there when he was young with his dad. The restaurant has been handed down since the 1900s. Also, no one can complain about steak and sauce.' They heard footsteps coming down the stairs.

Nick's mother was standing in the kitchen looking at them. 'I take it no one wanted to give me a glass of wine. I got a text from your mum, James, she's going to meet us there. Pour me glass of wine, Nick, please.' Nick went to the fridge to pour his mother a glass.

Sarah sat down staring at James. 'Tomorrow, I have got a new iPad coming from work. Can you set it up for me, James, there is some new settings which they want me to work out and advise with?' Nick handed his mother the wine.

'Can I have a look, Mother, and see what the iPad is like? I can give you tips. Being so young, I know how you can sell it to the young ones and business types?'

Sipping on her wine, she said, 'That is fine, Nick. As last time, just keep it between us and this time I can let you keep it. This is mine, I am happy with the last one. I always see them as the same.'

As soon as Sarah finished off her sentence, there was a beep outside. The West family went into the two cabs and headed off to the restaurant.

Arriving just before midnight, two cabs pulled outside the West family home. The family went inside and James's mum went in a different taxi home, Nick pulled Katie before going in. 'I know I say it a lot but I love you so much, Katie, you have made my life so happy and perfect'.

'Same here, Nick, every moment we do I love it. When people say they don't believe in love at first sight, I do. I don't know what I'd do without you. I was thinking about your bet.' Katie touched Nick's body, smiling at him.

Nick moved closer to Katie, holding her body. 'Well, I was thinking of the new move if you want to try, also you got your new outfit...'

'Nick and Katie, will you both come in. I don't want you two doing that stuff in public, people will talk.' His mother slammed the front door.

Both of them laughed, walking in the house. His mother hated any one knowing their business, Nick always thought she was paranoid. One time on his way home from the pub, Nick slept outside his front door due to losing his keys. His mother found him covered in sick with a note saying sorry. It was weeks before she spoke to Nick and their neighbours speaking about what he did. Arriving at Nick's door, when Katie pulled Nick to his bed touching his face, kissing him slowly. Nick was touching her body slowly, taking off her top when Katie stopped him. 'I will have a quick shower, get ready for you while you relax and wait for me.' Katie went over to her bag, slowly bending over.

'You know how to turn me on, I want to grab that ass and spank it.'

'I know you inside out, Nick, my super-hot body will turn you on even when we are old. I think I left my other bag in your car, can you bring it in for me please?' she asked, giving him a sexy look.

Nick agreed knowing what he will get in return, he picked

his car keys walking towards the door. Jumping down a few steps, Nick could hear his sisters talking in their room, Mickey snoring in his room and quietness in his parents' room. It was nippy outside as Nick picked up her bag, also took one cigarette out of his pack and went around to his garden wall facing the back street. He was lighting up his cigarette when he heard voices from his back garden, it was his mother and father. Nick thought they were in bed, he crept slowly to overhear. 'I can't believe it, James. Why would they do this, they know the rules of their probation.'

'Sarah, they will be caught. They have broken no rules, it was only for six months while they were released from prison. The only reason the police know they are missing is due to a murder on their street, it might not be them.'

'Of course, it was them, they have form. You don't know how it feels, I know you have tried your best but we can't stop them,' his mother said in an angry voice.

'There is a court injunction on them, you know they can't come anywhere near you. First thing I will do when I am back in the office is get an update on what's going on. Fancy a drink before bed?'

'I am fine, James, with my coffee, I thought it was over years ago. I never thought I had to see them again. I have always had this feeling about them, I could never trust them and need to protect my family.'

'Remember what I told you. We have no idea what they want, as far we know they might want to get on with their life. They want nothing to do with you, they might have forgotten about all this or don't care. You think too much about this, we need to move on and enjoy our life. We have four wonderful kids who need us.'

'I know, James, I am lucky to have you. It's been a while and nothing has happened so I will try and look forwards. From now on I will keep my past in my past and think about the future, I mean it was twenty years ago.'

'Do you remember what the meeting said, say it out loud or here quiet and it will help.'

'I know, James, but I can't bring myself to say their names or even the family name, I just can't, James.'

Walking back to house before his parents saw him overhearing, thinking what the hell were they talking about. Did his mother get into trouble before he was born? Or was someone after his mother and maybe she caused it? Was his mother involved in a murder when she was younger? Nick's mind was racing with so many questions but he knew he would find out. The only way he would find out was when he went to work with his father in a few weeks. Nick opened his door and saw Katie on his bed. 'I hope you're ready for me,' she said as Nick closed the door smiling.

Chapter 3

1st March 2019

Kings Cross station was full of passengers waiting to board their train, Nick was standing next to platform ten when Katie jumped from behind him. 'I nearly had a heart attack; my mother would have missed me you know.' Nick kissed Katie and picked her up.

Katie stopped kissing Nick. 'Such as drama queen you are. I do ask myself why I am dating you, such a mummy's boy.' Katie gave Nick a sassy look.

'I am the least of a mummy's boy, I got my independence without help from my mother and father. How long till Matt, Damon, Maria and Natalie get here?'

Katie and Nick walked over to the empty table. 'They are getting here soon. Matt was waiting for Maria and the other two coming from the other side of London. Wonder if Matt will get with Maria, it's about time they got together,' sighed Katie.

'It makes no difference; Matt is a shy person and will never tell her how he feels about her. He won't tell her unless he has a few drinks.' Katie looked at Nick in a way she knew something about them.

'Well Nick, I know more than you do about this. Matt slept with Maria a few weeks ago but he won't commit to her or make her his girlfriend. Maybe you can talk to him about it? Do not say I told you as I am not supposed to tell anyone about it, Nick.'

'So, you're asking me to be his right hand man but he doesn't know I am his right hand man? Well, it can't hurt, but it's more your friend than mine. Have you seen the two guys looking at you? Standing on the first level near the Italian restaurant, the last few minutes staring at you.'

The guys kept staring at them, the one on the left was wearing a navy-blue jacket and white shirt underneath. He was kind of a player by his look, his hair was short with no style on him. The other guy was bald, with a slight to medium build. He was wearing a plain shirt and leather jacket, both holding their coffees, still staring at them. 'Well Nick, I am a stunning lady with great hips and also ass. You are not getting jealous, are you, Nick?' Katie stared back at the guys.

'As they say, people can look but can't touch you, you are all mine. Those guys probably can't get any action and staring is what they are good at. We have to leave soon and the others are not here yet, message them please, Katie.' Katie got out her phone.

Nick stared at the guys. The guys had moved to a table and seemed to be looking at photos or paperwork. He was not a jealous type. The guy wearing the navy jacket looked at Nick. It was weird as the guy kept looking at him, maybe he was gay and fancied him and not Katie. After a few seconds, Nick looked around avoiding the guys when he saw Matt and the gang coming towards him and waving.

'You lot are bad time keepers, what took you all so long?'

'Well Nick, you can never rush a girl.' Maria smiled at Nick.

'Well we better be getting to the train, or we will miss it.'
Nick and Katie stood up.

The gang walked to platform ten, with Katie and Nick holding hands, Natalie and Damon cuddling while Matt and Maria walked in silence.

The train was travelling at a fast speed though the countryside of England, passing fields with grazing animals eating the fresh grass, passing motorways and rusty old buildings. The train was quiet going to Leeds, the gang was sitting in first class drinking champagne and nibbles. Damon was a tall guy with dark brown hair, blue eyes and made himself perfect. Damon was wearing tight denim jeans and a pale pink t-shirt, always wearing the fashion of the moment. His girlfriend was Natalie, they had been together for three years and called themselves childhood sweethearts. Natalie was a blonde girl, with blue eyes and a slim figure. She was a girly girl, always in short skirts and showing a little boob, they were always with each other and couldn't be without each other. Matt and Maria, or what Nick called the two M's. They both grew up together, same street, parents were best friends from a young age and had always known each other. They had fancied each other since around fifteen and neither had been with anyone, always them hanging out. There were a few people in first class, two elder men with their laptops out and paperwork. They seemed to be doing their business plans, next to them was a young couple cuddling each other while on their phones. Opposite the gang was a lone woman with a note pad, writing down notes with a hot cup of tea and a sandwich. The gang were laughing away when they got interrupted by the ticket man, after they showed their tickets, they continue talking. 'So last time we were drinking together, we had to carry home Damon. Any chance we will have to do it again?'

'You remember, Nick, that I didn't eat before as I was busy working and you were rushing me to get out, partly your fault. I am not drinking much nowadays; I am trying to keep fit and healthy. I said to Katie, you should join me, but Katie said you would not be able to keep up with me.'

'I never said Nick couldn't keep up with you, my words were, Nick could not keep up with your healthy eating and ways of living. Imagine Nick getting up at six in the morning to do one and a half hours of jogging, not in a million years, I am sorry, baby.' Katie gave Nick a kiss on the lips.

'One day I might prove you wrong, honey, I feel I am fit already and if I start getting a belly, I'll ask for help from you, Damon. Do we want another bottle of champagne?'

The group all agreed as Nick and Damon went to the train bar to order another bottle. Waiting at the small bar on the train the guys were in the queue. 'Have you seen Maria and Matt talking to each other since we got on the train? Why can't they just get together, we need to set up a plan for them.'

'Well, talking about them two, Katie wants me to help them out but I don't really know Matt. What about you?'

'Not really, I probably met Matt a few times as he spends most of the time with Maria. Maybe later, we can get him alone while the girls are getting ready and we can question him and maybe…'

The young lady behind the bar said, 'Next.'

'Can I have a bottle of champagne please, no glasses please'. The young lady prepared the bottle.

'What were you saying, Damon?'

'I was saying, when the ladies are getting ready, we should

give him a few tips on how to woo a lady.'

'Well, between you and me, we should be able to get them two together before we head home on Sunday. How many wingmen does one man need?' The guys paid for the champagne and they both walked back from the train bar.

Katie and Nick were cuddling up while staring out of the train window as the train was slowing down from an hour ago. 'So, are your parents looking forward to seeing me again, it was nice last time. Did your parents build their cover for the swimming pool?'

'Yeah, they got it built over Christmas. My mum was furious as they needed to empty the pool while building it but she is happy now. We can have a little swim before going out.'

'Hang on, I am confused. How can your mum be furious about draining the swimming pool when they are building a roof when it's cold in the north? It's not like she would have used it anyway.'

Katie struggled her shoulders 'That is my mum for you. She didn't talk to my dad for days but he liked it like that. My parents have a weird relationship, he will never argue back at her just take the blame and let her calm down no matter how long it takes.'

The train was slowing down more till it stopped at the station at Leeds, the gang got off the train walking toward the packed station. The station was not the same as London, it was darker and gloomier. The building was old, with broken windows and very cold. The breeze or wind blew through the station till they got outside, where they got into a large taxi to Katie's parents' house in Horsforth.

Katie's parents' house was beautiful, the black gates opened for them. Water feature in the middle with water spraying the grass around the house. The door was gloss white shiny, when opened by a maid. It was styled like an American house, white staircase in the middle of the room and plenty of doors leading to rooms. Katie showed them around while Nick went into the kitchen, the kitchen was open plan with a view to the swimming pool and the breakfast room. The kitchen was the size of most people's council houses, an island in the middle of a square shape kitchen. Nick's favourite part of the house was the garden. The garden overlooked the forest where Katie's dad walked the dog. Colin, Katie's dad, owns half an acre of the forest where he likes to do a bit of wildlife watching. Colin had a few bird houses, badger holes, and a few different kinds of species of bird in the forest. Nick left the kitchen after having a glass of water and met Katie in the guest room area of the house, or mansion, as Nick sometimes thinks of the house.

'I can't believe you live here, Katie, this house is amazing. Your dad must be doing something right in his night club.'

Katie sat in her living room which was next to her bedroom. 'My dad started off with one club but last three years he owns five of them in the Leeds area. It's the one thing he is good at, business. It was mostly me and me mum when growing up, but if not for my dad we would not be living like this. I got the plan ready for today, I got the hairdresser coming here at four today. My mum is cooking us a meal, you will like her curry. While you guys do what you want.'

'What do you want us guys to do for at least three hours?'

'Matt, my dad has a snooker room, mini bar and games room in the cellar. I am sure you will be fine without us girls while we look sexy for you.' Katie winked at Nick.

'These guys don't understand what it takes for girls to look glamorous, it's not just slap on a bit of make-up and skirt. Let's go girls, I hear, your mum has made us some cocktails.' The girls left the room and left the boys alone.

'Time, boys, I'll show you the games room, where no girls enter also it's the best room in the house.' The boys left to enter the games room.

The games room, or boys' room as Colin called it, was an enormous large space with a window looking up into the garden. The door was heavy oak and when they entered, they saw the red American pool table with leather pockets. In the corner was a bar with every drink available to them, dartboard next to it. In the white corner was Colin's PlayStation, X-box and Wii, with a large screen for football. Colin was a big supporter of Leeds, where Katie gets it from. The boys were dressed already with their shoes in the room, Matt and Damon were playing pool while Nick spoke to Colin. 'You got so lucky by winning that game, should have been Leeds but that's what we do. I do think we will win the championship. How is your career going in the law firm?'

'No, we were stronger in that game and Leeds were being Leeds. How long you been in championship for? I am starting next week with my father, he has got me a few cases to see that have been closed and how they defend their top clients. I was shocked what clients my father had in the past, I always thought he dealt with normal ones,' Nick said as both men drank their drinks and poured out new ones.

'I knew one client which your father told me about, where he was drinking and driving, a celebrity he got off a double charge. No prison sentence, just a fine and loss of license for six months. It's about the right clients and money they pay you, like my clubs. My last one I opened last year, I called it the mini celebrity circle. The celebrities pay three times more than a normal working-class family would. Also, when they drink there, it gets attraction from the press and then I am in the newspaper. It made me more money than my first one, in my first year.'

'It's like there is a connection between our two families, both minted and work with celebrities but in different ways. I remember my father saying he sends clients your way on a night out after court. How've you and Judy been?' Nick asked as Matt was behind the bar pouring himself a drink.

'We have been fine, Judy working hard on her health and beauty shop. Judy just opened her second shop and it's going well. Last time we spoke, we were talking about going on holiday in August and I got a destination, Australia. They do eight-bedroom villas, fully staffed for cooking and cleaning, what do you think?'

'I am up for that, only problem will be my mother. She is petrified of spiders. Matt, how was it when you went to Australia?' Matt looked over to Nick and Colin.

'I enjoyed it a lot, it's all in people's heads when they say spiders and snakes. The truth is, once people get over that, it's all easy and a lovely place. I went to Sydney a few years ago with my parents, our top place was the Sidney opera house.' Matt said as he continued playing pool with Damon.

'What's your plans for tonight, Colin, while I go clubbing in one of your clubs?'

'I was thinking of watching football then a movie when Judy is free from her friends. At least you're going to the club

34

where decent people go and no trouble, just remember when you're leaving to give the taxi receipt to my manager, we will pay.' Colin gave a cheer to Nick.

The door opened to the games room when the girls walked in, all looking stunning and glamorous. Katie was wearing a red silk dress with legs showing and a little cleavage, black shoes and red Gucci bag, walking over to Nick to kiss him. Maria was wearing a long black dress over her knees, and a white furry coat. Matt's eyes were glued to Maria, Nick and Damon winked at each other. Natalie was wearing a white dress, same length as Katie's with a red leather jacket and showing more cleavage. The other girls walked over to Katie and Nick. 'I have ordered you a taxi and it will be here in ten minutes. Please remember to look after yourself and be safe. You don't know who is out there.' Judy said as she took some pictures of the gang.

'We will, Mum, we have our blokes with us. Also, I still remember what you said when I was younger, if someone comes near you, kick them in the balls as they can't get back up straight away.' Katie gave her mum a hug.

'Your mum knows how to look after you girls, I was the bloke once when your mum kicked me there,' said Colin giving Judy a wink.

'Dad, I don't need to know that kind of information about you and mum, less details the better. We are going to wait outside.' The gang left the games room, leaving her mum and dad behind.

They arrived at the night club, Vivid. Vivid was a classy night club in the town centre with bright blue neon lights saying Vivid. Getting out the taxi was the gang, all holding hands including Matt and Maria. Walking to the door and skipping the queues, Katie spoke to the bouncer. 'Katie Turner, my dad has a VIP room; ready it for me and my friends,' she said as the bouncer looked at his clipboard.

The big bald man flipped the paper over and looked at Katie. 'ID please.'

As they all gave their IDs to the bouncer, he let them in where a lady was waiting for them. 'Come this way please to the VIP room, I will be your server tonight so, no need to go to the bar.' They followed her in her tight red dress and blonde hair tied up in a bun.

Damon looked at Nick when nodded at him, and winked. Walking through the crowd, the club was packed and music pumping away with everyone dancing to the tunes. The dance floor was lit up with flashing colours, mostly white and blue. Blue and white seats around the edge of the floor, the DJ box floating above the floor doing his decks, when they arrived in the VIP room with sliding doors. 'Hey Nick, did you see how fit our server was?' Damon said as he looked at her again.

'Yes, but I am more than happy with my Katie, you can look but can't touch or get numbers.' They both shut the doors to the booth.

The room had blue leather booths with a round glass table, on the wall was a window looking down onto the dance floor. The door opened with Lucy bringing in one bottle of champagne and twelve shots of tequila. 'These drinks are on the house from your dad, Katie,' she said as she placed them down on the table.

'Thanks, Lucy,' Katie replied as Lucy left the room.

The gang picked up the salt over their hands, licked the salt, drank the tequila and sucked the lemon. All of them pulled faces. 'Why is tequila so good. Let's do the second shot with no lemon or salt, or are you a bunch of pussies?' Damon goaded as he picked up his shot.

They all picked up the shots and slammed the tequila to their throats. 'That is worse. You need the salt and lemon to help out the strong taste. Girls, let's open the bottle of champagne.' Katie opened the champagne and poured out three glasses, while the boys opened their beer.

Within a few minutes Katie and the girls went to dance, taking their champagne with them and walking down the stairs. 'Matt, me and Nick have got a few questions for you. Are you ready?'

'I know what you're going to ask me, why I am taking so long getting with Maria.' Matt took a swift of his beer.

'Yes, Matt, I mean your face back at house when you saw Maria. On the train, you two were talking to each other most of the time. In your free time you spend so much time together, so what's going on?'

The guys sat on the booth as Nick opened another beer. 'Well, I do fancy Maria. There are a few things standing in the way, we have kissed in the past a few times but I am nervous about one thing, sex.'

'I am taking it you're still a virgin, there is no shame at nineteen. Sometimes when drinking is involved, sex is easy, the drink helps, have you two spoke about being in a relationship?'

'We have sometimes spoken about it, Nick, I think she is waiting for me to make my move. Maria wants to have sex with me again, I need to make the move.' Matt looks at Nick.

'I've got a plan, Matt, we will join our partners soon then you're going to take Maria back here. Talk to her how about you feel, get close like I am sitting next to Nick now. Kiss her, then report back to us. Any chance you kiss her passionately, there will be a chance you will get sex.' Damon patted Matt on the back.

The guys moved back to the window, where Maria waved at Matt to come down. Matt left the room, as Nick and Damon watched on. Matt walked over to Maria as she pulled him closer to him, dancing on the main floor. Both of them moved slowly over each other when Matt leaned in for a kiss, Maria responded back. 'I think we should join our girlfriends, Nick.' They both left the booth, taking their beers with them as Matt and Maria were walking towards them up the stairs when Damon patted Matt on the ass.

Nick was holding onto Katie on the dance floor, dancing to the rhythm of the tune and Katie kissing him. 'So, what did you tell him, Matt just kissed her and they both went to the booth?'

'Well, we found out that Matt has kissed Maria before, and was nervous about doing it again. So, we were like once you're in a good place dancing with Maria just go with your guts and go for it. Now they should be fine and move on. Your body is so nice in this dress, Katie. I can't wait till I get you back in the bed tonight.' Nick leant in for a kiss but Katie stopped him.

'Is that all you think about, sex? Well, we can't tonight as I've got no patches and left them back in London so, no sex tonight, I don't want a baby just yet Nick'.

'Fair enough, I don't think I am ready for that stage yet. I am going to get another drink; do you want a top-up?'

'Yeah, get another bottle from Lucy as well. Tell her to put it on my dad's tab. Love you, Nick.' Katie kissed Nick.

'Love you too.' Nick walked back to the booth through the crowd.

Nick opened the booth door when Matt and Maria were kissing on the booth, then stopped. 'Sorry to disturb you both, I am just getting Katie a top-up,' Nick said as he topped her drink up.

'I'll take it to her, Nick, and thanks, Nick.' Maria winked at him, leaving the room and Damon walked in.

'I am proud of you, Matt, straight away and no holding back. Why straight away and not wait till later?' All three stood looking at the girls on the dance floor.

'It was easier doing it straight away than waiting, the more I wait the more nervous I get. Who is that guy talking to Katie?'

The guys saw the man, wearing a navy-blue jacket and white shirt when he placed his hands on Katie's arm, he was trying to pull her away. Katie pushed his hands away but he placed his hands again on her arm. Nick ran to the dance floor from the private booth, trying not to hit anyone in the process. He hated anyone trying it on with his girlfriend but was still trying not to be the jealous type. Damon was behind when he held Katie by the hand and stared at the bloke who tried walking away with Katie with force. Katie got behind Nick and Damon, when the bloke turned around and stared at Nick. 'I know you. It's you from the train station staring at my girlfriend with your creepy friend. What is your problem, mate?'

The man from the train station didn't say anything as he ran through the crowd of the club as he went into the distance and Damon chasing after him.

Chapter 4

The Next Day

Nick was walking towards the swimming pool, leaving Katie asleep in her bed. She was petrified of last night's actions, leaving her scared after the man tried to take her. Entering the pool, the sun was rising upon the house. Matt was in the pool doing lengths, Matt stopped and swam to the edge next to Nick. 'How is Katie doing after last night? That must have scared her, did they catch the man?'

Nick jumped into the pool with his body floating. 'No. He got out of the fire exit and onto the back street, what a creep to do that. What I don't understand is, how he knew we were in Leeds, he was the creep looking at her at Kings Cross station yesterday morning.'

Matt took a sip of his cappuccino. 'I hope they find the guy. Did you phone the police last night, when we got back from the club? I heard Katie's dad was furious, I don't blame him, someone trying to attack his daughter.' The door opened and Colin walked towards the swimming pool.

'Morning, Colin, how are you after last night? It must be horrible what creeps are out there,' Matt said as Colin stepped into the jacuzzi.

'I am furious, I don't care that it happened in one of my night clubs, more that someone tried to attack my daughter.

My two daughters mean more than anything in the world. I am waiting to hear from the police, my manager has got the images of the bloke so should be near still. Are you sure it's the same bloke from the train station, Nick?' Colin looked shaken up still.

'Yes, I am sure, wearing same clothes also same looks. Have you spoken to my father yet for advice about this?'

'I am waiting for a reasonable time, Nick, I don't think seven at the weekend is a good time. I want that guy arrested and put away, no one does this to my family. Same goes to you, Nick.' Colin stepped out of the jacuzzi and into the swimming pool.

'Thanks, Colin, as soon as I saw it, I went straight over and confronted the man. I don't get why he thinks he would have got away with it. I am letting Katie sleep in, she needs the rest.'

All three of them swam lengths of the pool for thirty minutes when Judy walked into the swimming pool room wearing her dressing grown. 'Breakfast will be served in fifteen minutes, and Katie is awake. She is with Maria, she seems okay.' Judy left the room.

Nick completed a few more lengths of the swimming pool then stepped out, wrapped himself with the towel leaving Matt and Colin to talk. 'Oh, Matt, before I go. How was last night with Maria?' He gave Matt the happy smile.

'All you need to know, Nick, is that it was the perfect night and we are now girlfriend and boyfriend.' Matt winked at Nick.

Walking towards Katie's bedroom, through the long corridors, Nick found the room was empty. He found his clothes from his

41

suitcase when Nick's phone rang, it was his father calling him.

'Hi, son, I am so sorry to hear about the guy trying to attack Katie. How is she doing, also are you okay, son.' His tone of voice sounded worried.

'I am fine, Father, I was scared when the bloke tried to grab Katie away. Katie was okay after a while at the club. We just stayed in the booth room partying, just waiting for the police to come now for a statement then going out. Did Colin tell you about it?'

'Yeah, Colin told me about it in a message late last night, I am helping Colin and the police to find the person. I was ringing as well to say on Wednesday night. It's your nan's birthday, so we're going out for a meal. Katie is welcome to come if she not busy, also if she feels up for it.'

'Yeah, that's fine, I am free. Can't miss her birthday or I will never hear the end of it. How is Nan doing?' Nick put his socks on.

'Nan is good, spoke to her yesterday and was watching her quiz shows. Going to see her soon and take her shopping, I will pass my love on from you.'

'Okay, Father, speak soon.' Nick hung up the phone and walked to the breakfast room where he was hoping Katie would be.

'Where have you been, Nick, I was waiting for you.' Katie stood up and hugged Nick tightly.

'I was on the phone to my father, he sends love, honey. What time are the police coming?' Nick sat at the table next to Katie and her dad. Judy brought over Nick's breakfast, two juicy fat sausages, poached eggs, fried tomatoes, and large flat mushrooms. A bit of health and fat to help him build up, Katie was having eggs royale with green tea. Nick knew Katie was not herself, looking lost while eating her food. 'You okay, Katie? You seem a little lost. Anything I can do for you?' Nick touched Katie's hair.

'I am okay, I was glad you were there last night. That guy would not take no for an answer, and kept grabbing my arm. I am not hungry, sorry, Mum.' Katie pushed her plate forward.

Nick cuddled her as she sobbed into his arms, not knowing what could be done. He felt useless. 'Don't worry, Katie. We will find this man no matter how long it takes, I promise you, princess,' Colin said as he gave Katie a hug.

Judy took Katie's hand and left the kitchen as Nick finished off his breakfast, he was so worried and needed something to do to get Katie's mind free from last night. 'So, guys, what're your plans for today?' Colin asked as he finished off his coffee.

'I think we are going to go into town and do some shopping — Katie wants a new dress for my nan's birthday next week — then watch a film, something fun to cheer her up.'

'I will give you my credit card, tell Katie to get what she wants. Are you guys ready for a round of golf tomorrow? I got each of us a set of clubs. As far as the girl don't know, this place has a spa on the golf course. Keep that bit a surprise.' Colin put all the plates near the sink.

'Will do, Colin, I have not played for six months so might be a bit rubbish. Matt has never played so that will be fun.' Damon laughed with Matt.

'It will be fun, lads, trust me and...'

The maid spoke to Colin half way through. 'The police are at the door, Mr Turner, they are sitting in the living room.'

43

'Thank you, Tina'. Colin and Nick joined Katie and Judy to talk to the police.

The police were sitting on the sofa with paper and pen when Nick sat next to Katie waiting for them to talk. 'I am DC Smith and my partner is PC Willow, we are sorry to hear what happened to you last night. It may be too early to talk but the sooner we do this, we can catch the man. I am going to ask you a few questions and if you don't know then say don't know.'

DC Smith was an older man wearing an oldish suit, with a bald head and long black jacket, PC Willow seemed young. She seemed late twenties, blonde hair and in a police uniform. 'We got the CCTV from the club last night, thank you Mr. Turner for that. Getting all the information this early will help us out. First question is, do you know this guy, Katie?'

'No, the only time I've seen this guy was at Kings Cross station yesterday morning, staring at me.' Katie was holding Nick's hand tight.

'What time and place at the station was this, Katie?'

'I think it was around half past nine to ten, they were standing at the coffee shop called Shane's Coffee. That's all I know about him.'

'We got a description of the bloke from the CCTV. Do you know what accent the man had?'

'Yes, that was very clear. He had a Scottish accent.' Katie seemed to be holding it together.

'What did he say to you when grabbing your arm?' PC Willow kept writing.

'The man said, your dad is on the phone in the office in the club. I said go away as I didn't trust him and I know who works there. I had Lucy, my server, who would have told me.

After that he said, if you don't come you will get hurt, when he grabbed my arm the second time. That's when Nick and Damon turned up and the man ran away.' Katie sobbed into Nick's arm.

There was silence for a few moments when DC Smith spoke. 'Is there anything else or is that all you know?'

'One more thing, in London there was a second man. He was a bit rough, bald, wearing a black jacket and medium built. He was not at the club from what I can remember.'

'Thank you, Katie, that's all we need to know right now. If we need anything else, we will ring you, we have your London address. We are sorry for this attack, we will catch him.' Both police officers stood up.

'Will all this Information be passed on to my lawyer, Mr West in London? Mr West is dealing with this.'

'Yes, Mr Turner, Mr West will be updated on each item. Thank you for your time.'

Tina was standing by the living room door to lead out the police officers. Colin and Judy left to let Katie and Nick spend some time together.

The couple were standing on Katie's balcony, cuddling and smiling. Katie's mood had change since talking to the police; also, Katie heard she got her dad's credit card. She was staring into her dad's wild forest, seeing the wild birds flying around and back to their nests. 'When I was child, I could sit here and watch them all day, when I was sad. I love you, Nick, I could not ask for a better boyfriend.' Katie moved her hands to Nick's face and kissed him.

'It's my job to care and look after you, also spending your dad's money sounds fun. Any ideas what you going to buy for my nan's birthday?'

'Not yet but whatever I buy she will love it, first day I met her she loved me. Nan said, "You will always be part of the family". What do you get someone who is old?' They both laugh.

'You can't do anything wrong with my nan, I can't wait to see her next week. What time are we leaving to go shopping?'

'We have to wait for Matt and Maria, she's on the phone to her mum about them. Whatever you did last night, it worked.'

'I think it was just shyness, just needed a little push. I am happy you've got a little smile on your face.'

'My mum spoke to me, something she told me when she was young. Never let anyone get you down, first time someone tried to control me and I didn't know what to do. Mum said I've got a good man looking after me and some are horrible out there, I know I keep saying it but I love you.'

'I will always be here looking after you, it's part of being a boyfriend. Let's see what the others are doing.'

Nick kissed Katie to show her how much he loved her, touching her body slowly trying to get Katie turned on. 'I don't think so, Nick, maybe last night was a silly mistake with no patch on but no more. I wanted you close to me last night, we need to get the pill.' Katie went inside her bedroom.

Nick followed her into her bedroom. 'I know it was silly. We can go later and get the morning after pill. It was fun, the new move you wanted to do.'

'Yes, it was, let's find the others,' she said as they both left her room.

Nick picked up his cigarettes, placed them in his pocket as he was holding Katie's hands. Nick felt happy Katie was feeling better, while going shopping Nick was going to buy Katie a bracelet showing his love. They entered the living room where Damon and Natalie were sitting. Nick spoke to Damon about having a cigarette so they both went outside. Stepping outside when Damon gave Nick a lighter, he said, 'This feels good. I know it's a bad habit and one day I will stop. I can't believe I let that guy go last night. He was super quick,' Damon continued smoking.

'Don't worry, Damon, the police will catch up with him or them as there was another guy with him in London. We got her dad and my father on the case. Katie is feeling okay now. I think it was more shock at the start, shopping will make her feel better also…' The door opened and Katie appeared crying.

'What is wrong, Katie?'

'You need to ring your father immediately, it's about your nan, she's been attacked.' Nick dropped his cigarette on the floor.

What had happened to his nan, why would anyone attack an old lady. Was his nan okay? Rushing back in the house, through the corridors to get to Katie's bedroom. His heartbeat was racing wanting to know what happened. Grabbing his phone, he saw four missed calls from his father. Sitting on the sofa while the phone is ringing, 'Father, please tell me Nan is okay?' He was speaking fast to his father.

'Calm down, Nick, Nan has been transferred to hospital from her home. Nan is breathing but unconscious at the moment, she has been knocked on her head. The police are here looking for evidence, and the CCTV.'

Nick had calmed down knowing Nan was doing okay at the moment. 'Any reason why Nan was attacked, Father? I find it weird that my girlfriend and Nan were attacked on the same weekend.'

'The door was smashed in, the police are saying it happened last night around ten or half ten. I found Nan with bleeding from her head. We need to talk about getting you home safe, after two victims from the same family in two hours. I am sending up two security guards now to get you and Katie home, do not leave the house, Nick. It may sound silly but who knows what is going on, it may be different crimes or the same.'

Nick was worried now as what could be going on, was someone after his family? Or two completely different crimes. All Nick wanted to do was see his nan and everyone safe. 'I promise, Father. I am a little scared of what's going on, are the rest of the family safe?'

'Yes, Nick, we have a police guard outside our home for a while. I need to ring your mother to tell her you're safe, promise me you'll stay in.'

'Yes, Father.' Both hung up the phone.

Arriving back at Kings Cross station two days earlier than expected, Nick and Katie were sitting in first class alone with one security with them and one on the door. This was a weird experience for them, people looking at them when they got on the train not knowing what's going on. Some of the public, were saying they were famous, only if Nick was. Most of the journey they were quiet, Nick was worried about his nan. His mother kept ringing to see where he was, not that he could make the train go faster than it was. The only good thing about his nan's house was her CCTV, hoping they will get a perfect image of the man. The train stopped at platform two when the doors opened, Nick had to wait till the platform was empty by the security guard. They both got off the train with one of the security walking in front and other one standing back watching out. Being back in London, Nick felt safe walking with the security team. All four went through the ticket barriers when Nick saw the coffee shop where the guys were standing and staring at them a day earlier. Kings Cross was semi packed with public looking at them as they exited the building. There was a police car waiting for them as they sat in the back, with the public staring at them. 'Hey, Nick, do people think we are criminals walking through the station and back into a car?' Katie laughed with Nick, smiling a little.

'Well, it's a different image, next all we need is the press and photos.'

'I've never been in the paper before, has your father been in the paper due to his work?'

'Yes, a few celebrities with my father talking to the press about them being not guilty, it's funny sometimes seeing him on TV talking.' Nick put his arm around Katie.

'I'd rather stay out of the press, I don't think I can deal with the press around me all the time. I think we are home now.'

'Best thing about living in central London, always a train station near your home.'

The police car arrived as the police officer opened the door for them as they entered Nick's parents' house, and his mother grabbed him to give him a cuddle.

Same evening, Mother decided to order a takeaway as soon as Father was back from the hospital, the family were waiting for news about Nan. The house was quiet with Nick playing games with Mickey, Jade and Ellie sitting with Katie in the living room and mother on the phone to her friend. The police officer was still guarding the door for them. Nick left Mickey to finish off the game to see who it was, when hearing the door. Opening the living room door to find Father speaking to Mother, Mother was giving him a cuddle. 'Any news, Father, on Nan?' Nick asked as he sat on the other side of the room.

'Nan is still unconscious but breathing by herself, there is no damage done to her brain. Just a bit of swelling, I am going back up in the morning for an update. How is Katie, Nick?' Father got up and walked to the kitchen.

'Katie is doing well, she's more concerned about Nan. We are getting hungry, Father, can we order food?' Nick's belly had slight pain.

'Yes, Nick, I am doing it now,' he answered when there was a knock on the door.

Mother went to answer it. 'All done. Going to be forty-five minutes,' he said as Mother walked in with two men in suits.

The first man was young, around early thirties, and in a smart suit. Second man was late forties, grey hair and sort of old man look. 'I am DC Walker and my partner is DC Anchor, I am here to give you an update on your mum's attack this morning.'

'Take a seat please, DC Walker and DC Anchor, would you like a cup of tea or coffee?' The police sat on the sofa.

'We are sorry about your mum's attack, we now have a time and image of the person; thanks to your mum's CCTV. The attack happened at half past ten with the attacker using a crow bar to open the door. We don't have that weapon at the moment, I am fine at the moment for coffee.'

'Was this weapon used to hit my mum over the head?'

'We have spoken to the doctors at the hospital and the guy did hit your mum over the head, there was blood on the table where she fell. There were no fingerprints upstairs only your mum's, and downstairs as we discovered the man was wearing gloves.'

'Did you get anything from the CCTV cameras? There are two, one facing the door and one on the door showing anyone knocking.' James' feet were moving up and down.

DC Walker opened his briefcase and pulled out a brown envelope. 'I have these images of the man who attacked your mum. They are perfect pictures of the guy, we should be able to get him.'

DC Walker passed the pictures to father, he looked at the pictures trying to hold back his feelings. Mother had a look and shook her head. Mother passed them back to DC Walker when Nick spoke. 'Can I have a look please, DC Walker, I've got this funny feeling in my stomach about this.'

'What do you mean, young man?' DC Walker looked at Nick.

'My girlfriend was attacked yesterday night, on the same night as my nan and there were two guys at the station but only one of them in Leeds.' DC Walker passed the pictures to Nick.

Nick took the pictures out of the envelope and saw a bald man, slight medium built and leather jacket. 'This is the guy from the train station, the other guy attacked Katie in the Leeds. I don't get it, two guys attacking two family members on the same night.'

Nick gave the pictures back to DC Walker with his thoughts in progress. 'DC Walker, if you talk to DC Smith in Leeds he has been working on Katie's case. I think these two attacks are connected. What is the next step?' James looked at him.

'I will be talking to DC Smith and working together on this, we will keep the police officer on the door till further notice,' he said as Nick got up from the sofa.

'I am going to see Katie.'

'Keep it quiet from the girls, please, Nick.'

Nick nodded, leaving his parents and police officers to talk more, he felt someone was attacking his family but was not sure why.

Chapter 5

4th March 2019

Spring was upon London, the sun rising when Nick's alarm clock was going off. His hands slowly moving from his bed to stop the noise, Katie moved around and placed her arms round Nick. 'Don't put the alarm on snooze, we need to get up. My driver will be here soon.'

Katie's dad had organised a driver and protection for a while due to the attacks on her and Nan, until there was more information on who done it. 'I am glad you've got protection, I was going to be worried about you being at university, and them guys out there watching you.'

'I know, Nick, I am little nervous about been alone. Once I am with Maria and Natalie, I'll be fine, I am not leaving their sides while at university.' Katie continued cuddling Nick.

'I will be messaging you just to make sure, I hope you don't mind. I can't believe today is my first day working with my father at his office. I can guess I will get boring jobs today.' Nick jumped out of bed and stared out of the window.

'We all have to start somewhere and one day you will have people working under you, maybe even one day your father might change the family business to West and Son Solicitors.'

'Sounds like a great name, I have been thinking about doing something but it's dangerous, it can get me into trouble with my father.' Nick sat on the bed next to Katie.

'I don't like this idea, Nick, but tell me anyway.'

'Well, the other night I was smoking a cigarette round the back, I overheard Mother and Father talking about something that happened in the past. It sounded like Mother was in trouble years ago, these people were sent to prison for murder and have been released.' Katie took Nick's hand.

'Wow, I was not expecting that. I don't think your mother would be involved in murder? Maybe someone got murdered and your mother was a witness, do you know much about her past?'

'No, we have never heard about her side of the family or what happened in her past. The only thing mother has said was she was adopted when she was young, maybe when mother was growing up, she was involved but police went easy on her giving information. Father does deals with people so they get lightly sentenced.'

'I don't know but that does seem over the top. Sarah doesn't seem the type, I am not sure if you should do some digging. It seems risky.'

'Then why two attacks, two people from the same family? Also, what she spoke about the other night, it's all weird. Put together and Mother might have been a part of the gang.'

'I think you're jumping the gun, two attacks in different areas and remember we don't have the same surname so it might be nothing. Please, Nick, do not go searching on your father's laptop on this. It can end badly also for you and your father's career with data protection.' Katie was giving Nick the serious look.

'One last thing, in my nineteen years we never heard anything from Mother's past. Not even from her adopted parents, we don't even know their names. If we are in danger, I think we have a right to know, that's all.'

'Let it go, Nick, your mother will tell us whatever her problem is when she is ready,' she said, giving him a stern look.

'I promise you. Want to join me in the shower? I need my back rubbing.' Nick took off his trousers and entered the shower wondering whether to go digging or not on his mother.

Walking down the stairs from Nick's room with Katie behind him, Nick was wearing his dark grey suit, jet black shirt and shiny shoes. Nick felt weird wearing a suit, usually he would wear his smart causal gear going to university, but this week was work experience. His mind was still thinking about whether to do some digging about his mother's past. All thoughts were coming to his mind, they know everything about Father's side, family tree and jobs. His grandad was a solicitor, and his great granddad. Nick would be the fourth generation of solicitor in his family but on Mother's side, nothing. Entering the kitchen, he found everyone at the table. Same routine for most of them, mother going to work to sign off new gadgets, Jade and Ellie going to school but this time Mother would be dropping them off. Mickey going to primary school with father dropping him off, and Katie going to university.

'Morning,' he said and the family said morning back.

Nick poured himself some cereal, also some coffee from the machine and sat next to Mickey. 'How're you, little bro?' Nick asked as he tucked into breakfast.

'I am good, I got dressed all by myself this morning. Mummy was busy.'

'Your mummy told you get ready. You are six years old, Mickey. Sometimes you need to grow up and do stuff yourself.' Mother seemed to be in a funny mood.

Mickey pulled a face behind his mother's back as she poured herself another coffee. 'You okay, Mother?'

'Yes Nick, I am petrified of you all going out and not knowing what and who is out there. So, I am little bit funny this morning, the police are taking their time finding these two blokes. I am supposed to sit here and wait,' she said, leaving the room with her phone in her hand.

'Leave it, Nick, let her be alone and calm down. Mother has been like this since she woke up, Jade and Ellie. There will be a car after school to pick you up for the next few days, after you will get Mickey from school. No friends till further notice. PC Khan will be on the door all day.'

'But, Father, we had plans to meet in the park with our friends. We will be safe, maybe the police man can come with us?'

'No, unless you tell your mother, I would not right now. Nick, can you go hospital before work, I can't do it. I've got an urgent meeting with a client at nine, I will message my PA to say you're going to be late. Is that okay?'

'Yes, Father, can I stay for a while and spend some time with her? It will be nice. Will Nan be out before her birthday?'

'No, Nan will be in hospital for at least one week. No, take the stuff and get to work. There is a long list of jobs you need to learn today before starting your week task.'

Nick agreed as one by one they all left the room for the day, grabbing his keys to his car when he had a tap on the shoulder. 'Remember that Nan is still little confused in her head. Sometimes she doesn't make sense, just ignore it.' That gave Nick an idea about his Nan.

At the hospital, St Pancras Hospital parking was a nightmare, also being central London. Parking his blue Audi a few streets away from the hospital, carrying his nan's personal stuff, thinking of a few questions he could ask his nan. His nan had been around his mother's life since their marriage so she might know a few things, or who these guys are. Nick had a feeling they were connected to her but needed proof to find out. Walking past the main entrance of the hospital, Nick sanitised his hands and walked through the long corridor with doctors and nurses walking around. The hospital was old fashioned with the windows being single glaze, all the doors had been badly painted over so many times. Nick had been here a few times with injuries, last time was when he fell off his bike and broke his arm at around fourteen years old. After five minutes of walking and reaching the ward, Nick pressed the buzzer and waited. How long do you wait till you buzz again, or was it rude? After a few minutes, Nick buzzed again when a nurse opened the door. 'Visiting hours are between two and eight. Please come back later.' The young blonde nurse looked at Nick.

'I am not visiting, I am just dropping off some items for my nan. I can't stay anyway.'

'Okay, come in. You are cute seeing your nan, I wish most young people were like you. I've given you five minutes so you can speak to her, she is in room four. Down the corridor and left-hand door.' The nurse smiled at Nick.

'Thank you,' Nick said as he smiled at her and walked down the corridor.

The ward smelt of old mist, not knowing what the smell

was made Nick feel sick. At room four he opened the door and saw his nan sitting up in bed staring out of the window. 'Hi, Nan, how are you? Father sent me up here with a few items for you,' he said when Nan saw Nick standing next to her.

'You are a good boy, my first grandson. I hope my magazines are in the bag, I am so bored watching the birds feed their young. They look so happy.' Nan kept staring at the birds.

'I am not sure, Nan, Father packed the bag last night for you. Should I empty the bag for you?' he asked, still standing over her.

A few seconds went past when Nan spoke to Nick. 'Yes, Nick. I am sorry dear, these drugs are making me away with the fairies. The stupid man hit my head and I'm still a little sore, I have that image in my head and it's not going away,' she said while Nick placed her things in her cupboard next to her.

'Do you think you know the guy who attacked you, Nan? Did you know Katie got attacked as well?'

'I am sorry, Nick, I don't know who the person was. I did hear about Katie, it's weird two attacks, same time, same night and different places. It's just one of those things that happens in life.'

Sitting next to Nan holding her hand, Nick said, 'I am worried, who these guys might be, Nan. They might come back or next could be one of us. Mother is worried about all this.'

Nick was hoping this might open Nan up, he felt guilty using Nan for information. 'Mother will be fine, Nick, your mother is tough as old boots. She knows to deal with people like that, so trust me and relax.' Nan stared at Nick.

'What do you mean Mother knows how to deal with people like that, Nan?'

'When your mother was young, she hung around people like them. She learnt how to deal with thugs when being threatened.' Nan looked round back to the window.

What did Nan mean, was his mother part of a gang? Did mother stop thugs and sort them out, why was mother being threatened when she was younger? 'You're confusing me, Nan, was Mother part of a gang when she was younger?' he asked, holding onto her hands.

'Nick, you're asking too many questions and my head is hurting. You've always been a pest asking too many questions and still are. Just relax and look after her, they can't hurt her. They are in prison, in Scotland. One more thing, your mother was…' the door opened with a doctor walking in.

'Oh, it's a bit early for visitors. I am Doctor Hardy. I need to talk to your nan. May I ask you to leave, please?' The doctor was standing there and waiting.

Nick kissed his nan on the head, walking out of the hospital even more confused about his mother's past. Was his mother part of a gang? What went wrong? Did they get caught and his mother got away with it? Maybe they want revenge on account of what went wrong. Walking to his car, he texted his father saying on my way.

Heading back to work from his lunch break, Nick bought a sandwich and a cappuccino. His first few hours of work seemed boring, learning what sections of the office to deal with. Nick was on the top floor, criminal law. Luckily, after his lunch he was working with his father's assistant, working on a current case of drink driving and hitting a member of the public. He was sitting in the staff room messaging Katie about what his nan had said about Mother. The staff room was quiet, a few comfy sofas with a small television on the wall. There was a window looking out to Regent's Park, an empty park, today being cold and raining. Closing his eyes for a minute, he heard the door open. Nick opened his eyes to find his father standing over him looking cross. Had he found out about what Nan said this morning, or that he played with his Nan to get answers out of her? The room was silent while his father made a cup of tea. 'I am so pissed off, Nick, I can't believe what happened this morning.' Nick stood in silence not knowing if he had pissed his father off.

'That stupid appointment this morning, the guy has changed his mind and is now pleading guilty to GBH. We worked so hard trying to help and get his sentence lighter.'

Nick was in the clear with his heartbeat slowing down. 'So, what is the point of you, if they don't listen to you?'

'That is what I been trying to tell him, pointless man. Whatever happens I still get paid, how was your Nan early this morning?' he asked, looking at Nick and sitting next to him.

'Nan was good, a bit out of the world. Nan kept moaning her head was hurting, and the doctor turned up as I was leaving. I didn't talk much to her, didn't want to push her much,' he said, drinking his cappuccino without looking at his father.

'You are a good boy at heart, there was me thinking, you were going to ask questions about what happened. You were always the kid who asked questions about anything.'

'I think it's time you got back to work, Nick, you've got some underlining to do on the case. It will get better over time, you start here and before you know it, you'll be higher up and doing cases.' Father left the room, leaving Nick alone.

Nick was sitting at his office table with three files, two marker pens and a laptop. Nick's boss was sitting opposite him working on the same files. He opened the files, reading through them seeing what happened to this guy. The guy was over the limit by double the amount in Croydon, CCTV showed him getting in the car and starting it up. The guy drove away until he hit a woman aged thirty-one crossing the road, the man hit her going at forty miles per hour. The lady was taken to hospital straight away with head injury, she recovered but it left her with slight brain damage. 'How do you get someone off this charge, all the proof is there of being guilty of all this.'

'You see, Nick, our job is to defend the ones who are guilty and try to reduce their sentence. Our job is hated by some people due to defending the people who are guilty. This guy might be in the wrong, but his past is horrible. He was abused as a kid, into foster homes, and is being treated in a mental home so we can use that in court,' he said, looking at Nick.

'But is that just finding a way out of his crimes.'

'We get paid lots of money to do this, it's about you not feeling guilty to get someone off,' Dave said as he walked out of the office.

He was looking through the files when a thought popped into Nick's head, so he opened the laptop and logged in with his details. Feeling Dave could be back anytime, also not knowing where to start. Clicking onto the files, Nick found more than he expected, when looking for West. Getting to the W page where there were over one hundred cases. Nick went back to the main page and put Sarah West in the search page, where he found a case on his mother. Clicking onto the case, 'access denied' with a password come up. Knowing his father's password would be impossible so he tried all his siblings' and even his mother's name. A thought came into his head what his father said to him a few years ago, numbers. Always set numbers as your password as most people pick pet names or children's names. An idea popped into his head of birthdays, putting in his siblings' birthdays from Nick to Mickey with date of births, 'access denied'. When thinking of his parents' birthdays and grandparents, Nick was in. It took a few moments before it clicked, he had access to his mother's files, this was the golden ticket. Clicking into the files, the date showed 1998, Glasgow crown court. Nick's eyes were skimming the files and looking for keywords, a few names popped up: Donald McDonald, Gary McDonald and Sarah West. The victims were Lucy Swell, raped by Gary McDonald and accessory to murder. Donald McDonald attempted rape of Lucy Swell and murder of John Klien. He was searching for more paperwork on the laptop when he came across Sarah West. There were notes on Sarah being in court, Sarah knew the victim that got raped, didn't help her as she walked away from her. Then Nick came across more information about John. Sarah knew John got killed by them, she also hid the weapon used to kill him, then handed it in to the police with her fingerprints on it. He was reading more when he heard Dave outside the door. If only Nick had more time but getting caught would have been risky, so he closed the files also making sure it was password protected. The door opened when Nick closed the laptop. 'How're we getting on, Nick?'

'Really good, his state of mind was not stable when he got

into his car,' he said, hoping Dave would not expect anything dodgy.

'Perfect, Nick, see, anything is possible with a history check of the client.'

Getting up from his chair and walking over to the coffee machine, he wondered if his mother was a killer, or even worse part of a gangster mob from Scotland. Were they looking for revenge on his mother, did she make a deal with them to get them jailed and not her? Maybe Mother's past, being adopted, helped her avoid jail, the only thing going through Nick's head was, his mother might a killer.

Chapter 6

18th March 2019

Nick was lying on the sofa looking at his family pictures of when his parents were young, his mother looking all innocent. His mind was racing backwards and forwards thinking his mother couldn't be involved with gangs, that was not his mother. His mother was kind, had a really nice heart and to take a man's life, it was crazy. It was nearly midday when his father called a family meeting, Katie was running late. Katie had gone home for a week, to see her family, Nick had not told anyone about this information that he'd found out yet. Daydreaming of what and how he was going to tell Katie, he knew was she going to be mad at him for digging or not telling her. The living room door opened when his sisters walked in and his parents. 'Get your feet off the sofa, we only got it clean this week.' Nick sat up on the sofa.

'Sorry, Mother, I forgot. We're just waiting for Katie to come, she's in a taxi and be a few minutes.'

'That's okay, Nick, I am going to make coffees, do you want one?'

'Yes, please, Mother.' Nick kept looking at his mother.

Maybe Mother was forced into the gang when she was young, you do hear of gangs grooming girls into doing criminal stuff. Maybe Mother had changed since her days in

Scotland. Whatever it was, they wanted her for something. The living room door opened again when Katie walked in and smiled at Nick, going straight over to him for a kiss. 'I have missed you so much, I hated not been around you.'

'Same here, Katie, how is your family doing?' he asked as Katie sat next to Nick.

'Good, it was good seeing my little sister. Emily just got home from Germany after her dancing competition, she came second. Not bad for an eight-year-old. I think we better join the rest of the family,' she said as mother was staring at them.

They were sitting next to each other when Mother placed Nick's coffee in front of him. 'We have called a family meeting as the police have giving us an update. The police can't find the suspects on who attacked my mum and you, Katie. I am sorry, they only have images of them with no names,' Nick's father said.

'So, is that it, case closed? Nothing is going to happen to them?' Nick spoke to his father.

'I am sorry, Nick, about this, they are not known to the police. They have never been in trouble so no finger prints, remember how many people are in the world and they are looking at two men. I have pushed them to do more but they won't, they have put it down to two separate incidents. There is nothing to worry about.'

'This is a joke, what is the point of the police?' Nick was getting angry at his father.

'Nick, it's the end of the case. What do you want them to do, stop everyone in England? The police protection has ended so we are living normal lives again.'

The table went quiet. 'Changing the subject, Father. Is Nan coming home today?'

'Yes, Jade, Mother is picking Nan up later. Nan will be staying with us for a while, she is a bit nervous about going home alone. You can come with your mother if you want, girls.' They both nodded.

'Is this meeting over with, Father?' Nick asked, giving his father a stern look.

'Yes, Nick.' He left the table with Katie following him.

Walking half way up the stairs, Katie asked 'What is wrong, Nick?'

'It's Mother, it's all her fault and she's not telling anyone about it.' Katie's face looked lost in his words.

Katie shut the bedroom door and took Nick to the sofa to calm down, she kept cuddling him when Nick spoke to her. 'Mother was in court for murder and a rape case with two other guys.' Katie looked shocked.

'I think we need to start from the top, I am not happy you went digging into your mother's past but happy you were not caught out,' she was saying when his bedroom door opened.

Jade walked in with a cup of coffee. 'I think you need this, Nick. I can't believe you flew of the handle with Father. Ellie has gone with Mother as I want to know what is going on,' she said, staring at them both.

'I can't, Jade, you're a bit too young to know. I am sorry.'

'Well, you're going to tell me what is going on, I will not tell our parents. I am not Ellie.' Jade sat on his bed.

Knowing Jade was right and not going to go away, Nick knew it was the time to tell them everything. 'First things first, Jade, get a note pad from my desk. We are going to write this all down.' Jade went to get a note pad.

'The other night I heard our parents talking about some

guys who have been released from prison, she was worried and scared by her voice. The guys went missing as there was a murder on their street when Mother said they had form for it.'

'That means nothing, Nick, maybe she was friends with them? A bit over the top, Nick.'

'Jade, there is more but I am taking it from the top. The guys got a court injunction so they can't go near us or Mother, she can't even mention their names.'

'That is weird, why would they have a court injunction when we don't know anything about it?' Katie spoke back.

'See, Katie, that is weird. Second, two attacks on the family with someone after Mother.'

'I don't think they are connected to us, it's two different situations. On that one, you are jumping ahead, men do attack women all the time. I say write that down as a question mark till we have more proof, unless you do, Nick?'

'No, Jade, I don't have proof on that one. This next one is proof, I spoke to Nan about the attack and she said interesting things. Nan said Mother knows how to deal with thugs and being threatened, at the same time Nan said they were in prison in Scotland,' he said, looking at Katie.

'Okay, that bit is a bit weird. May be your mother got into trouble, when she was younger, but in Scotland. No one has mentioned Scotland before in the family, where was your mother born, Nick?'

'Mother has always said she was born in London but adopted with a new family in London. Nan's been in Mother's life since they got married.'

'Yes, brother, but maybe she moved to Scotland with her new family? It's getting weird and not making sense.'

'This next bit and the last bit are true, I went digging on

Father's work files. There were two guys, Donald and Gary McDonald, who raped a girl in Scotland and killed a man. Mother walked away when a girl called Lucy Swell got raped. Second, when this guy got murdered Mother hid the weapon to help them. This was in the reports in Scotland and court of Glasgow, this is the one with proof.'

There were silent in the room, no one was talking as Jade kept writing down all the information. 'That bit confirms Mother was involved in murder and a rape case, our mother doesn't seem the type to do that. Why is Mother not in prison?'

'Well, it could be that she helped the police, they give lighter sentences for helping and that is why they want revenge because she snitched on them. Katie, what do you think?'

'I am confused now, there are a lot of secrets your mother is holding back. We need to find out more, but how?'

'I tried to do more digging but Dave, my boss, was in the same room all the time after that. That's why these two guys are connected to Mother who tried to hurt our family, I bet the police know but can't connect it yet. We need to be careful now.'

'Nick, how long ago was this?'

'It was twenty-one years ago, two years after I was born, Jade. Maybe Mother was let off, helping out the police. Funny nothing happened, only after they are released.'

'Also, Nick, the guy who attacked me had a Scottish accent. Your mother knows all this and needs to tell us if we are in danger, maybe you should later tell her.'

Their faces after Katie said tell Mother was shocked. 'I don't know. Mother is a scary person and I am not sure, but then we do need to tell the truth on what we know.'

'Rather you than me, Nick, I just sit and watch Mother

shout at you. How are you going to explain you went digging on files that were private and confidential?'

'Oh yeah, I can't mention that part but that is the biggest proof. I've got a plan, I will ask her later about her family and her childhood. We can see her response, after that then I will see how far I take it. Today after dinner I will ask mother about all this,' he said, feeling nervous and scared to ask his mother.

Sitting in the garden with the temperature being fine to sit in with Katie reading her book and Jade on her phone to her friends. The garden was modern with less maintenance to do, a large sitting area with artificial grass for Mickey to play his football. The sitting area was covered by a roof which Nick had open today. 'I still can't believe you, Nick, what you did. Risking everything just to find out about your mother, but then I am thinking it was worth it,' Katie said, putting the book down.

'Sometimes you need to be risky to find out deep information, at least we know what Mother was when she was young and why this is happening.'

'I still think there are other reasons to this, did you read the whole thing?' Jade asked Nick.

'No, I didn't have that much time to read the file, I only got half way though. I think what I saw was enough, also...' Nick stopped when he saw his father opening the back door.

'I have just signed a parcel for you Nick, I'll leave it in the kitchen for you.' Father closed the back door and disappeared.

'Aww I got a present from you, Nick, I do love you,' Katie said, kissing him all over.

'Nope, I didn't order anything as I am saving money for

our holiday this year. I'll open it soon, maybe my other girlfriend bought me a gift,' he said, looking at Katie.

'You're so funny Nick, you think other girls like you. You're lucky you got Katie, and that is pushing it.' Jade kept laughing at him.

'You're so right, Jade, I could do better than you Nick but I felt sorry for you. Only joking, sweetheart, you're my true love,' she said, stroking his face with a kiss.

'You girls think you're so funny, I don't see you with anyone, Jade. Maybe the boys don't find you attractive, that must be bad,' Nick said, laughing at himself.

'For your information, I do like someone but I am waiting for him to ask me out, we spend a lot of time together at school.'

'Does he have a name then? Father will be happy knowing someone is taking the pest out of the house.' Katie slapped him on his arm.

'That is not nice, Nick, your father is back again opening the back door.'

'Nick, Katie and Jade, do not leave this house. Mother has been attacked trying to pick up Nan and they have taken Ellie.'

Father went back inside with no one saying nothing, it was happening again.

Within thirty minutes there was a policeman back on the door while Father went to see Sarah, Mickey and Nan. Ellie had been kidnapped, Nick didn't know what to do or say. Katie was keeping Jade calm in her room with Nick in the living room. Was he the same guy who attacked Katie or Nan? Worried what was going on, Nick kept ringing his father but was getting no answer. Time was getting on; it was five o'clock when he heard the front door open. Rushing to the front door when Mickey ran straight towards him, father was holding Mother with Nan behind him. Not knowing what to say, he took Mickey in the living and kept cuddling him. Seeing no Ellie, Nick wanted to cry but was holding up for his siblings, his parents went straight to the kitchen with Nan. Hearing footsteps from the stairs, Katie appeared with Jade, Jade went to mother for a cuddle. 'Please tell me they know where Ellie is,' she begged crying into her mother.

'I am so sorry, Jade, there is no news yet. I tried to grab Ellie when I saw the men grabbing her but they were too strong for me. I didn't get enough time,' she said with both of them crying.

Nick entered the kitchen giving his mother a cuddle. 'It was two against one. Don't blame yourself, you did what you had to do. Do you recognise the blokes who did it?'

Nick was hoping Mother did, they might find Ellie quickly without her getting hurt. 'I don't want to talk about it right now. I need some space.' Mother left the room with Father.

'Mickey, do you want to play in your room for a while?' Mickey nodded when leaving the room and going upstairs.

'I know what you're going to say, Nick, the two guys are the same people who attacked me and Nan. You don't know at the moment and we have to wait till the police get here. We don't know if Mother saw their faces yet or the full story, go and spend some time with Mickey and I will stay with Jade.'

The next day the house was quiet with Ellie missing now for sixteen hours, not knowing who had her or what they were doing. Nick was praying in his head it was not the McDonalds due to their history of violence. All Nick wanted to do was ask his mother about her past but knew it was the wrong time. The house was quiet when walking downstairs to the living room. It was slightly open when hearing voices in the room, Nick stayed on the stairs trying to listen in. 'We have CCTV from the hospital car park showing the two guys running towards you wearing masks, we have spoken to police officers in Leeds about the van the suspect got away in and it's the same van. We are sorry to tell you this.'

'So, the two incidents are now connected to Ellie getting kidnapped? What are your plans now, my daughter has been missing for sixteen hours; and alone with them.'

'We are doing our best, James, we need to ask you, Sarah, a few questions on this if you don't mind.'

'Okay, I will answer them, best I can.'

'When did you notice the guys at the time of the attack?'

'I was walking to the car holding on to my mother-in-law, Mickey screamed when I saw the two guys holding onto Mickey. I let my mum go when I scratched him, he let go when I said to Mickey run inside the hospital.'

'We took the skin and blood from your nails but unfortunately we have no records on them, carry on Sarah.'

'The other man grabbed Ellie when she kicked him in his privates falling to the ground, I grabbed Ellie when the other man pushed me to the ground with his mask in my hands. He grabbed Ellie and ran towards the end of the car park, leaving me and my mother on the floor.'

'I am sorry to ask more questions; can you describe the man when the mask fell off?'

There were a few moments when Nick heard footsteps behind him, it was Jade. 'Keep quiet, the police are talking to

Mother about what happened yesterday afternoon. So far there's nothing really to tell you.' They both went quiet when Mother was talking.

'The guy was five foot nine, short brown hair with a Scottish accent. He was wearing blue jeans with a black jacket, that's all I can tell you.'

'Nick, that must be the same man who attacked Katie. I am not being funny but there can't be that many Scottish people living in London.' Nick nodded while trying to listen.

'I am going to show you a picture of the guy who attacked Katie in Leeds a few weeks ago, this might be the same guy.'

There were a few minutes silence when Mother spoke. 'Yes, this is the same man. What does this mean? What do they want?'

'We are not sure right now, we are looking at new leads. We have the number plate of the van so we can pick it up on our cameras, we will keep his DNA from his skin and blood on record and will update you as soon as possible.'

'I want to ask you more about the man, do you know him or have you seen him in the past? We have read the files from Scotland which could be connected but we can't work out how, Sarah?'

'When I pulled the mask off, there was an image in my head as I have seen a different kind of face before but it can't be. The person is dead.'

'Sarah, who is the person you are talking about?'

'The face reminds me of a person I know from Scotland, Gary McDonald. It was a young version of him then I remembered he had a son but he died in a robbery job. It sounds crazy but it's his young version.'

'Oh my god, all this is connected to Mother's past and still she has not told us yet. Nick, what are going to do?'

'I don't know yet.'

'We are running searches on him and the rest of the family. Yes, you are correct, Patrick McDonald died doing a burglary job. Gary and Donald are missing at the moment and we can't trace their steps. Is there anything we can do to help your family?'

'Find our daughter and bring her back, she needs to be with her family. Ellie is so sensitive and won't cope, please find her.'

Nick and Jade decided to move upstairs in case the door opened. 'So does this mean the McDonalds have Ellie?'

'I am taking it as a yes, these two men are missing and a mystery Scottish guy has Ellie. No one knows who he is but I think they are connected and working all together. We need Mother to come clean to us about what is going on, she can't leave us in the dark even knowing we know.'

'Let's go and tell Katie, at least we know they are looking again. You know we are house protected now until further notice.'

They walked to Nick's room, not knowing what the future held for the family at that moment.

Chapter 7

20th March 2019

Standing in the kitchen watching the rain pour over the garden, Nick was thinking about how his sister was coping. Was she safe with them, were they feeding her food or starving her? Then other thoughts popped into his head, were they torturing her, beating her up or worse? His little sister meant the world to him, not knowing where she was, was hurting him. The family was not the same with a sibling missing, it was like a part of the puzzle was missing. 'How long have you been awake for?'

He turned around to find Jade sitting at the table staring at him. 'Too long. I can't sleep knowing Ellie is out there alone in the cold and rain.'

'I am having same thoughts, I have never left Ellie. We have always been together, same school, same friends and bedroom. Ellie is my missing best friend. I can't talk to Mother at moment. It's you and Katie.'

Nick walked over to Jade to cuddle her. 'I am always here. Big brother will always protect the family, I am here day and night,' he said when Mickey walked in crying.

'Come here, little bro, what's wrong?'

'Don't tell Mummy and Daddy, I have wet the bed again. I didn't mean to, I had a nightmare the naughty man was coming back to get me.'

Nick walked over to Mickey and sat him on the chair. 'Don't worry about the bed. How about Jade takes you back to your room, changes the bed and pyjamas. Then bring it to me and I will wash it for you.' Mickey cracked a smile.

Jade left the room with Mickey, leaving Nick alone with his thoughts, making a fresh batch of coffee when he saw two empty bottles of wine in the bin. Putting the cold coffee beans in the bin, he knew his mother was going through a rough time. 'Ah, I love a fresh cup of coffee in the morning,' his father said, appearing from out of nowhere.

'Give me a heart attack, why not. Is Mother awake yet?'

'After her third bottle last night I don't think she will be for quite a while, it's hitting her hard, more than I thought.'

'I can only see two bottles in the bin, Father, where is the third?'

'On the bedroom floor. We have to let Mother ride it out. Don't mention anything about the drinking.'

Nick agreed then poured out two cups of coffee, when there was a knock on the door. Father went and Nick followed, hiding behind the wall. It was DC Walker. Nick wondered what he wanted this early in the morning. 'Sorry to disturb you this early but we have news.'

'Come in, before we go in can we not mention anything about names yet. We have not told the kids yet about who it might be.'

'Yes, James I can do that for you.' Nick quickly got back to the kitchen table.

DC Walker and Father walked into the kitchen as they both sat down. 'We have some news on the van used to kidnap Ellie West. We have found some hair in the back of the van and it matches Ellie West, it was found in a town called Bushey, near Watford. They moved her to the blue Ford but had fake number plates. The blue Ford seems to be around fifteen years old, we are searching the area but we think it was a decoy.'

'Through my experience, they could be anywhere in England. So, two days on and still nothing on my daughter.'

'We have a few leads but they seem to be keeping a low profile, driving and less CCTV. We will catch them, in my time of dealing with kidnapping they will be in contact and will be asking for something.'

'Great, so we have to wait for them to contact us, it's been two days. Can't we do a press conference or police appeal?'

'I am sorry, James, it's a bit early for that. We don't want something big at the moment, we prefer keeping it low at the moment. If we went to the press, it might bring out all kinds of stories which might be true or not. It will be a decision made by you and Sarah. Are there any questions I can help you with?'

'No, DC Walker, I am sorry for my tension with you. I know you're doing your best to get my daughter home and safe.'

'I will see myself out.' DC Walker stood up and walked out of the house.

Sitting in silence with his father not knowing what to say, Nick wanted his father to tell him the truth but was not sure how without getting in trouble. How hard was it to find these guys? We live in world of CCTV, phone signals, people see everything even if one person saw them. 'Father, is there anything we need to know about what is going on?'

'No, son, you know what I know.' Nick knew his father

was lying to him.

'I am going to see how your mother is, can you sort out Mickey please. I heard he wet the bed.'

'I have sorted it, Father, Jade is getting him changed and I am washing his stuff.'

'Oh, okay. Message from your mother, can you take your parcel to the room. It's been sitting there for days,' he said with a change of tone in his voice.

'Yes, Father.' He left the room, walking past Mickey and Jade without saying anything.

'What is wrong with Father?'

'Just being grumpy as always, let's get these washed, Mickey. I am going to cook you a breakfast, what do you want, little bro?' Nick asked, messing up his hair.

The day got boring with nothing to do, watching television even got boring. Mother was still asleep with Father walking up and down the stairs doing everyone's heads in. Katie was at university today, Nick was not allowed to go in. Jade entered Nick's room and sat herself on the sofa. 'I have worked something out. Without Ellie to talk to or Katie, you're going to talk to me.'

'Oh, God help me, just don't talk about girl stuff, boys, makeup or shoes. I know nothing about shoes just that you wear them.'

Jade laughed. 'You are funny, Nick. Maybe that's why you're the oldest and I am not.'

'Not really, Jade, I was born first so maybe that's why. If you are bored, why don't you open my parcel before Mother chucks it at me.'

'See, Nick, you are funny,' she said, leaving the room

giving Nick some peace and quiet, that is why he needed Ellie.

Ellie kept Jade company and also didn't bother him. Nick closed his eyes but within a few minutes Jade was back being loud. 'That peace didn't last long, so what is in the parcel then, Jade?'

'Hold on, boy, I need to relax before I open it. The box seems light to handle, seems loose items in the box, not breakable which is a good sign. The box is waterproof so they don't want any water in it.'

'Are you going to open the box or do you want to play with it, Jade?' Nick giving Jade a stern look.

'That is disgusting, Nick, I do not want to play with the box.'

Nick watched Jade open the box with a face of disappointment. 'It's nothing, Nick. Just old newspapers which smell and a white envelope. I'll just put it in the recycling bin,' Jade said as she got up from the sofa.

'Wait, pass it here. You said old newspapers and white envelope?' Nick jumped out of his bed and sat on the sofa.

Jade joined him with the parcel and looked in the box. The box contained old newspapers articles with a funny smell. Reading headlines of the article, one of them said 'McDonalds attack again'. The second one said, 'return of the McDonalds'. Looking at them, there was one saying Sarah kept secrets about McDonald. 'I think we have more proof that Mother was involved in the Scotland case,' Nick said, looking at Jade.

'Who sent it, who would send this to you? Maybe they want you after all?'

'Why would they want me? I have nothing to do with them, Mother was the one who was working with them.'

'Should we give this to Mother and see what she says

about it, or read it first? Should we open the envelope?' Jade was holding it with Nick staring at her.

'No, we read some of the newspaper clips, then open the envelope. I think we should stop touching the box and newspaper clips, get some gloves. The reason is when we tell Mother, we need to give the box to the police for fingerprints. It might lead them to new names.'

Getting two pairs of gloves out of his drawers, Jade picked out the first newspaper clip.

August 18th 1982

Trouble on the block.

After twenty years of trouble with the McDonalds, Donald and John. We all thought the police stopped their trouble, drug dealing on the estate, carrying out attacks on anyone who got in their way. The newest member to join the gang was Gary McDonald. He was arrested last night on an attack, a boy of twelve. The boy is in a stable condition but the next twenty-four hours are critical. Gary has been released upon questioning. The police say they have no proof Gary attacked the boy and no witnesses to the attack. A member of the public had this to say: 'We know John set this up. John is getting his son to do his dirty work. Of course, John gave Gary an alibi of his whereabouts. We are back to square one, again, McDonalds back in full business.'

The police are trying to get a court injunction on Gary but we need someone to come forward. They will give you full protection but who will come forward?

August 20th 1982

A boy is killed on Bedmoor estate.

Forty-eight hours after the police ask for the public to come forward on the attack, a young boy aged fifteen has been found dead and placed in a bin. The police can confirm that this boy was talking to the police but refuse to say what details he gave to them. Gary, John and Donald have been interviewed but they have an alibi on the night. Who is helping them out? Is the new McDonald taking over John's patch as he is getting older? A member of the public spoke to us: 'McDonalds have eyes and ears everywhere. It doesn't matter what we say, they know and before you know it, we get a knock on the door. We need the police to stop this, our kids are at risk. They are recruiting kids to spy, attack, or anyone who goes to the police. We can't live normally with McDonalds still living on the Bedmoor estate.' We sent a reporter onto the estate to see if a McDonald would talk to us, a young guy said to us, 'You are not welcome here, holding a gun to our face.' The police went straight round, searched the flat but found nothing. What is next for these poor residents?

Nick stopped reading and placed the newspaper clip with the first one. 'I would not want to live next to these people. I have seen films about gangs but never thought people lived like this.'

'I agree with you, I would move away from these people and Bedmoor estate. Wonder where Mother will come into it?'

'Mother was born in '77 so Mother would been six years old, not old enough. It's sound's horrible, recruiting kids to do adults jobs. Do you think Mother lived on this estate? If she did, that means she knows what Gary and Donald are like.'

'If Ellie is with Gary, he is a known killer and not shy to do it. I am scared for her life now, I hope she is fine,' she said, holding onto Nick's hand.

'I don't think they want to kill anyone, they want revenge and are waiting for something to happen. That is my gut feeling, Ellie will be fine,' he said, cuddling and making Jade feel safe.

'Your turn to read the next one.' Jade picked it up.

12ᵗʰ September 1982

Evicting day for McDonalds.

We have some good news for the residents of Bedmoor estate, the McDonalds have been evicted from their flat. We are not sure where they are going but it's far away from Bedmoor, we have been told. John, Mary, Donald and their little girl have until 12ᵗʰ October to move out. Gary McDonald has been put into youth offenders for GBH on a fourteen-year-old girl. The girl recovered from her injuries and is now in police protection. The police will now work with Bedmoor estate to reduce the crime and make it a nice place to live. Anyone with information, call the police and it will be dealt with.

'So, I am now confused, Nick, if they got evicted how comes Gary went to prison later on in life?'

'Maybe Gary stayed in Scotland after he got out, I feel sorry for that little girl John had. I bet you John got his little girl to do some dirty work when she got older.'

Jade placed the newspaper clip with the others when she spoke. 'Do you think that little girl is our mother?'

'No, I don't think so, when I was reading her case file, there was no mention of her being family to them. It said Sarah West when Mother was in court.'

'Okay, so they convinced mother join the gang when she was older. It does make more sense, how many more till we open the envelope, Nick?'

'Let's read a few more then we open the envelope.'

Jade agreed, when passing Nick, the next newspaper clip.

January 10th 1985

Return of the McDonalds.

There have been reports the McDonalds have returned to Glasgow, the council will not comment how they were allowed to return. The police refuse to comment on this case as well, all the police work done on Bedmoor estate will be undone. We have an update by a mystery reporter on Bedmoor estate, the person won't give his name for safety. 'The McDonalds are back but this time they are more dangerous, there has been a death in the family, Mary McDonald. Mary died giving birth in the early hours of yesterday, John abused anyone last night who got in his way. Mary was holding the family together, Mary gave alibis to her family. John was out drunk last night when he attacked two adults, the guys had done nothing wrong. They have been back for forty-eight hours and are causing crime again on the estate. Mystery reporter, more reports to come.'

We are getting more reports on how dangerous these guys are becoming, we asked the police if they will re-question the McDonalds about the attacks but they gave no comment.

January 20th 1985

Donald Prison sentence.

Court day today for Donald McDonald for GBH on a young man in his late twenties. Donald was found guilty of

GBH and sent to prison for two years. The CCTV saw Donald hit the man with a baseball bat across his knees for which the guy needed an operation to correct. The police released a statement: 'Installing new CCTV cameras across the estate has encouraged members of the public to come forward. We will protect the community; any more attacks will be caught on CCTV. Donald will be serving two years for GBH, any more violence from the McDonalds, they will be getting prison sentences from the court.'

We have another secret mystery report from the estate. 'The attack on the young lad was caused by Donald drinking too much and fighting with his brother over the death of Mary. Day by day the family are breaking apart, no one is thinking about that little girl who lost her mother at eight years old. What future does she have? No one sees the little girl, she needs protection against her family. Since my first report, John has been going mad about who is reporting on his family. His words were to the estate, anyone doing this will be killed. I am a little scared but this is the risk I need to take for this to stop. I will give you all one bit of advice, do not go through Merry Lane. They do their dealings and beat you up if you don't pay as they know there is no CCTV on that street.'

What another great report on them but we do advise him to be careful, we don't want another death made by the McDonalds.

'Wow, they all have form on GBH. Wonder why he would risk his life for people to read his stories, maybe he wants to be a reporter.'

Nick was silent for a while when something clicked. 'Hold on, Jade. In Father's files a newspaper reporter was killed by them with Mother's help. This guy must be John Klien, he was murdered by them. It's all coming together now, John was helping out the police by becoming a mole on the estate.'

'Yes, Nick, you're right. Poor bloke but he must have known the rules by doing this.'

Placing the two clips with the rest, Nick picked up the next one.

28th July 1990

> *Drugs and fights still continue on Bedmoor estate.*
>
> *Another attack on the estate, with Gary being mentioned. The two boys were walking home from school when Gary and his gang walked up from behind them. A witness watched it happen but in the last few hours, the case was dropped. The police released a statement: 'The attack that happened on Bedmoor estate was a mistaken person. Gary McDonald was at home with his alibi, we are still searching for the boy's attacker. Anyone with information needs to come forward and help us.'*
>
> *Five years on from the mystery writer from the estate, we have our first report in a while. 'We all know the truth about what happened to the young boys, it was Gary McDonald. A few hours later, a few boys knocked on their door and threatened them to change their statements. Gary's alibi was from his kid sister, even his sister is scared of him. What are they doing to her? Someone needs to save her from this dreadful family. Being thirteen should be fun, will someone save her?'*
>
> *Thank you for another inside report, the police comment on this guy's letter: 'This guy is helping us out but we need the*

public to come forward to get the family arrested. Someone needs to be brave: we will protect you.'

September 19th 1997

   Is the mystery guy dead?
   A guy was found dead this morning in a bin on Bedmoor estate, the guy has been named as John Klien. John was a news reporter when he was younger and lived on the same block with the McDonalds. We have been told John was a friend of the family, maybe they found out he was the reporter. We have a statement from the police: 'A guy was found murdered this morning. The guy is called John Klien, we are looking for anyone who was out last night between ten and twelve, the body was found with two stab wounds in his chest. We have a few a people under caution but we need the public to help.'
   Too many people are dying from the McDonalds with no proof, is it time to put the McDonalds behind bars. Time to act now and clean up the streets, call the police with any information small or large.

Nick put the newspaper clips back in the box, and closed it. 'All this shows us nothing about Mother being involved, unless there was a reason why she was not mentioned in the press. What do you think, Jade?'

   'I think the young girl of the McDonalds is Mother, I don't think she was a part of the attack on John. The girl is the same age as Mother, she was not mentioned in anything also Gary had a sister who helped him give them an alibi. I also think Mother was scared of her family, and that's why we don't know much about her.'

   Nick sat in silence, thinking Jade was wrong. 'No, Jade,

86

you're wrong about this. Mother was born in London, then adopted in London. We would know if we had killers in the family, don't you think?'

'Okay, then how comes Mother was in court in Scotland? You can't explain that part, it all makes sense now,' Jade said, staring at Nick knowing she was right.

'Maybe Mother moved to Scotland with her new parents, once adopted people move from the area so the real families can't trace them. Have you not seen where they trace their adopted families? I still think mother was part of a gang.'

'Well, there is only one more thing we can do, ask Mother the truth now we have this information. Are you ready?'

Both of them stood up when the white envelope fell on the floor. 'Oh, we forgot to open the envelope. Do you want to open it, Nick?'

'I am not sure, maybe we let Mother do it. It is about her,' he said, looking at Jade.

'No, we need to know everything before we tell Mother and she can't skip on anything about her past.'

'You do have a fair point,' he said as they both sat back on the sofa.

Nick opened the letter, showing cut-out letters, stuck on white paper. 'Jade, this is big. The note says, "If you want your child back, give us fifty grand in cash. We will be in contact soon. If you call the police, your child will be gone forever. Gary McDonald".'

Both of them were in silence, staring at the letter in shock. A few minutes had passed when Nick spoke. 'Time to tell Mother now.'

They both left Nick's room flying down the stairs till they arrived in the living room. 'Why are you both running down the stairs?' Mother asked, looking at him.

'Are you part of a gang, Mother? I had this box delivered the other day showing newspaper clips of Gary, John and Donald McDonald. They did murder and attacks on people in Scotland, did you work with them when you were younger? We don't know much about your past so what happened, Mother? There is also a letter saying they want fifty grand for Ellie.'

Mother took the box into the kitchen with the letter, pulling out all the newspaper clips then reading the letter. She was staring at the box when Father walked into the kitchen looking at the letter, Father whispered something into Mother's ears. Father got his phone out and called someone. 'DC Walker, can you come around as soon as possible, we got a letter from Gary McDonald.'

Walking into the living room with Mother holding his hands, he said, 'It's time we told you the truth about what is going on. This is not easy for Mother, we tried to protect you from this, but they got to you. I will let Mother tell you the rest.'

Holding onto Sarah's hand, she said, 'I was not part of a gang when I was younger, nor was I adopted. The person who has Ellie is my brother, Gary McDonald. John McDonald is my father and Donald McDonald is my uncle.'

Chapter 8

21st March 2019

The night before was tense. Mother stayed in her room all night, as Mother was not ready yet to tell them about her family. That night Nick could not sleep, lying in bed knowing his uncle had his little sister. He'd got it wrong that his mother was a part of the Scottish gang but needed answers about what she did. What happened between them in the last few years in Scotland, the biggest secret the family ever had. Nick now knew there was another family out there. Was his grandad alive? Was his uncle that evil to kidnap his niece and get revenge on his mother? How much did his nan know about the family, and why didn't Mother tell them anything? Turning around in his bed, staring at Jade on Nick's sofa. Jade was nervous about being alone in her room. 'Morning, honey, how is Jade doing? She was turning all night and talking in her sleep.'

'I think Jade was fine once she fell into a deep sleep, she is so lost without her sister. I understand the twin thing, she really misses her now,' Nick said, turning back round to give Katie a kiss.

'Jade is so luckily to have a big brother like you, she needs you more than ever. I can't believe that parcel sat in the kitchen for two days before you opened it.'

'I know, if I'd opened it straight away, we might have more clues but I was stupid to leave it till yesterday. I hope there are clues for the police to help them, Ellie needs to come home. No one knows where they have her, it could be Scotland or anywhere,' he said, staring up into the ceiling.

'Don't think like that, Nick, it was not your fault. Today, Mother is going to tell the truth about her family. I can tell last night at dinner she was not ready for it, I can feel it's going to be painful for her. Imagine twenty years of not talking to them then she's got to tell us everything. Be nice to her later.'

'I will be nice, I just want all this explained. There are so many gaps to the story which are confusing. I've got a feeling this will be emotional.'

Jade was turning again when she opened her eyes. 'I am sorry I fell asleep on the sofa. I didn't want to be alone right now,' she said, looking at them both, and then walked over to the window.

'It's fine, Jade, we are here to help each other at a time like this. I think we have a few people outside the house, it's the press.'

All three were looking out of the window with around five or six people taking pictures of the house with the policeman at the door. 'I think the press know about the kidnap, why can't they just leave us in peace.'

'It's their job, Nick, to find stories. A young girl has gone missing. The press will be all over this, they won't be going anywhere. Let's find out if your father knows they are outside.'

All three left the room, walking down two sets of stairs to find Mother on the phone and father next to her. 'What is going on, Father?'

His face was disappointed. 'The press know that a known

murderer has kidnapped Ellie. We are waiting for DC Walker to turn up.'

'I don't get it, Father, but why Ellie? She is just a normal fifteen-year-old girl.'

'It's more because of the name McDonald, we are finding out how the press got this information. This should be under wraps with the police only knowing.'

'DC Walker will be here soon, he has said not to talk to the press. DC Walker will talk to them, in the meantime, I need a coffee,' he said, staring at Nick.

Nick walked into the kitchen as Katie followed him, saying, 'I will take the day off university today. You need me today and I can be here for Jade. In the note it said no police, I am not being funny but when a kid goes missing what are they expecting? Do you think it will not be on the television?'

Pressing the coffee down in the machine then pouring out four coffees, Nick said, 'I've got a funny feeling it will go public. It's not a bad thing, I don't think, then everyone will see the pictures of who kidnapped Ellie.'

'Yeah, true, they have to feed her somehow and go into the public street. Where have your mother and father gone?'

'They have gone to get changed, DC Walker wants them outside when he speaks soon. Apparently, it will help the case and more people will help.'

'I think we should get changed before DC Walker comes,' she said when they all left the room.

The family sat around the table waiting for DC Walker. When the door knocked, Father stood up and went. It was silence around the table with Mother shaking her hands. Jade placed her hands onto hers and looked into her mother's eyes. Mother

91

smiled when Father walked in with DC Walker, sitting at the end of the table. 'Sorry, I am running late, I had to find out what the press knows about this case. All they know is that Ellie West has been kidnapped, no further names mentioned so far. We don't know how they found out but my boss thinks this might be good press, with pictures of the McDonalds who kidnapped Ellie,' he said, taking a sip of coffee.

'We are sorry there has been no further update on Ellie, the car disappeared one mile, where the van was discovered. We've got some information on the box which you gave us yesterday, there was four sets of fingerprints on it. As well as Nick's, Jade's and yours, Sarah, but that is due to you touching it.'

'Gary McDonald and Donald McDonald were found on the box and surprisingly John McDonald, which is a new name added to the list.'

'Hang on, how is it possible my father's fingerprints are on the box? Is my father still alive?'

'Yes, Sarah, your father John is alive. We have sent two police officers to his care home in Scotland to question him. He is added to the list for Ellie's kidnap, I don't know how you're feeling that John might be involved as well.'

'I am not sure how to take it, my father involved in the kidnap of his granddaughter. I don't expect anything less from a horrible man. Who is the fourth person with fingerprints?'

'That could be anyone's, post office or even the mail man. That's all the news I have to give you, we need to talk about the press conference. We believe with pictures being in the newspapers and television, it will help the public if they see them. We are going out at just after one so it will be live on the television, are you okay with that?'

They were staring at each other when father spoke. 'Yes. It's the next step and if it helps bring back Ellie then it's worth the shot.'

'That's good, bad news about doing the press conference is, the press will be outside till we find Ellie. It will take time getting used to them, my advice would be not to talk to them and walk straight on. Let me speak to the press, you both stay silent. Are you ready?'

Leaving the table with DC Walker, Nick, Jade and Katie went in the living room, turning on the television. Nick put the news channel on with a blonde reporter talking in front of their house. 'We are standing outside the house where a girl was kidnapped three days ago. We are waiting on information about who is responsible for this, so far that is all we know.'

The door opened with DC Walker and the parents standing at the door. 'Ellie West was kidnapped on the eighteenth of March of this year, the young girl has been missing for three days now with no trace so far. Ellie was taken in this white van, which was parked at St Pancras Hospital where Sarah was picking up her mother-in-law. Sarah was pushed when the two guys grabbed Ellie, here is what the van looks like. They drove the van to Bushey near Watford where they changed into a blue Ford. The license plates are fake but this is the picture of the car, since then there has been no sightings of Ellie. We have four people responsible for the attack, these two people Gary and Donald McDonald but these two took Ellie from the car park. The same two people who attacked Katie Turner, Sarah's son's girlfriend and James' mother, Irene West. These four people are very dangerous to the public, do not go near them. Call this hotline number or 999. Gary and Donald have form for murder and GBH, we need to get Ellie home soon as possible. Any questions?'

The blonde reporter jumped up. 'Yes, you.'

'Is there any reason why this girl has been taken?' asked the blonde reporter.

'Ellie was taken due to Sarah helping out the police twenty years ago. We are working with the police in Scotland as Ellie may have been taken there. Next question.'

'Can you tell us what happened, twenty years ago between Sarah and the McDonald family.'

'No, we can't reveal what happened at the moment. I have one more question from the public.'

A young man raised his hands. 'Yes, young man.'

'Do you think the young girl is alive, after three days missing? The statistics show most people who are kidnapped are found dead.'

'We are more than certain Ellie is alive, this is not a missing case where a normal person takes a young girl. This case is more personal to them, we are waiting for them to contact us.'

DC Walker walked into the house with Sarah and James, Nick turned off the television as they entered the living room. 'Just a few more things to say before I leave, the newspaper will print stuff you don't want to hear. I would advise you not to buy the paper, they will now do digging into the McDonalds' history. The chances will be high, also finding you're family to them.'

'How comes you didn't mention Sarah was family to the McDonalds to the press?'

'It will cause bad press straight away, James, newspapers will twist what we say. It will come out, my team already have a statement ready when it does come out. We are protecting you before they find out, where you changed your maiden name, they might not find out, Sarah.'

'Thank you, DC Walker, we can't ask any more from you.'

'We are here to help, James. I will make a move. If we get any update, we will be straight round.'

DC Walker walked out of the house, leaving the family in the living room. 'I am going to lie down for a while.'

'I will come with you, Sarah,' Father said as he left the room.

The same night, the family was sitting at the kitchen table with Mother putting all the plates in the dishwasher. Father got out two bottles of red wine, waiting for mother to sit at the table. Tonight, mother was going to tell the family about her past. Mother was quiet with Nick concerned about her. There was a knock on the door and when Father went to answer it, DC Walker walked into the kitchen. 'I have never known anyone who comes day and night to this family,' Nan said to him.

'I know, I am not here to talk. I am here to listen and to see if I can get any clues from your past. I think this might help us catch them.'

'I will do my best, DC Walker, what I am going to say is what happened to me since I can remember when I was young. It's not going to be easy for me so don't talk to me while I am telling the story.'

They all agreed when father poured out a wine for him, Mother, Nan, Nick, Katie and DC Walker. 'Nice wine, James.'

'Father only buys the nice wine, can't stand the rubbish wine,' Nick said as they all laughed.

'My first memory of my family was when I was around four and five. I remember when my older brother came home with a black eye. My father was furious someone had attacked his son. My brother was around twelve years old. He went out for a few hours with my uncle Donald, a few hours later they came home with blood on their hands. He rented out a garage at the end of road, at this point there was no CCTV. The next day, our door was knocked down by the police, around ten police officers searching our home. I don't remember what they found but my father was taken away, I lost count of how many times our door was knocked down. I remember the council always fixing the door frame. My father was home the next day. My mother spoke to the police saying Father was home all night, that was the first time I heard my mother lie and not for the last time. The boy had lived but we never saw him again, that is when Gary turned into another person. My father spoke to him about taking over the family business, it was selling drugs and weapons.

'My father had a friend who dealt with the guns but he never used them, Harry King was his name. His way was stabbing people in the leg when they didn't pay. Gary stabbed a few druggies in the leg, I remember once he told me to walk to the park and drop it down the drain. A few months later, the police searched the flat as Gary attacked a boy. The knife was in the drain straight away as father told him to beat him as he owed drug money. The boy was a runner for us, he lost some drugs and would not pay it back. My father gave him an alibi, which was normal for him. The boy survived, he went to prison a few years later for dealing drugs. He didn't mention any names to the police but the flat was searched again. The reason why no drugs were found was my father's best friend kept them in his flat, his name was Colin Smith.

'After Gary attacked another boy, we got moved to Watford. Before we moved to Watford, I overheard Gary telling my father he had killed a boy. Apparently, it was an accident when he slipped on the stairs. Same again, more police saying Gary pushed the boy to his death. My mother wanted a fresh start with no trouble. We had a four-bedroom house which was nice. I remember our neighbours being nice and friendly, I played with their little girl Daisy Smith. Her mum didn't like my brother, kept calling him names. It was three months before my father and Donald found a supply then dealt drugs again.

'Day and night, I heard the door open. It was not long till the police found drugs in Gary's room. He was arrested, the judge gave him two years in prison but it didn't stop. Donald took over, recruited four young boys to do his dirty work. There was not much violence in Watford, more drug dealing. Donald was never home. I asked my father where my uncle was, he kept saying he was out in his den. Stop asking. When I was seven years old, my mother told me she was having a baby. I was so excited to have a younger sibling to play with, Daisy was happy too. Some of my childhood was spent with Daisy and her mum in her café, until I got told we were moving back to Scotland. I was crying for days, I made my first friend and now my father wanted to move back to Scotland. I don't know how Father managed to get us back there, but moving day happened when Mother was eight months pregnant. Gary followed two weeks later when he'd been released from prison, this time Gary had completely changed. Gary was more tough, and people walked on the other side of the street.

'One night, my mother was giving birth when my uncle

was looking after me, Gary had a friend round. I saw in the doorway Gary knocking him out, pulled a knife out and stabbed him in the leg. That was the first time I saw violence, I was scared and cried all night. Next morning, Father came home from the hospital with a bottle of whiskey, I remember asking where my baby sister was. Father pushed me into the wall, hurting my arm. All day I didn't know where my mother was or my sister. Gary sat down with me, telling me Mother had died with my sister. I cried for days with no one to talk to, Father got arrested for attacking two boys. Donald gave him an alibi, which I knew he was lying about again. My mother's funeral came, not many people turned up. I sat next to Gary and all he did was give me a pat on the back. Things were turning for me as I made a new friend on the same block, Lucy Swell. Lucy was the same age as me. Father didn't care what I did. I spent most of my time with Lucy. Her dad was a gentleman, John Klien. My brother killed him but that is later.

'In the same year I lost my mum, my uncle went to prison for GBH. Donald hit the man with a baseball bat, apparently the man said my mother was better dead than alive with you damaged thugs. Donald got two years, that's when my life got bad. I was eight years old, I had to clean my father's flat and start cooking for him. I didn't see Lucy much after that, only when I went to the shops. You remember that a mystery man wrote to the newspaper, it didn't click with me until he died. I was posting letters for John, he was the one writing to the press. For five years Father made me clean the flat till Gary had a girlfriend, Julie. The violence kept happening, drug dealing but not getting caught. I would hear people talk about my family but what could I do? Nothing. Lucy was back in my life and we spent more time together. I stayed more at her house then mine, her father didn't mind. He treated me like a daughter, my real father only wanted me to give them an alibi.

'I was happy for the first time until 1997. I was walking home from the shops. I was twenty years old. I had a date with James, we'd meet in town when he was working in a lawyer firm. James said I was pretty and the only girl for him, you said love at first sight. I never said anything to James about my family at first. James went to university in the area so that's how we met. I knew James was the one for me. Walking back from the shops, I saw Donald waiting at the top of the stairs. He said to me "walk on, girl", pulling a knife out of his pocket. At this point I was scared, opening the door but looking to find a girl on the floor. Gary's pants were on the floor with the girl's knickers at her ankles. I noticed the pink bag and blonde hair; it was my friend Lucy. I wanted to help but Donald still had the knife in his hand, I didn't know what to do. Lucy was my only friend, Gary had a girlfriend and a baby girl called Lily McDonald. I heard Lily had an accident and died, not sure when. I was shocked when I found out, I didn't attend the funeral as I left Scotland for good. Lucy didn't see me for a few days but spoke to her father. We both knew who it was, Lucy went to the police, reported it, but didn't want it going to court. Klien was not happy with what was happening. I was stuck in the middle of my family and my best friend's family. I said to Klien it will end soon and I will help you, I didn't know Gary was listening to our conversation. Lucy Swell was found in the forest, she had hanged herself. Lucy left me a note saying look after my father. She couldn't cope any more. Each year I think about her.

'A few months later, Klien gave me a letter. His words were do not open it till later in life or when something happens to me. I didn't know what he meant by this so, for safe keeping I let James keep it for me, me and James were dating for six months and coming to the end of his university. I didn't know what to do, leave with James or stay. My mind was made up, I didn't want my family. A week before I was leaving, my father was drinking more, and more. Gary was having another child, I was packing my bags when Donald opened my bedroom door. Donald told me to hide the knife, as he didn't get time to drop it down the drain. I hid it in the bag I was leaving with, didn't know whose blood was on the knife. The next day, I went to see James with my bag but upon my return the police were searching the flat. I heard John Klien was found dead, Donald had killed him last night. At this point I told my family I was going to the shop, I didn't return in case Donald wanted the knife back. I stayed with James, crying my eyes out knowing they'd ruined my life again. I went to the police station and told them everything about Lucy Swell's rape case, and Donald killing John Klien. I knew it was dangerous snitching on my own family but it was something I had to do. John and Lucy were like a second family to me.

'Within a few hours the police had arrested Donald and Gary. The police offered me full police protection while the case went to court in '98. I needed to be brave and put an end to this. While I was with the police, I told them all the houses where Father was dealing drugs, kept the guns and weapons. It was in a warehouse round the back on the estate. They found it all but no proof linking it back to my father, he kind of got away with it. My family had been attacking and killing people for over thirty years. With Lucy's statement before she committed suicide and my eye-witness to the account they both got sent down. Gary got sent down for rape and Donald for attempted rape. The second case was straight forward, they found hair from Gary on the body. Donald's fingerprints were on the weapon which I handed into the police. They both were found guilty of murder, justice was served for my second family.

'Walking outside the court in Scotland, I was a free woman from my family. That was the last time I saw Gary and Donald in court. Their faces were horrible, I could tell they hated me. Outside the court, I met a woman called Hazel Swell. She thanked me for all I had done and getting Lucy's rapist sent down. We had a cup of tea after and she showed me pictures of Lucy when growing up. I had one last thing to do, I had to see my father and pick up my last few things. I left behind my mother's jewellery, she left me this diamond ring which I have upstairs in the box. I got police-escorted to the estate, because of my father's temper I had police with me. Entering the flat one last time, my father looked at me in a disgusted way. His words were that I betrayed the family, my mother would be turning in her grave. "All I have left is Lily, Julie and my new grandson. I don't want to see you ever again, you are not my daughter any more." Leaving the flat for the last time felt good, I had my boyfriend James waiting for me with his mum. I was going to live in London, and start a new life.

'Leaving the estate, I saw Lily running towards me. I loved my niece; she was going to be a bright star. I hugged her when she run back to her mum Julie, it was the end of my life in Scotland. When I arrived in London, I had an appointment with the solicitors but I didn't know why. When John Klien died, he left me everything. His business, all the money in his account, it came to three hundred thousand pounds. I was shocked I got it all, I felt blessed and this was the new start to my life. James gave me the letter which John gave me, I still remember the words today. "To Sarah, if you are reading this then I have died. I hope they caught the killers and they are behind bars. You were like a daughter to me, best friends with my daughter. I hope they get put into prison for raping my daughter in the future. I am giving you this necklace as it belonged to Lucy, she would have wanted you to have it. Love John." I still have the necklace in my jewellery box, I was never abused by my family just not loved. Never did they hit me, they wanted to control me but it never worked out and Bedmoor estate become a McDonald-free zone. I know I should have told you all this years ago but I was scared to, I am sorry.'

Chapter 9

22nd March 2019

Four days Ellie had been missing from her family, last night's conversation with Mother telling her story and Nick was shocked by it. Jade stayed in Nick's room another night, spending most of the night talking about mother's past. The tension in the house seemed to have gone now with everyone on the same page. Nick was walking upstairs with two cups of coffee. 'Here you go, Katie,' he said, passing it to her when sitting on the sofa.

'Thanks, my honey bun,' she said, kissing Nick on the lips.

'I heard Mother going out with Father, not sure where they are going. I feel so guilty for thinking Mother was part of a gang and involved in murder and rape. Her family seems rough as anything,' he said, sipping on his coffee.

'Remember, Nick, that her family means your family now, it's weird your uncle murdered innocent people. I don't think it'll be long till the press works out how it's all connected, I feel sorry for your mother. Twenty years of nothing then all this.'

'I know, we've got more family members now. Do you think Mother wants anything to do with her father? We know we have another grandparent. I don't think I want to meet him, he sounds like a horrible man.'

'I agree with you, Jade, Grandad John is one person I don't want to meet. I do think he's a part of this kidnapping, he wants revenge like Gary and Donald. Last time he spoke to Mother, she ripped her family apart. I am going to see Nan,' he said, leaving the room to find his nan in the kitchen.

Nan was staring into the garden watching Mickey in his play house. Sitting opposite Nan and holding her hands, Nick said, 'It'll be fine, Nan. We are all protected here with the police, no one else is going to get kidnapped.'

Nan looked at him. 'This is not the end, Nick. I remember your mother being with them and how scared she was. James said Sarah was the one, I didn't believe him at first but I am glad I went with my gut. Your grandad said, that girl needs to be saved from them. I am glad I saved her but this time I can't help, I can't do anything to help.'

'No, Nan, you saved her from these evil people. The police will catch them and bring Ellie back, it's about time and waiting. I feel guilty about what I said to her, I said she was part of the gang. Next time I read all the notes, where is Mother?'

'Mother is at mine getting some things, they have an unmarked police car driving them there. I remember sitting in court and staring at them, their faces were like they didn't care about what they did. Laughing in court, talking while people were on the stand. One stage, the judge nearly suspended court because of them. They had a really fancy lawyer, which I don't understand how they afforded, he was really good at lying for them.'

Getting up from the kitchen table and pouring himself and

Nan another coffee, Nick said, 'Maybe they had hidden cash when the police searched the warehouse and flats. Donald seemed to be clever until handing the knife to Mother, maybe it was dirty cash?'

'No, Nick, this lawyer was the best in Scotland which cost more than people's wages back in them days. When your mother got on the stand, they shouted some horrible names to her. I could see she was shaking, but Sarah was brave and told them everything that she knew. I thought the Lucy case would have been found not guilty due to only one person seeing the rape. Gary was telling the court she wanted to have sex with him, and she enjoyed it. It was so sick watching this all, but he was found guilty. The killing of John was easy due to fingerprints on the knife and hair, we thought that was the end of them.'

'Hope they catch them all and get life this time, I can't believe Mother has to go through this again. Is there anything I can do to help her?'

Sipping on more coffee and holding onto his hands, his nan said, 'Just be here for her. That's all she wants from you all. Just let the police do their work, hope we get an update later from DC Walker with good news.'

The garden door opened. 'I am hungry now, Nan,' Mickey said, closing the door and sitting at the table.

'You say it how it is, Mickey, don't you,' Nan said, laughing at him with a smile.

Pouring Mickey some coco pops with some orange, she said, 'If I was younger, I would go searching myself. I can't sit here and watch this all. When your mother lived in London, she told me all the places where they hung out. I know the police are doing their best. The problem is, when police are around, they will stay hidden, once gone they will come out and do their work. It's common sense.' She walked into the garden with a cigarette.

Nick felt maybe he could do what his Nan wanted to do, he was young. Nick could blend in with normal people, picking up a cigarette and joining his Nan outside.

'I told you to give up, Nick, these are bad things to put into your lungs. You should listen to me,' she said, giving him the serious look.

'I will one day, Nan, maybe we should give up together. A time like this will be hard. What places did they hide in Scotland?' He was trying to dig out information on them.

'When they lived in Scotland, they had dens and hideaways. Gary used his best mate's garage on the estate, Harry King. The other person was Smith, can't remember his first name. His parents had a caravan site on Dumbarton. Also, his father worked at the port, Greenock.'

'When they lived in Watford, was there anywhere they hung out?'

Putting out her cigarette, she said, 'Not really, Nick. They hung out on the Bushey golf course, the forest next to it where they did the business but nothing really. It was more Scotland…' Then Father knocked on the garden doors.

The family was sitting around the table waiting for Jade to join them. There was a box on the table which seemed old and falling apart. Jade joined them when mother opened the box. Were more secrets about to come out about Mother? Nick thought his mother could have rested when Mother pulled out a picture from the box. 'After yesterday's story I thought I should show you a few things about your family. This is a picture of your grandparents holding me as a baby. I must have been around three years old living in Scotland.'

The picture showed a young nice woman, long brunette hair and blues eyes, must be his nan. His grandad with short brown hair and ginger beard. The baby wearing a red dress with white tights. 'I have the same looks as you mother. The eyes are the same. Was Nan happy here?'

'Your nan was always happy with us kids, she lived every moment with us. She tried to keep us out of it but my father always made us join the family business. Mother let us have a childhood, the day she died was the hardest for me. I had lost my childhood being with him, my father. This next picture shows the whole family.'

The picture was in Nick's hand when mother spoke. 'On the top row is your grandad and nan. Second row is Donald and his girlfriend at the time, in front of Donald is me and my brother Gary. We went on a caravan holiday in Scotland, Dumbarton.'

'A holiday in the same country as you live?'

'Yes, Jade, my father didn't like to splash the cash. He kept it locked up to buy more drugs and make more profit. He ruined so many lives with his drugs. The next thing is a teddy I had growing up, his name was Mr Huggles. After my mother died this kept me happy,' she said as Father held her hands.

'When did Nan die, Mother? You don't have to tell us.'

'I don't mind, Nick. My mother died on the ninth of January '85 with my little sister. I don't know what my life would have been if they'd survived, would I still be in Scotland trying to protect my little sister or here with James? Every year I light a candle for her death, the white one. I remember Nick saying what is that which is on the wall in the living room, I can now tell you. MVM 85, Mary Violet McDonald and the year she died. You girls have Violet as your middle name after your nan.'

'That is so nice, Mother, maybe next year we can do this as a family. Have you got any photos of you and your mother we can put up?'

'Yes, Jade, I do, this is the reason I went back to the flat for the last time. I was collecting a few items but was caught out by my dad, he would not let me leave with it. Yesterday I said about my mother's engagement ring and Lucy's necklace.'

'You are sure, Mother? We can wait till you're ready. There is no rush,' Nick said when he looked at his mother.

'It's okay, Nick, it's time we all know what is going on and what items I have of our family. This ring with the diamonds on it was your nan's engagement ring, it was bought by blood money but still my mother's. I want to pass it on to you girls for the future. This necklace was from Lucy. The two hearts mean love from her mum and dad.'

'This is so nice from Lucy's dad, I read the other day that one best friend means more than having loads. Is this ring expensive, Mother?'

'Yes, it's worth around two to three thousand pounds. I don't care about the money, what it means to me is worth more. When I got the money from John Klien, I didn't waste it I brought a house and went to university. John wanted me to have a fresh start and that's what I did. One day I was going to tell you about Lucy's necklace. I also want to hand it down and what it means.'

There were a few minutes where Mother went outside with Nan, Nick could see it was getting to her. Nick could not image how hard it was, talking about her bad times. 'Will Mother be okay, Father?'

'Yes, Nick, she will, this has done her good getting it off her chest. Imagine twenty years of holding it in, the last year has been bad. When we found out they were getting released from prison, it set Mother off.'

'I can't imagine, once the guys are caught this will be over.'

'We hope so, Nick, Mother can't live with this forever,' he said as mother walked back in with Nan.

'I hope you all understand why I am telling you about these guys, they are evil. I can't say for definite but this item maybe why Nan got attacked.'

Mother pulled out a pocket watch, it was in a leather case. Pulling the pocket watch out, she said, 'This is what Gary might have wanted from me. This is a pocket watch belonging to one of my grandparents going back four times, on my mother's side. I am not sure if it's true but it was something to do with some war. He was in the Scottish army, each member had one. I never really understood but a few years after Gary was in prison, I went to get the watch checked out. This is a rare item of the Scottish army; the price is out of the world. Gary saw it a few times in Mother's room and wanted it after Mother's death, but Father took it from him. Back to the last day of seeing him, I took it off him as it was my mother's, not his.'

'Wow, this is amazing. The design of the watch, it has to stay in the family. So, Gary thought Nan might have it in her house?'

'Maybe, Nick, it's the only thing he wanted from the family. He must have guessed I would not be hiding it, so he tried the next person close to me. I feel sorry, Nan, you got attacked for me, that is another reason why I've been feeling down.'

Holding onto Sarah's hands, Nan said, 'Don't blame yourself, Sarah. It was hidden well. I will always protect you till the day I pass away.'

The rest of the box was about old photos, Mother's baby things and keys. The keys didn't lead to anything, just old doors, Mother said. Sitting at the table when the door knocked, Nick went to answer it. It was DC Walker standing there with the press taking photos. Nick shut the door and walked into the kitchen with him. 'I am sorry to come around without phoning but we have an update on the case.'

'Can I get you a coffee, DC Walker?'

'Yes, please, James,' he said while he sat at the table.

'Since we released the photos there has been a few sightings on the kidnappers. I'll get straight to the point,' he said as Father gave DC Walker his coffee.

'Yesterday night, a member of the public saw one of the guys. The bald guy who attacked Irene West and in the car park. The Scottish police arrested him last night, found on Bedmoor estate. His name is Billy King, does that name mean anything to you, Sarah?'

There was silence in the room till Sarah spoke, 'No. But I do remember a Harry King from Bedmoor estate, he was friends with Gary. They worked as partners dealing drugs, Harry dealt with the weapons being transferred around Bedmoor estate. His father was called Bill King, friends of my father.'

'Yes, you are correct. Harry is currently in prison with his father Bill, we are looking around Scotland for Ellie. We are thinking Billy is working with them as his dad is in prison, he has no records with the police. So far, his answers have been no comment, but we know he is involved in this.'

'So, Billy has given no help to the case, DC Walker?'

'I am sorry, James, he will not be released by any chance. By the end of today he will be charged with attacking Irene West and kidnapping Ellie West. We don't think the judge will give him bail. Billy will be looking at twelve to fifteen years in prison, his case is being heard in Glasgow. They have been trying different ways to get him to talk, giving him a softer sentence if he tells them where Ellie West is, nothing is working.

'Second, the blue Ford was found in Scotland but destroyed. There was hair in the boot and it's Ellie's. The area is being searched. We are checking CCTV from Watford to Glasgow to work out where they went.'

'You are trying your best and getting the first one is a good sign, only three more to come. Has anyone said where the rest are?'

Sipping on his coffee, DC Walker said, 'Yes. The other man with no name has been spotted in Watford a few days ago. We are checking CCTV of the shop, it was a few hours after they swapped from van to car. Still not sure if they are still in the area, at moment it's between Glasgow and Watford.'

'Thank you, DC Walker. Do the press know yet about Billy King?'

'No, I am about to tell them now. I be back as soon as possible with more updates.'

DC Walker stood up, leaving the kitchen. Mother cried when Father took her upstairs. Nick and Jade put on the television. They could see their house on the television again.

'This morning in Scotland, Billy King was arrested and questioned on the kidnapping on Ellie West. So far, we have no new information as Billy is refusing to answers our questions. In the meantime, Billy King has been charged with kidnapping Ellie West and GBH on Irene West. All this happened in twenty-four hours, we keep asking the public to keep an eye out. The blue Ford which the kidnapping happened in has been found in Bedmoor estate. There was hair found and it matches Ellie West. All CCTV will be checked from Bushey, to Glasgow. The main two areas are Glasgow and Watford, any information please call…' Nick turned off the television.

'At least they are getting somewhere now, four days in and one person is caught. They are using the same areas where they lived, which is good so getting closer.'

'That is true, Jade, I am going to ring Katie and give her an update on what's happened today, while I am gone. Read the newspapers and see what they are saying,' Nick said, leaving the living room.

A few hours went by when Nick was waking up from his bed, tiredness kicking in after searching online all night about the McDonald's family. It was five in the evening when leaving his room and making his way downstairs. Nick could hear Father talking to Jade, with Mickey playing with his toys. He entered the living room when Jade left Father to enter the kitchen, sitting next to him. 'How is Katie?'

'Katie is good, having a meal with her friends at university then coming home. Did you find anything from the newspapers?'

Jade opened her iPad, showing Nick the news article from

the newspaper.

Three days ago, a young girl was kidnapped from picking up her nan from hospital. Ellie West was taken from her mum and push into the van. The van was spotted in the town of Bushley near Watford. Her parents want her back as soon as possible. Gary and Donald McDonald have a criminal background from murder to rape. Both men were sent down for rape back in 1998, which is the same year they murdered a guy called John Klien; they both got twenty years in prison. Gary's sister, Sarah West, helped the police by putting them away. They were known to run the estate Bedmoor from the seventies to '98. Ellie West is the daughter of Sarah West. It is simple: these guys want revenge on Sarah but are taking it out on a young girl, their own niece!

'Well, that didn't take them long to find out Mother is related to them. Does Mother know about this yet?'

'Yes, I have shown Father, before you came downstairs. She's taken it okay so far, the rest of the report is pictures of the guys and where they lived before.'

Nick looked into the garden where Mother had stopped crying and Nan was pouring her a glass of wine. Sitting at the table feeling useless, Nick had a plan but was not sure how to tell his mother. 'Is there anything on Billy King, from the Scottish newspaper? A clean record from living on Bedmoor estate, not a chance. What about his social media sites?'

'You don't think I have not checked already? I found him so I checked his friends and not one looking like the other guy. No newspaper reports on Billy King, only his father Harry King. They mention warehouses in Scotland where he hid his

113

weapons and little drugs. Their known places were port Glasgow where he had his warehouse, and he hid at the golf club where the police found him and has been in prison since.'

'I don't get it, how is Billy King connected to our evil family? There is a twenty-year gap between them, in prison and no younger family members alive of the McDonalds.'

Standing up, he walked into the garden giving his mother a cuddle, 'We are here for you, Mother. Did Father take the box back to Nan's house?'

'No, we've got it here till further notice. We got a police guard so it be safe. Is Katie having dinner tonight?'

'No, Mother, Katie is having dinner with her friends at university. She'll be home around seven. You okay about the news arcticle in the paper?'

'I am fine about it; it was all in the paper years ago so would have been easy to find. Finding one guy is the start, I am so proud of you looking after your sister and brother. I am sorry if I am not been able to look after them.'

'It's fine, Mother, I am the big brother so my job is to protect them and make sure they are fine. I am worried about you, Mother,' Nick said, holding onto her hands as Mother had a tear in her eyes.

'I have your father and Nan to look after me. I am paying for a holiday for you and Katie to go on, first class and five-star hotel after all this.'

'No, you don't need to do that, we all need a good holiday after all this. Ellie needs it more. Ellie has been through so much. Do you think Ellie is in Scotland or Watford?'

Mother was silent for a few moments before answering back. 'My gut feeling is they have taken her to Scotland. I know what they want, they want me to get her. Four days and only a note, I am not paying them a penny. If I have to go and meet them, I will do it. We will hear from them soon.'

'I've got an idea Mother. Will you let me go to Scotland? I am young, not acting as a policeman. I will take a friend with me, keep in contact with you. I want to go to Scotland and get my sister back,' Nick said, staring at his mother in her eyes.

Chapter 10

23rd March 2019

The breakfast table was quiet with Nick waiting for his mother. After telling his mother what he wanted to do, she ignored him and went straight to bed. His plan was to search Scotland and help the police, another pair of hands would help them. Maybe DC Walker would convince his mother that a normal member of the public looking was helpful. Hearing footsteps on the stairs, his father walked into the kitchen, walking over to the coffee machine. 'I don't want to hear it, Nick, it's a silly idea for you to go to Scotland. You don't understand how dangerous these guys are.'

'I can help the police. I am bored out of my nut doing nothing and sitting here. I can blend in more than the police,' he said, looking at his father hoping he would change his mind.

'The answer to this, no. Mother would never let this happen, they have one of our children. We are not handing them two, we will wait for the police to find Ellie.'

Nick was about to talk when his mother entered the kitchen when father poured a coffee for her. 'Don't mention anything about Scotland, Nick, to me, the risk is too high. Thanks for the coffee, James.'

'I didn't say anything, Mother, I was going to say morning to you before you bit my head off. I know you don't like the idea of my going to Scotland.'

Mother looked at Nick in a suspicious way. 'I know you inside out. Trying to butter me up so I change my mind, this is why I am the parent and you're the child,' she said, drinking her coffee as the post box dropped.

Father went to get the post as the kitchen stayed in silence, while Mother was making herself some toast. Nothing was going to change her mind, but Nick was not going to give up on this. Walking back into the kitchen, Father passed the post to Mother. He decided to ask more later, getting up from the kitchen table when Mother dropped her coffee on the table. Her face seemed shocked. What was going on? Father took the letter from Mother, reading it when he picked up his phone. 'What is going on, Father?'

Passing him the letter, as Nick read it, he said, 'Time is running out, Sarah. We want fifty grand in our account in seventy-two hours or say goodbye to Ellie.'

Within the letter was pictures of Ellie tied up, her face looking bruised. Red eyes, dirty skin and hands tied up with rope. 'Father, who was that on the phone?'

'It was DC Walker, he said don't touch the letter any more. He is on his way over. Sarah, are you okay?'

'I am a little shaken, we've got seventy-two hours or they are going to kill Ellie. We need to get them the money, it's only money and I'd rather have my daughter alive. James, transfer the money straight away,' she said to him, sitting next to her.

'No, Sarah, let's wait for DC Walker to give his advice. If we give them the money, it won't end there. We don't know if they would release Ellie. Relax and wait for him to come. This is what they want. Have another cup of coffee.'

Nick went to wake up Jade and Katie to tell them the

updated news.

The family was sitting at the table waiting for DC Walker. Mother was still shaken up from the letter. Mother refused to eat breakfast. Someone was knocking at the door. Father went to answer it, hearing DC Walker's voice. Walking into the kitchen, Father passed him a coffee. 'I am starting to like it here, coffee each time. I am sorry to hear you got another note, this may a bad thing but a good thing for us. What I mean is that Ellie is still alive, we need to take the letter so we can get some fingerprints off it. The bad thing is this won't tell us much about where they are at the moment, I am sorry.'

'Can't you tell where the letter came from, where Gary posted it from?' Jade asked DC Walker.

'I am sorry, Jade, someone posting letters can't be traced. If you get special recorded, we can trace it. This envelope has been sent in the post, I don't think they would do special recorded as it would show them where they sent it. I don't have any more updates…' DC Walker's phone started to ring.

Walking into the living room, he left the family at the table. 'What are we going to do, James? The time is ticking away. I hate the feeling my daughter's life is now a ticking bomb, we need to pay them.'

'What did I say, Sarah? We pay them the money and we don't know if they will give us our daughter back. Let's see what DC Walker has to say about this ransom, we need to have faith in the police,' he said, cuddling Sarah.

'I do have faith in the police but my brother knows how to avoid the police, he's been doing it for most of his life. Only once he got caught, that was because of me. I gave them to the police, if I didn't give them to the police, this would never have happened.'

DC Walker walked back to the table, looking at them. 'Sorry about that, the police have been giving information about Gary McDonald. Donald has been spotted on Bedmoor estate walking to the shops, Glasgow police are checking the CCTV in the area. Also, Gary has been spotted in Watford, the woman said he was buying food. When the woman said Gary, he ran away from the shops. I have got a team searching the area, two reports from different areas. From my experience, one of these is fake. They know we are searching two different areas and testing us, but we always check everything.'

'I do thank you for doing your best, my brother is the best at avoiding the police. Where do you think Ellie is more likely?'

'I think Ellie is in Scotland, they know the area very well and have more connections. The car was found with her hair in it which they thought they'd got away with. Gary will have more eyes and ears, telling him everything. We are controlling more police up there now, but if they are in two different parts of the country, it will be harder to locate Ellie.'

'What if you had extra help? I can't believe I am saying this but it makes sense. What if Nick went to Scotland and acted as a normal citizen?'

Nick was shocked Mother was going with his idea, letting him go and help the police. This was his chance of helping out and getting closer to them. 'I am not sure about this, letting Nick go to Scotland would be dangerous. I would need to ask my boss, if they knew Nick was walking around, they would use two children against you, Sarah.'

'But you can trace him, leading Nick to them like bait.'

'Thanks, Mother, I am not a maggot fishing for fish. I gave

119

Mother the idea last night as I could get involved in the community, also, I am not a member of the police.'

'I can see the idea but you would be risking yourself. I will need to call my boss. Give me a few minutes,' he said, leaving the table and walking into the garden.

'Sarah, I thought you were against the idea. Using Nick would be dangerous, they could get two of our kids. Please explain and I will think about it,' James said, staring at Sarah.

'Imagine this, Nick doesn't look like a policeman. He can get information and blend in with the crowd, the police can help him with anything. I've seen it on television, tracking devices, emergency phones. What about giving Nick seventy-two hours to see how much digging he can do?' she said, holding onto James' hands.

'I am not sure, Sarah, putting Nick out there would be risky. Imagine if Nick got hurt by them and we never saw him again.'

'But, Katie, the police would have tracking devices to know where Nick is, I know this is hard for you, he's your boyfriend. I would not have asked.'

Katie kept quiet holding onto Nick. 'I would never put myself at risk if I knew where they were. I can get the police there quickly and not go in. How about I make a promise, I'll phone you every night once I am safe. Second, if I don't get anywhere after three day I will come home.'

Mother and Father left the table leaving the kids and Nan alone, no one talked at the table. Nick was a few moments away from going to Scotland, hoping his parents and police would agree. 'I would ask someone to come with me, of course, Katie, I would not go alone. I know the best person for this trip, Damon. Damon sent me a message a few days ago saying if I needed him, he'd be there.'

'I do get why you want to do this, sitting here doing nothing makes you feel useless. I am worried about your safety not knowing who is out there. I'd be lost without you if anything happened, you're my world, Nick.'

'I will always be safe and…' he was saying when the garden doors opened and his parents came back.

All three of them sat at the table staring at Nick. 'I have spoken to my boss about this and DI Watson agrees your help might come in handy. With this new note, time is ticking now whether they mean it or not. But it's down to your parents, even knowing you're over eighteen.'

'Thank you, DC Walker. Mother is it fine if I go and help out the police?'

'Me and your father have been talking about you going to Scotland, we agree you can help out the police but there are a few conditions. One, you ring us at least four times a day so you're safe. Second, you listen to the police and if they say that's it, you're out. Third, you take someone with you.'

'I will ring DI Watson and get you ready for Scotland.'

Midday had arrived with the house full of policemen, all with different tasks to help out Nick. The police agreed Damon could be Nick's partner going to Scotland, as Damon was strong and could protect him more if there was trouble. They were leaving in an hour, but waiting on DI Watson to come. Nick felt happy he was helping out but at the same time scared of what could happen if it went wrong. The last hour Nick was spending time with Katie making sure she was fine, Katie didn't want Nick to go but she knew this could help the family out, getting Ellie home. Jade was scared for Nick, leaving her upset. Since Ellie had been missing, Nick had been her help but he knew Katie would be there for her. Walking down the stairs, he left Jade in his room. Jade didn't want to say goodbye to him, she spent her time playing with Mickey. Arriving in the living room, he found his mother and father talking to DC Walker, two policemen sitting on the sofa, suited man on the phone and Damon waving at him. 'Ah, this must be Nick, I am DI Watson, before you go, we need to tell you a few things. You will not be taking your car, well, at first you will. You need to listen to us carefully to what we say, Nick.'

'Yes, I will listen carefully to what you say,' he said, sitting next to DI Watson.

'First things first, you need to wear this watch at all times. It's a normal watch but inside is a tracking device. This will show us where you are for the next three days. Next thing is this phone. There also a tracking device inside it, if you get into trouble or need to come out, dial 999. Don't talk, we have it registered so when you do press 999, we know your location. You can take your other phone but only use it at the hotel or where you will be staying.'

'Yes, DI Watson. What if I lose them both? What do I do next?'

'You will need to ring us, using your personal phone when safe to do so. We will work out why you lost it and if it is safe for you to go undercover again. You are getting three days to get anything information you need on Ellie, then report to DC Walker. You can't wear your fashion clothes, so we have arranged for normal clothes. They are in the boot of your car, which is on the back street where no one saw us. You're leaving at one so you will be in Scotland by night. The first night you will be staying in Bedmoor estate. We have undercover police around you. You won't know who they are but they know you and have seen a picture of you.'

'Is it dangerous staying there on my first night?'

'It's not as dangerous as it used to be, I would advise you not to go out at night, day time only. Here is a list of areas you need to check without being noticed. Any update on their whereabouts you will find out first. Last thing is, you will be leaving in your car and driving up north till you get to Birmingham. There you will switch cars to another one, we don't know if they know your car. Also, you can't be seen in your flashy car on Bedmoor estate, any questions, Nick and Damon?'

'Yes, I have one question, what happens if Gary sees me and I don't have time to use the phone?'

'We will have you on the tracking device, if you are in a place that seems dodgy, we will know and the police will be straight there. Any more?'

'Nope, I get the plan. First, we go to Birmingham for a car swap, then drive to Bedmoor estate where I be staying for one night. What about our second night, DI Watson?'

'We will plan it out as the day goes on, it's down to you to get information on Gary and his whereabouts.'

'Okay, one more question. What will happen to my car when I leave it in Birmingham?'

'We have a look alike which will drive your car home at dusk so if they are watching the home, they will see you here and not in Scotland.'

'Fine, can we go yet?'

Cuddling his mother, Mother wished him luck in Scotland. 'I will bring home Ellie before Mother's Day, promise you, Mother.'

Same with his father, holding on longer. 'I am going to miss you son, be brave and bring your sister home if you can.'

Katie hugged him tightly. 'Take care, honey bun. Message me when you can and there will be a surprise when you get home.' He kissed Katie loads.

DI Watson followed Nick to his back garden where Nick left through the gate, with Damon. He walked through the alley way and saw his car, opening his car when both stepped in driving off to their first stop in Birmingham.

Five hours into the drive, passing Blackpool the boys were only three hours away from Glasgow. Spending most of their journey on the motorway, it was boring, nothing to look at except cars and empty fields. The change over at Birmingham went straight forward, changing from his blue Audi to a fifteen-year-old Nissan. 'I'll say one thing about this car, it has a bit of speed,' Damon said, testing the car to see how fast it went.

'Be careful, Damon, the police have tracking devices on us. They might be able to see how fast we are going,' Nick said, putting his feet on the dash board.

'Nah, they can't do that I don't think, well at least the car does over one hundred miles per hour. We are stopping at the next service station for change over, that okay?'

'Yeah, that's fine, I had my little sleep. This drive is so long, why do people drive to Scotland when a train takes five hours and you're able to drink?'

'I would not even go to Scotland, what is even up here? It's always cold and rains most of the time,' Damon said, laughing at his own joke with Nick shaking his head.

'That is what every English person says about Scotland,

it's just colder up here they say. They have the Loch Ness monster, great whisky and a football league.'

'No, Nicholas, the monster is made up so people come and see a nice lake. The football is based on two teams which win so if you don't support them what is the point. When was the last team to win it without Rangers and Celtic? I give you the whisky one, most of the whisky comes from Scotland.'

Nick got his phone out, searching Scottish football. 'The last team was Aberdeen back in '84, so thirty-five years of the top two winning the league. That does seem a bit boring, also the only country which drinks iron brew,' he said as both stared at each other quickly.

'Have you ever tried iron brew, it's not nice. Back to football, I support Chelsea so we win cups every year. Also, different teams win the league back in England, did your mother tell you what team your family supports in Scotland?'

'No, she didn't tell me, I don't think that it is a question to ask her now. Both teams are based in the same town but Rangers is close to my grandparents' house.'

'While we are in Scotland and before we leave, we should see both stadiums and see which one is the best. No one can beat Stamford Bridge,' he said, laughing at Nick.

'I can't say much about it, Queens Park Rangers are okay they just need a bigger stadium. Oh, look, we have reached Scotland. Welcome to Scotland, wonder how many people can read Scottish Gaelic.'

'I don't think many people can and wasting money like the Welsh language,' Damon said as the boys entered Scotland and their journey started.

The boys were a few miles from Glasgow driving past nice

125

country lanes, hitting a few towns. The towns seemed nice, people looked after their houses. A few more miles into Glasgow they saw a different look. The town centre looked packed with shops, people all around. A few pubs were closed down and some boarded up. The closer they got to their destination it got worse, parks with teenagers playing in and hanging around. The houses got smaller with one in four boarded up. Nick looked at his notes to see where they would be staying. 'We are staying with someone called Hazel Rightworth, she works with the community to make it safe. Her address is Block D, twenty-one Walter Road. The satnav is saying we will be there in ten minutes. I am not liking this, it's not getting nicer. I hope my car will be fine.'

Damon looked at Nick in a weird way. 'Nick this is not your car. If they take the wheels, it be fine. I've seen it in films,' Damon said with a small laughter.

'Oh yeah. That's only in films they do that. As long as we stay safe and don't walk around in the night. I think we are entering Parkhead West, the estate is around here.'

The boys kept looking around when they both saw the sign, Bedmoor Estate. The first thing they both saw were cars been abandoned in a small car park, young men hanging around street corners talking to girls. Damon turned into the estate. The estate seemed run down, lots of grey buildings looking more dirty grey. Windows were broken in some of them, a few of them were boarded up as well. They could see people standing outside smoking in their dressing gowns, children running around on the pavements and roads. Damon was driving slowly, avoiding hitting the children, turning the corner when they saw two burnt-out houses. Passing the park with young men passing drugs to them, they looked around fifteen. The park had broken bottles everywhere, at the end of the park they saw men go into some park house. The satnav spoke to them saying you have reached your destination. The boys parked their car into the bay, opposite the park. Sitting in the car getting their things together, Nick said, 'I think this is a good spot.'

Looking over the park and the large grey buildings holding lots of flats, Damon said, 'Let's get inside before any one spots us sitting here.'

'True, Damon, remember we have to say Auntie Hazel when she opens the door. DI Watson told me in case we get anyone earwigging.'

The boys got out of the car, grabbing their bags from their car boot when Damon knocked on the door. Hazel opened the door greeting them.

Hazel was in her late sixties, with grey short hair. Her house was comfy, nothing too fancy just basic living. Sitting in their room for the night with the light off and staring at the block of flats. Their room was basic with two single beds and a wardrobe. 'So, from the plans DI Watson gave me, I think that top flat up there is where Billy King lived. He lived alone but lights seem to be on, I wonder who is up there now?'

'Maybe he had a flat mate, he might know a few things. What are we going to do tomorrow?'

'Just walk around the estate and see if anything is suspicious that we can tell the police about. I am going to ask Mother later where she lived and take a walk up there. Something might turn up, but I've got a feeling Ellie is not here.'

Looking out the window, he saw a guy passing drugs to

another man, the man passed him some cash. 'Why do you think that, Nick? Why are the police not walking the streets? They are dealing so easy. I thought your mother said it got better after her brother got put into prison.'

'Maybe when the main dealer goes to prison, their patch is free for the next person. I think the person who made the call about Gary made it up. Police might be scared to patrol the streets at night, I would be. Let's move to the front window,' he said as both boys moved.

The front window faced the park, looking pitch black but not the park house. 'Hazel, can you come up? We've got a question for you.'

They heard footsteps leading towards them then Hazel appeared. 'What is that house in the park?'

'That house belongs to the caretaker of the park, closed around ten years ago when gangsters took over and used it for selling drugs. Every night you hear all sorts walking to the house getting drugs. The police searched it a few weeks ago but they are still dealing from it. We've been asking them to knock it down but it's a listed building. Stay far away from it.' Then Hazel left the room.

'You're thinking I should go and have a look. We've got a list of faces and I've got a good memory. I will buy drugs but bin them after?' Damon said, looking at Nick.

'I am not sure, it's too risky but it's worth a risk if you want to go, but we are being tracked and they will know you walked to the house at night.'

'I promise I will be safe, or do you want to go?'

'I will go, Damon, this is what I wanted to do.'

He was leaving the bedroom, and putting his coat on when Hazel saw him. 'I'll be back in ten minutes. I'll be safe, Hazel.'

Hazel looked at him. 'I promised your mother I'd keep you safe. If you're not back in twenty minutes I will be calling the police.'

Nick nodded, walking out of the door and into the freezing night, it was colder up here. This is what Nick wanted to do and do some digging in the area, seeing the park house in the distance. His hands were shaking with fear walking to the house, coming closer to the house seeing how run down it was. He felt this was a bad idea, but it was too late to return to the house. After a few more steps he reached the house. The smell was strong. It was the smell of cannabis. He walked up the steps then opened the door. The inside looked like an abandoned house, broken chairs, tape on the windows with three men sitting on the sofa. 'What do you want? Class A, B or C, boy?' The man spoke to him.

'Class A, cocaine. Just enough for me and my mate.' Nick had controlled his shaking when the man stood up.

'You're a new customer, never seen your face round here before. Don't sound Scottish, it sounds like you're a Londoner. How do I know you're not the police?' The man stood up holding a knife.

'I am here visiting my Aunt Hazel, been long time since I've seen her. I hate the police, been stopped too many times,' he said as the man walked over to him with the knife.

The man touched Nick from the arms to his legs still holding his knife. 'You're clean. Class A, did you say? That'll be thirty pounds. I do take English money, boy. So, if you're from London you must have heard of that little teenager going missing.'

'Yeah, I heard about it on the television. Well, if you betrayed your family what do you expect? Gary knows what he is doing and I hope he gets what he wants from Sarah.' Nick hoped he said the right words.

The man threw him a small bag of white powder. 'I like your words. I remember a few months ago when Gary came here, he knows what he is doing. That girl will not survive after his little girl, his plan was to kill her anyway. I am here all night if you want any more.'

'Where is Gary now?'

'No one knows where he is but I can say, he is not in Scotland.'

'Thanks,' Nick said, leaving the house.

'Call me David, my friends are James and Henry. What was your name by the way?' Nick stood there not knowing what to say.

Nick remembered Hazel talking about her sister's children but couldn't remember if it was Calvin or Ben, taking a risk with one of them. 'It's Calvin.'

The silence in the room was killing him. 'Yes, I remember now. His mum is called Carol, nice woman she was. You be back soon,' he said as Nick left the house.

Chapter 11

24th March 2019

First night in Scotland was something different for them, waking up in a cold room. Something which the boys were not used to, it was colder up here than London. Looking out the window and seeing people leaving the park house, it seemed to deal drugs all day and night. It took Nick hours to sleep after last night's actions, but knowing it paid off. Was David telling the truth about Gary not being in Scotland? Was Gary in Watford, and Nick was in the wrong place? Nick spoke to DC Walker straight away with the news about what happened that night, DC Walker was disappointed about what Nick had done but it did help in a way. Nick turned around to see his phone ringing. 'Hi, Nick, it's DC Walker. The information was good, the guy you spoke to was David Gilford. He has links to Billy King, meaning he might have information on him. We have the police going to his house this morning, we can't arrest him for drugs due to you visiting him. Once you're out of there, we will arrest anyone in the park house, second thing was the CCTV in the area. There is no sign of Donald there, we are looking at Watford more but keep looking for any clues of where he could be. All good this morning?'

'Yes, DC Walker, no trouble from last night. I am going to keep my head down and see if any one talks to me. Does my mother know what happened last night?'

'No, I have just told her someone spoke to you about this. Your mother would pull you out knowing what you did last night. Any sign of trouble, you know what to do.'

DC Walker cut Nick off when leaving the room to get some breakfast, finding it weird being in somebody's house. Passing the other two rooms with nothing in them, Hazel did have a basic house. Entering the kitchen with a small table in the corner, Hazel was cooking bacon. 'I love the smell of bacon in the morning, I am sorry about last night but it did pay off. Can I ask you a question or two?' Nick went to sit down.

'Yes, you can, it's fine about last night. I called the undercover police to watch out for you so you had protection, I had no choice. You can ask me a question.'

'You said last night you had to protect me as my mother said, did you know her? You must have been in your twenties when you knew her. Why is your house very empty? Not being rude…' Hazel passed Nick his bacon sandwich.

'It's not rude, Nick, the reason is because I am moving near my sister Carol. Most of my things have gone all ready, I wanted to stay a little longer to help the police. I have been a part of this community for over forty years helping out anyone who needs it, this is the last thing I am doing to help them. I have been told if it gets too dangerous for me, I will be moved immediately. Your first question about Sarah, I have known that family since before she was born. I have always tried to look out for her. A few times when she was younger, I saw her at the shops and I would talk to her. A few times Sarah would come over to the house for dinner,' she said, standing up to walk to the kitchen cupboard.

'Here are a few paintings your mother did when she was

younger. Sarah was always happy till her mother died. I didn't see her for a few years till she got older, the day she reported her family, everyone on the estate was shocked in a good way about what Sarah had done. There are a few problems on the estate but not as bad as it used to be. What you're doing is a good thing to help your family, I can see so much of Sarah in you. You have her eyes, hair and nice personality.'

'Thanks, a lot of people say that. I want to bring my sister home for Mother's Day, it will be the best present for her. My family needs to be all together. Something that David said yesterday doesn't make sense. My cousin Lily McDonald, what happened to her? It's like he's getting revenge for that,' he said, sipping on his coffee.

'I remember what happened to her but can't work out why Sarah is getting blamed, she was gone after it happened. Lily got hit by a car on the estate, she was running in the road when a speeding car hit her. It was the most upsetting thing I've seen, that little girl had a full life ahead of her.'

'I need to find out more about this, what happened to the guy that hit my cousin?'

'Well, there was a search for the guy once he was on bail, his name was Steve. Steve didn't show up for court and has since been missing. Rumours here are that he was killed on the estate and they buried the body.'

'Wow, I heard so much dangerous activity on this estate about stabbings and murders. I am surprised people still live here, I think I will keep my walk safe. Any advice for me, Hazel?'

'Yes, only one, if you are caught or in danger. Run to the fields on the right of the estate, it will take you to the Main Street.'

He left the table with his coffee, planning his day on the estate.

Shutting the door, Nick and Damon started their walk around the estate, they started walking towards the end of the street. While walking they passed the park house which seemed quiet, with a few cars parked outside. 'Nice cars, I am not being funny but nice cars on the estate would mean drug dealers. What did you do with the drugs last night?'

'I gave them to Hazel last night, she passed to them to the undercover police. They are hoping to find fingerprints on them linking it to David. I may have got someone arrested. Also, he knows Gary so he might know where he is.'

They were going past the house when the path led two ways, one towards the block of grey flats and other one leading to another park. The guys decided to walk past the park with older kids hanging around. There were three young men, sitting on the bench as both of them tried not looking at them. 'I am guessing they are waiting for customers, what kind of people buy drugs this early in the morning?' They saw a woman in her late forties walking over to them. Clear as daylight, the woman handed them cash but he didn't see what kind of drug it was.

'Okay, I take it back. What is our plan, Nick?'

'Well, I was thinking we can go to the shop to buy a newspaper, it's a normal thing to do, I guess. But I think we have gone past the shops.'

Stopping, they turned back. 'Let's go back and walk back to the block of flats. At least it looks safe. Did you find out where your mother lived?'

'Yes, block B, three Carter Road. I want to have a look

later today.'

Walking through the estate, they found broken bottles smashed everywhere, needles in street corners when walking past a group of girls. 'Hey, boys, you free now to buy us some cigarettes? We will pay in sex or blow jobs,' they said as the boys stopped.

'Sorry, girls, we are not into that sort of stuff and you're all underage.'

'What boys turn us down? I am fifteen so nearly legal. The only boys that turn us down are gay boys, walk on, gays,' they said as they boys carried on walking.

'Wow, I am not sure if I am offended by being called gay or I that won't sleep with them. I have seen a completely different way of living. Do men actually sleep with young girls here?'

'From my mother's stories, that's what people do round here. I've seen it on television but never been spoken to like that. Me, gay? No. I think the shop is around the corner.'

Turning the corner, they arrived at the shop. The shop had it shutters down with the door boarded up, with a spray sign saying open. The boys walked in finding the shop keeper yelling at young kids, walking past them to pick up a drink and newspaper. 'Get back here, you little bastards, I will tell your parents.' Nick could see the shop keeper saying underneath his breath, 'What is the fucking point?'

Putting the items on the counter, Damon paid for them and walked out of the shop, seeing broken windows all over, the reason why the shutters were down.

Sitting in Hazel's kitchen, they were seeing if there was anything new in the newspaper, the front-page showing Billy

King as one of the kidnappers. Turning to page four, the headline showed 'One out of four caught':

Last night the police confirmed Billy King was refused bail and will wait in custody till his court case. Billy King pleaded not guilty to GBH on Irene West, kidnapping and false imprisonment on Ellie West.

Standing in court with no sign of emotion to the family, James West attended court on behalf of his family. Leaving court, James West didn't want to comment on what he thinks of Billy. The police gave an update on the case. The family received a note in the post yesterday saying they have seventy-two hours to hand over fifty grand. The police are confident that Ellie West will be found. The search is still happening in Watford and Scotland.

'The rest is nothing really, just repeating what we know already. I don't get how he can plead not guilty with all the proof the police have, at least he'll be with his dad and grandad in prison.'

Hazel brought in two coffees for the boys, sitting on the sofa behind them. 'How was your walk, boys? I still see you're alive so okay.'

'Yeah, it was good, saw a few drug deals, girls asking for sex for cigarettes and a shop keeper losing his hair on kids. I take it a normal day for the estate,' he said, looking at Hazel.

'Sounds normal, the problem is there is nothing for them to do. Kids aged thirteen upwards either deal drugs for their boss or ask men for sexual favours. I tried helping them but nothing works.'

Drinking his coffee which was too hot at moment, Nick said, 'I feel for them with nothing to do. I've got twin sisters and would hate them to do stuff like that, the way they asked was normal. Any man can take them and abuse them, like my Uncle Gary.'

'Gary was one of them, I saw on many occasions Gary taking young girls back for sex. He supplied them with drugs or what they wanted. I know you don't want to hear this but I am scared for Ellie being with him. I pray every day that the girl comes home soon.'

Nick felt sick in his stomach knowing what Gary was able to do. 'I hope Gary hasn't done anything with Ellie. That nonce, needs locking up for life. Drink up, Damon, we need to get back out there. Let's go out and get some lunch.'

Walking though the fields from Main Street, it wasn't that bad and there were nice people in the street. The fields seemed to be fine until you got closer to Bedmoor estate, you could see a few beer cans in the grass, empty wine bottles and cigarette boxes everywhere. The estate was making the rest of the town a mess. 'How can people make this much mess.? Even in London people put their rubbish in the bin. I can see we are back now,' he said, seeing a sign saying Bedmoor estate.

The boys walked under the bridge where a few young men were standing in the middle, walking past them without making eye contact. A few seconds after they were in the clear, Nick said, 'God that was scary. Even I was shaking walking past them thugs. How anyone can live here without being scared, I do not know.'

'I know what you mean, I can't wait till I can leave here but we've got no information today. We need someone to confirm if he is here or not,' he said, sipping his last bit of coffee.

'Where are we? Never been this bit of the estate before.' Both boys looked around.

'I know where we are, Carter Road. This is where my mother lived with my grandad, let's take a look.'

Damon looked at him with a suspicious look. 'Will this be safe, Nick? We are in a closed place where we can't run if we get into trouble,' he said, throwing his cup in the bin.

'Yes, no one knows who I am. As far as some know I am Calvin, also we need talk to people and see what they know.'

Damon agreed then they both entered block B, with a smell hitting them. The smell of piss. The floor was covered with rubbish and yellowish puddles in the corner. Nick pressed the button for the lift when Damon stopped him. 'Why are we getting the lift? It's in an old building and the chance of getting stuck is likely, can we take the stairs?'

'Such a pussy, let's get the stairs then.'

Opening the door to the stairs, they found more yellowish puddles on the stairs and needles in the corner. The walls had spray paint on them, till Nick saw one saying, McDonalds rule. Looking at the door numbers they saw a sign saying one to ten, arrow pointing to the left. Turning left to open the door to find his grandad's flat. 'This is where my mother lived, imagine living here twenty years ago and how it would have been. I wish my grandad was still here, I would talk to him.'

'We are both lucky we live in a nice area and houses, I don't like it here,' Damon said when a door opened.

They turned around to find an old lady staring at them. 'Get out of here now, I don't have any money so fuck off.' The lady was holding a baseball bat.

'We are not here for trouble, we are here looking for answers. We are good people and don't want to harm you.'

138

Nick looked at the old lady.

The old lady put the bat down looking at him, she looked at his face when stepping back. 'You should not be here, Nick, your family are at great risk. What do you want?'

'How do you know who I am?'

'You are a Sarah look alike, I watched her run up and down here when she was younger. I played with her and looked after when the police were knocking down that door,' she said, pointing at number three.

'I just want to know if you know anything about Gary and where he is? Have you seen him?'

Looking around, the old lady spoke quietly. 'Yes. Gary was here last month hanging around David and his gang. They hang around the park house, since the reports of young Ellie getting kidnapped. Gary has not been spotted round here. Come with me, Nick.'

The old lady closed her door when walking back to the stairs where the sign of McDonalds rule. 'Do you remember or know what happened here and why that stupid name is still there?'

'Is this where Lucy got raped by Gary? And John got killed by Donald?'

'Yes, Nick, that poor girl. Did nothing wrong and that man raped her here. The council keeps removing this but someone keeps putting it back. I will tell you one thing, get out of here. If I recognise your face then someone else will. All I know is that Gary has not been spotted for a month.'

The old lady walked away from them when two girls were walking up the stairs, Nick and Damon hid around the corner hoping not to be seen, when they were talking. 'I need to tell my mum to stay safe, David's gang are out looking for the

Nick boy. They are bloody angry right now, I can't believe he is here, he looks so cute.'

'What has Nick done wrong to them?'

'Well, I heard David got arrested on drugs and knowledge of that Ellie girl who went missing and…' Nick could not hear anything else as the girls walked away from them.

'Shit, how do they know it's me? We need to get out of here as soon as possible, let's look out the window and see if anyone is outside.'

Both boys went towards the window where they saw four people sitting on the wall on the entrance of the building, suddenly they heard a voice. 'Come on, Nick West, we know you're here. Doing dirty with the police, what a naughty boy you've been. Come and get your punishment.'

Moving away from the window, Nick got his phone out. 'You call 999 and don't talk. The police will know we are here and I'll call DC Walker. The phone was ringing when DC Walker answered. 'We are in danger. The estate know who we are, Damon has called 999. Can you get back-up? We are in my mother's old flat area,' he said, trying to calm down.

'Don't move, stay where you are. I will ring for back-up immediately. Do not move, Nick.' DC Walker hung up.

Damon was near the window watching the lads. 'They have moved on. If we run for the fields we can get away. Do you want to try?'

Two things were running through his mind, stay or run. What if they caught him, what would they do to him? 'I say run, I am fit but DC Walker said stay where you are. The police are on their way.'

'What if they come inside? We've got more chance running.'

Nick agreed, walking down the stairs, checking the windows each level they went down. No sign of them, they both reached the ground floor as Damon opened the door to find no one outside. 'Remember the way back to the field. If they get me, run, Nick. I can defend myself. If they get you, I will come back, yes?'

They both agreed, walking out of the building when turning left and seeing the field, it was near then he fought. They both started running when two guys jumped out in front of them holding a knife. 'Ah, Nick West, nephew of Gary McDonald. What a nice surprise, how is Scotland for you?' he said, walking around him keeping the knife near him.

Nick remembered two of the guys from the night before, James and Henry. Feeling scared with the knife near him, he looked at James. 'Scotland is all right, nothing special,' he said, trying to stop his hands from shaking.

Two more guys were walking towards them holding a knife, not knowing these guys or seeing them before. Nick knew running was out of the question. Fearing the worst with four knives near his body, he felt he was going to get stabbed by them. 'Last time I saw you, you were buying drugs off David. That was all good except the fact we know who Calvin is, silly boy. Calvin was a good boy, didn't do anything wrong but you never forget a face. A few hours ago, David got arrested by the pigs. We are not happy with that, anything to say, Nick?'

'I am sorry,' he answered, not knowing what to say.

'Then I saw a photo of you, in the newspaper the other day. There are two things we can do. One, we will take you to Gary so you can get killed with your sister but your friend dies first. Second, you both die here together. Not a great ending whatever happens, as they say life is short,' he said as the knife

141

got closer to Damon.

'Why don't you let us go, I'll say nothing and that's it. Simple solution, and no one goes down for murder.'

'Oh, boy, we run this estate. We will kill you here, no one would say anything. How about I ring Gary and ask him, he would love to know I got his nephew. Hold them both, Henry and Frank.' The man got something out of his pocket.

He pulled his phone out and started talking. 'Hey, Gary. You're not going to believe this but I have your nephew here, Nick. What do you want me to do? I can kill him where your family name is or bring him to you. It might be another reminder of Sarah for her.'

Standing there with three men holding a knife at him and Damon, the three men smiling at them showing their yellow black teeth. The only hope was the police. Where were the undercover police DC Walker talked about? 'That's fine, Gary, I will drive Nick to you. See you soon.'

Putting his phone back in his pocket and facing Nick, he said, 'Well, I have good news and bad news. I am not going to kill you, Nick, Gary wants to do it. Unfortunately, for your friend, his life is now dead. You can watch if you want, Nick, what is the verdict?'

Looking around wondering if the police were here yet, Nick heard a gunshot. Closing his eyes when falling to the floor and hearing the police in the background. Opening his eyes, the man who spoke to Gary was on the floor bleeding from his leg. 'Henry, take my phone and tell Gary what has happened. Run now.'

Nick didn't know what to do but stayed on the floor. 'Stand up, Nick, I am DC Hill. Both come with me immediately.' Nick walked with DC Hill.

Chapter 12

24th March 2019

A few hours later that day, Nick and Damon were in the hotel room in central Glasgow. Feeling better being off the estate and safe away from it. Damon was shaken up but felt good to be safe from Bedmoor estate. Lying on his bed thinking it could have ended differently, both murdered or watching his friend get killed. He was closing his eyes when he heard his phone ring, standing up to get it. It was his mother calling doing facetime. 'Nick West, I have never been so happy hearing your voice. What you did was a stupid thing, I could have lost you. Not only you, Damon as well. I am not sure what to think. Katie was worried about you when she heard.'

'I am sorry, Mother, but I was only doing what it takes to get Ellie home. I knew calling the police before I got outside gave me more chance. In the last day, I have managed to get people arrested for involvement in the kidnap and am getting closer,' he said, smiling at his mother.

'That is why I can't be angry with you, you got close to Gary's gang who are involved in the kidnap. Even DC Walker is impressed, we are waiting for an update on the three men who got arrested. The fourth man got away.'

'The only problem is, Henry who got away has given Gary the heads up. It was going well but then that happened.

How is Katie?'

'Katie is good, been a little ill since you've been gone. I am looking after her, she'll be down soon to see you. When the police were chasing the fourth guy, the guy threw the phone in the water. The main thing is, the police found the phone so they're hoping to get it working. The police hope they can get the last number he rang on it so they can trace the signal to where Gary might be.'

'Oh my god, I didn't think about that. So, we might know where Ellie might be soon.' Nick smiled knowing risking his life might have worked.

'Let's hope, the conference is not till later around nine with DC Walker. Did you manage to talk to anyone on the estate?'

'Yes, we spoke to an old lady who lived near you on the estate, it was number eight. The old lady knew you as a child.'

Mother seemed to be thinking about the old lady, 'Oh yes. Betty, I can't believe she is still alive. My father didn't mind me hanging around her flat, she was nice to me. How was she?'

'She seemed fine, walking well and in good health. She showed me the area where Lucy and John got hurt by Gary and Donald. There was a sign saying, McDonalds rule, it was horrible. It was like it was a happy sign.'

'Nothing surprises me with Gary, he will never change. Here is Katie.' Mother passed the iPad to Katie.

'I am proud of you, Nick, getting this far with the case. I was like your mother, angry at first but it has worked out for the best. Did Mother tell you I was feeling ill?'

'Yes, how are you feeling? I wish I could be there to help you. I feel happy with what me and Damon have done so far. I know it was risky but it paid off. How are Jade and Mickey?'

'They are fine. Jade was worried about you, the same as us. How did it all start?'

'Well, it all started by me buying some drugs, which I didn't use. That person was talking about Gary, the next day his gang caught us when James was ringing him. This is such scary work that the police have to do, I don't think this is the career for me. Damon is loving this, he's a bit shaken up after the knife threat but okay now.' He sounded happy with himself.

'Sounds like you're having fun, for me it's more nervous what is going on. I can't wait till you get back, I am missing some fun,' she said, winking at him in the camera.

'Maybe later, we can have a camera fun,' he said, licking his lips.

'Nick and Katie, less dirty talk while your parents are nearby, please,' Mother said as Nick laughed.

'Sorry, Mother. What are you plans for tonight, honey?'

'I am watching a film with Jade after DC Walker gives us an update. One of her favourites, after that we can facetime. What about you?'

'I am not sure, probably have a few drinks with Damon. Might try the different whisky as I am in Scotland, or watch an action film.'

'Don't you think you two have had enough action for one day, Nick? You men like action too much. Remember you're not real policemen.'

'I can show you if you want,' he said, winking at Katie.

'Nick, don't make me say it again,' Mother said as Katie laughed.

'I'll speak to you later, love you baby,' he said as Katie ended the facetime.

Putting his phone to one side when the door knocked, he got up again to open the door. It was DC Hill with Hazel. 'Can we come in?' He let them in.

DC Hill and Hazel sat in chairs as Nick sat on the bed. 'We have brought you your clothes from the house. Unfortunately, the car has been burned out by the estate gangs, so we will give you another one tomorrow. How are you feeling?'

'I am feeling good, happy the case is getting somewhere. Can I ask why it took so long for the police to come? DC Walker said they would come immediately,' he said, looking at DC Hill.

'They didn't, Nick, they were waiting around the corner. The four undercover police were waiting for me to say yes and go forward. We would never let you or Damon get stabbed, there were four undercover police with guns waiting to shoot them. We would have gone in sooner but when they guy said about ringing Gary, we knew we had to wait. Using the signal, we should be able to know where they are soon.'

Nick's mood changed a little knowing his life was less in danger, just waiting for the right move. 'Ah, I get it now, let's hope we get the results. When do you know when is the right time?'

'I just know, Nick, I had four undercover police waiting to shoot them all in the legs. That's what I am trained to do.'

'Fair enough, what will happen to you, Hazel? You can't go back there.'

Hazel looked at Nick and smiled. 'My time is up on the estate. I can't do anything else now, I am going to spend my new life with my sister. I am happy with the outcome, I hope you find Ellie soon.'

'One more thing, do you know where my grandad is? I want to visit him. This is a safe trip. If you want a policeman with me, that is fine,' he said, looking at DC Hill.

Sitting in the back of the undercover police car, DC Hill was driving him. He spoke to DC Walker before and agreed the plan, maybe his grandad knew a few things. Whether he was going to tell him was another story. Nick was nervous meeting him. Not knowing what he was like, and never seeing a picture of him when he was older. Mother said he was never happy, grumpy most of the time and would moan a lot. Wonder why he was never happy? DC Hill spoke to him about the last time she saw him and questioned him. Saying I don't talk to pigs, he was rude to her and she got nothing from him. Maybe with Nick going to see him, he might say a few things or slip up. The car arrived at the care home, looking all modern and clean. First time Nick had seen anything newish since arriving in Scotland. Stepping out of the car, she said, 'I will come in with you, but will sit in the staff room so he doesn't think I am here. Remember he will be rude, this is his fifth care home in three years.'

'That's fine, I can let things go over my head. Nothing he says will hurt me,' he said as they both entered the care home.

The electric doors opened and a middle age nurse stood in front of them. 'Hi, I am Hilda. I am the nurse in charge of John McDonald. John is in his chair at the moment in his room. He doesn't know you're here, all he knows is that he's got a visit from someone. John is rude most of the time, he can't move much so he can't get violent but the chair will be on the other side of the room. Are you ready?'

The both nodded to nurse Hilda, walking through the care

147

home smelling of flowers. His sisters said once that old people homes smell of wet feet, when they'd done their work experience. They walked through lots of rooms with older gentleman watching television, some sleeping in their chairs and one playing chess talking to himself. 'I will be in here, Nick. Put this voice recorder in your coat pocket. Anything you both say will be recorded. Good luck, Nick.'

Nick placed the voice recorder in his pocket, walking past a few rooms when arriving outside his room. Nurse Hilda walked back when Nick walked into the room, seeing a grey old man sitting in his chair looking at him. 'Hi, Grandad, nice to meet you at last,' he said, sitting on the chair which was uncomfortable.

'I don't have any grandchildren, only Patrick McDonald and you're not him,' he said, giving him the stare look.

'I am your grandson Nick, Nick West. My mother is Sarah, your daughter.'

John looked at him in disgrace. 'Ah, my disowned daughter. Whatever you want, I don't care and you're nobody to me like she is, now get out,' he said, shouting at him.

'I am not going anywhere, Grandad, whatever my mother has done it's got nothing to do with me. I am still family and didn't do anything wrong. I am here to see you and get to know you,' he said, smiling at him.

John looked at him for a while with no talking, pulling out the newspaper from his bed. 'This is why you're here, your sister is missing and you want me to tell you where they are,' he said, looking away from him.

'Why do you keep looking away from me? This is your granddaughter who is missing and you're not going to help us. What kind of man does that? Where is your family love?'

'Family love, your filthy mother abandoned her family to marry that man. Look at you, spitting image of her making me feel sick. The only blood I have left is Gary, Donald and Patrick. You're English blood, not Scottish. You have wasted your trip here so piss off back to London.'

Nick thought what his grandad said didn't make sense. 'How do you know I am from London, Grandad? I never told you also Patrick is dead like most of the family.'

Within seconds his face turning angry he spoke back. 'Patrick is not dead. You're a…' John stopped half way but continued.

'Yes, Patrick is dead, my mind plays games with me. I know you're from London as my son told me, why don't you fuck off to London, rich boy,' he said, picking up his cup.

Nick watch what he was doing in case his grandad was going to throw the cup. 'So, you've been taking to Gary since getting out of prison, I bet you know where your granddaughter is. For once in your life help us out, I don't think your mind is playing games with you. I bet Patrick is alive, you know everything that is going on,' Nick said, staring at him, making him angry.

Nick had learnt in making him angry. 'You're an evil boy, like your mother. I might attend your sister's funeral and say hi to my daughter. The day she left is the day you all died to me. Sarah needs to pay for Lily's death. Her fault she died.' He was coughing and trying to calm down.

'My mother left before what happened to her, she's not involved in her death, old man. Won't be long till you go, Grandad, sounds like you're dying. Tell me where they are, maybe things can change and imagine having us in your life. Your daughter back, four grandchildren to visit you.'

149

Sitting in silence looking at him, John sat looking out the window. 'Imagine, Grandad, sitting in the park with us, Mickey is only six so you can play with him. It would be so nice getting to know you, move to London and have your family with you,' he said, hoping his grandad would talk back.

'Playing the guilty card, are we, boy? People like you die where I am from. You're a backstabber like your mother, nothing you say will change my mind. Even if I did know where my son is, I would not tell you or the filthy pigs.'

'I was on Bedmoor estate last night, I was there less than twenty-four hours and got four people arrested, all linked to Gary McDonald.'

John looked at him with another disgraced look. 'Working with police, are we, boy? I get your game, wind me up so I say where they are. Not going to work, people like you are filth.'

'Well, Grandad, you did say about your favourite grandson being alive, also you know where they are. What's wrong? Don't like it that you have a grandson who is nice and wants to help people?'

John was getting angry when Nick saw him pick up his cup again and threw it at him. Nick ducked his head, missing him, kicking his table across the room and trying to get up. Picking up his walking stick but fell to the ground with Hilda walking in. 'I tell you something, boy, I can't wait to see the newspaper about your sister. Tell my daughter to have a nice life,' he said with nurse Hilda nodding at him to get out.

Walking to the staff room from to find DC Hill, he passed the voice recorder to her. 'Coffee, please.' Nick sat back in the chair. A few moments of silence when nurse Hilda walked in. 'Your grandad will be fine, nothing new with him. I hope you got what you wanted from him.'

150

'Yes, I did. How do you cope with him? Grandad is not normal.'

'You learn to deal with them. Good luck finding Ellie.' Nurse Hilda left the room.

Sipping on his coffee, he said, 'Grandad knows where they are but is not telling me. There is one thing he said, he kept mentioning Patrick McDonald. I've got a funny feeling he is alive somehow, he is the one you need to find.'

DC Hill sat next to him 'Why, Nick?'

'Gary and Donald are known to the police but if Patrick is alive, no one knows this. That is the key to find my sister,' he said, finishing off his coffee.

Back at the hotel, Nick was sitting next to Damon having dinner. Nick was telling Damon about his grandad and what happened. 'Wow, all this in two days. I think you were right to help the police out, even when we are stuck in bad situations. What is next for us?'

'How about a bit of resting from being action men, I need some rest. I have had a knife to my body and cups thrown at me in one day. Also, DC Walker will tell us, we are hoping to get a phone signal from Gary's phone. That is the massive clue, if Gary is dumb enough to stay there, they will get Ellie by the morning.'

'I hope so, also, we are in the time frame still, it's only been forty-eight hours. Let's go and pick a film for tonight, I smuggled some booze for later,' he said as the boys' food came.

The time was nearly nine o'clock with Damon on facetime with Nick's family for an update, pouring themselves a drink.

Damon had ten different kinds of whiskey for them to try, with Nick talking to his mother. 'I can't believe my father, he knows and won't help out. To be honest I didn't think you'd get anywhere with him. Not changed one bit at all. We are just waiting for DC Walker to come. At least this time it was in a safe environment.'

'Also, we may have another name out there, Patrick McDonald. I may be wrong but I've got a feeling he is alive. I am not sure how he's done it. I am happy we are getting somewhere now with Ellie. We've got twenty-four hours left to find her and we are getting close,' he said as his mother smiled at him.

'I am so happy I changed my mind about you going to help the police. DC Walker is impressed with how much you've achieved in so little time. I am proud of you, also Father is proud about how much you done in two days. I think DC Walker is here,' she said as she left the camera.

Nick waved at Katie and she was smiling back at him. It was a weird feeling seeing his family this way and not sitting with them. Jade waved at him with little Mickey pulling faces, making Nick laugh. Seeing them showed him how much he missed his family, he couldn't wait to get back home. On the camera was DC Walker sitting next to Katie, waving at him. 'I am sorry this is late for everyone but we do have some updates from Nick's work in Scotland. Good work so far from both of you, next time less dangerous situations,' he said, looking at Nick and Damon.

'We didn't mean to get in that situation, David's gang knew I was not Hazel's nephew. We are lucky we had the tracking devices also the support of the undercover police on the estate.'

'The main thing is you're both safe, right with the new people been arrested. David Gilford, we found nothing on the phone except calls from one number which is not registered. The drug bag you bought from him, had his fingerprints on it and he's been charged with dealing drugs. An hour later we raided the park house, finding three big bags of cocaine, two bags of cannabis and four bags of heroin. David's fingerprints were found on all bags, very good work Nick. Onto Ellie West, we have no proof he is involved in the kidnapping of Ellie. He will be charged with drug possession. The four guys that cornered you both have been arrested, the fourth guy got caught later that day. The guy that spoke to you, Nick, holding a knife to you was James Smith. James went straight to hospital after the gunshot but will be fine. We have recovered his phone, it's damaged but we're waiting for the phone network to release his call log. We should get this in a few hours, and he will be questioned tomorrow night.'

'What proof do you have on him to do with Ellie kidnapping?' Nick spoke to DC Walker.

'If we can prove from the network that James called Gary, he can be charged with accessory to kidnapping also his fingerprints are on the drugs, the last charge will be handling a weapon. James will be lucky to get out anytime in the future. The other three guys will be charged with handling a weapon. All houses are been search by Scotland police. DC Hill will inform us if they find anything. Last thing is your visit to John McDonald.'

Nick could see Katie and Jade's faces when DC Walker said their grandad's name. They seemed shocked by what he said. 'From my visit with him, I believe he knows where Ellie is but didn't say a thing. Grandad mentioned about Patrick

McDonald, his words saying he is not dead. I think the other guy who kidnapped Ellie from the car park is Patrick, it was like Grandad was proud of him. I know what you mean now, Mother, about him, he was rude about us as a family. Grandad doesn't care about us or who is killed,' he said, taking a sip from his drink.

'Your grandad will never change. Patrick is dead, DC Walker.' Sarah looked at DC Walker.

'Yes, on record he is dead but from the voice recorder Nick handed back to DC Hill, it sounds like he is alive. DC Hill is looking at his case at the moment, it was a two-man robbery job where the shop keeper shot one of the suspects. Two things can come from this, Patrick swapped his ID round so he is alive or Patrick was shot in the shop. DC Hill is getting the photos of the suspects with their criminal records. With your help, Sarah, you said the fourth guy was a younger model of Gary so I will show you the photos in the morning.'

'That is fine, DC Walker, if the fourth guy is Patrick that means three family members are holding Ellie.'

'It does sound that way to me, if Patrick is the third person that means he's been able to walk around us without getting notice. We have to wait for the report first.'

'They must really hate me to do this,' she said, crying into Father's arms.

'It would be perfect for Gary and Donald to have someone like that helping them, I am sorry. I will be in contact with new information as soon as I know. Nick and Damon, have a good night sleep. Just relax tonight till I ring you. All keep safe.'

Chapter 13

25th March 2019

The hotel breakfast room was quiet with Nick and Damon waiting for their breakfast, with two police officers near them. It was six in the morning with the sun rising in the sky, they had a plan to start early today. 'That was the best sleep I've had in ages, I love hotel beds. It's different from your own. Where do you want to start today?' he asked as the waitress brought over their breakfast.

'Well, I was thinking of searching the port where Gary had a few mates down there. Also, the caravan site which my nan told me about. After that I am clueless unless DC Walker has an update on the phone signal.' Nick was eating his bacon.

'This is the last day before they do something to Ellie, I promise you Nick that we will find her. I have been best friends with you since primary school, known your sister since she was little. Do you remember the day in school and the promise I made you: whatever happens, we will always help each other out no matter how dangerous it is,' he said, looking at Nick?

'I do, Damon, and thank you for your help so far, I would not have got this far without your help. I have no idea what we are going to find today, that guy James would not travel far if he was taking me to Gary. He must be around Glasgow? Where is my newspaper I asked for?' he asked, looking around still eating his breakfast.

'Who do you think you are, Nick, demanding things? You are not in London,' Damon said, laughing away.

'Well, I'm not allowed to leave the hotel till DC Hill tells me, I am now a wanted man putting five criminals away. I still don't want to be a police officer, too risky.'

'For me it's changed my views, I never wanted to be one but I might apply after we finish the case. I am being serious; originally, I wanted to be a fitness instructor but I want to help families and catch criminals,' he said, finishing off his breakfast.

Putting their plates to the side, the waitress passed them the newspaper when she cleared their plates. On the front page was an image of Nick. 'We have made the front paper with the four guys holding knives to us.' Nick showed Damon.

'Oh God, some scum bag took photos of it and sent it to the newspaper. How low can you get? They are saying the police are using us to get to Gary, what a load of shit. You offered to help them and it's working.'

Opening to page four and five, the press made a two-page spread of it.

Nick West and his friend were held with knives by four men from Bedmoor estate, the police only made it by seconds before they were going to get stabbed. Nick West is the sister of kidnapped Ellie West. What was he doing in a dangerous place where the police should be doing their jobs? A few people spoke to us about the attack. We knew Nick was in town acting on behalf of the police. What are they doing, losing another victim to the family? Police should be disgusted by what they are doing, using bait to get Gary to come out. The police have refused to comment so far on what is going on. Four men have been arrested for the knife attack on Nick with one suspect in hospital having been shot by the police. Why are the police shooting in a close place? The police are losing their self what is going on?

'This is all wrong, it's common sense why they don't know what is going on. If they knew it would blow my cover on the estate, since then I have helped them get closer to Gary,' he said, passing the newspaper to Damon.

'I am upset that I am only mentioned as a friend, I do have a name. Did you ever think you'd make the front pages of the paper?' he said, laughing at him.

'You are funny, I'll ring the newspaper and let them know who you are. There is more at the bottom.'

I am sitting here with a lady who saw what was going on: 'I lived near where Nick was staying. Nick was staying with Hazel who was helping out the police, there was also undercover police living here as well. You can tell by the way they walk, watching out for Gary. This is more than police work, Nick walked one night to the drug house. Buying drugs and working for the police, never trust police. Next morning, acting all innocent then that afternoon the park house gets raided, he got caught buying drugs so police had to act. It's corrupted by the police, this lad bought drugs and is he getting arrested? No. One rule for them and another for us.'

'Wow, this lady doesn't like you. We were helping the police, also we managed to get the park house raided. What does she want?' he said, passing the newspaper back to Nick.

'DC Walker will put this right for us. Me arrested for buying drugs? Maybe they should knock down that estate, that will show them. Let's get ready to leave, DC Hill will find me,' he was saying when a suited man was walking towards them.

'Nick West?'

'Yes, I am, how can I help you?' Maybe he saw the newspaper about him.

'DC Walker is trying to ring you; can you ring as soon as possible?' Both boys left the breakfast room to fetch their phones.

Entering Nick's room to find his phone, eight missed calls. This must be urgent, he thought when ringing DC Walker back. 'When did I tell you to leave your phone alone? Anyway, we have an update on your sister, we tracked where they have been hiding. It was in a forest in Watford, an old house they used to deal drugs in. Unfortunately, by the time we got there, they'd all gone,' he said as Nick put the phone on loud speaker.

'What do you mean they have gone? How can no one see it?'

'I am guessing the guy who got away with the phone, after the police shot James. A call was made from the phone within one minute to Gary's phone. The police are searching the forest for clues now, we don't think they got far.'

'So, what do you want us to do? We can go to Watford and look around.'

'Yes, that is the plan, we have booked you on the plane, leaving in two hours. The car will be outside in five. Any questions about this?'

There were a few but the newspaper came into his mind. 'Yes, in the newspapers I am front page. What will happen?

They are saying the police are using us as bait.'

'I have seen it and we will leave it, the press always write bad things about the police. There is no time to do a statement, we are so close to catching Gary and getting Ellie back.'

'Will me and Damon get a car so we can drive around town?'

'Yes, a car will be waiting for you when you arrive at London Heathrow airport. We have less than a day to catch them, every man we need to help and search the area.'

'We don't have our passports to get on the plane. How does that work as I have no ID as well?'

'It's police business so we can get you on your flight, see you in Watford.' Nick hung up on DC Walker.

'We've been searching the wrong area the whole time,' Nick said, standing up and kicking the chair.

Damon stood up, standing in front of Nick. 'No, Nick, last night's actions did it. If we didn't get ambushed by the thugs, the police would never know where Gary was. It was worth coming here, let's pack and get that plane back to England. I never thought I'd say that.'

Arriving at London Heathrow airport, they stepped off the plane with an undercover policeman. Walking through everyone, skipping the ques at passport control, showing his police badge and paperwork. This was the quickest Nick had ever been through the airport, walking past anything to declare, both of them laugh. They entered the main airport then arrived at the front to see daylight, the time was nine and back in London. 'This is your car, all the information is in the glove box. DC Walker wants to meet you first.'

The boys stepped in the red Vauxhall then drove off from

the airport. Nick felt weird being back in London, safer than being in Scotland. Only a few hours ago waking up in Scotland then driving on the M25. Watford was only thirteen miles from the airport. 'Imagine we are a few hours away from getting Ellie back home. I am happy that I joined you Nick on this journey, I see what you mean now by not sitting at home and doing nothing.'

'I am glad my mother let me do this, at first, she was a bit taken back by what I said. Just need an action plan now, less then twelve hours to go,' he said looking out the window onto the M25.

'What is the plan for today or are you waiting for DC Walker to tell us?'

'I am not sure, I think we should have a new plan. I think we should have a new approach to this, go and see some people who knew them. Go past the house they lived in and see what we can see.'

'What do you mean by that?'

'Knock on their door, ask them nicely what we can see from the top floor. After that my mother mentioned about her friend next door, she ran a café back when my mother lived here. Then I am not sure, someone must know about their life and where they did stuff.'

Turning off the motorway, they entered Watford. Bushley was just a few miles away where DC Walker was meeting them. 'This town is not bad, much better than driving into Bedmoor estate. Why didn't they stay here, but then Grandad loved his Scotland too much,' he said, looking at the street ahead.

'Also, Nick, you would not have been born. James would never meet Sarah, how history works. I remember once when

160

Natalie lost her mum last year, I was her rock. History is there for a reason and see how much couples go through to make them stronger, I can't wait to kiss her again,' he said, turning into the forest, finding police cars everywhere.

Getting out the car when DC Walker waves at him, he walked over to him to find his mother with him. 'Nice to see you here, Mother. What are you doing here?' he asked, giving her a hug and kiss on the cheek.

'Father said I could come and help the police on the search in the cabin. Father is at home with Jade, Mickey and Katie. I have gone in there but nothing where it could lead them. I am so proud of you what you've done so far,' she said, hugging Damon.

'I have always said, Sarah, Nick is like another brother to me. Always be here for him and your family, I am making sure Ellie is found today,' he said, smiling at Sarah.

'I know, Damon, thank you. How was meeting my father, Nick?'

'It was horrible, the way he talks about you. His own granddaughter and not caring, how can anyone act like that also the…' DC Walker stopped them.

'I am sorry to disturb you talking, we have the photos from Patrick McDonald's case. Are you ready?'

They all nodded walking towards the police tent, Nick was holding mother's hand when they reached the desk. 'I have here three photos, first two when they walked into the shop. The other one is the man dead. When you're ready have a look.'

Nick looked at the pictures with the first two looking nearly the same, only difference Nick could see was the earring being tiny. The other picture was a man who got shot by the shop keeper. 'I can't see any difference in the pictures. I am sorry, DC Walker.' Mother sat in the chair.

'What one is Patrick in the first two pictures, DC Walker?' He pointed to the first picture.

'The second guy is Finley Holland, since that day the Scotland police can't find him. Gone right under the radar, they think he went to Spain.'

Nick looked at the pictures when he noticed something. 'Look, DC Walker. In the first picture Patrick was wearing his small diamond earring, but in the picture of him shot dead, it's not there. Patrick is alive, Patrick is the third person.'

DC Walker looked at the pictures for a while then looked at him. 'You're right, Nick. Somehow Patrick managed to declare himself dead. I'll call my team now and let them know. Great work, Nick,' he said, patting him on the back.

He was walking away on his phone when his mother looked at the photo. 'You are suited for this job, Nick, you see more details than most policemen. Patrick must be trouble like his father.' Then DC Walker walked back over.

DC Walker put the photos in his briefcase then looked at them. 'We are getting a team to let the public know that Patrick McDonald is another suspect. Late last night we raided the cabin but it was left empty. We've got a team doing fingerprints on everything that was in there. We've got CCTV on them leaving this spot and getting into the car. We do know the car has not been picked up on the motorway so it's still in the area. We've got extra people searching the whole town's CCTV for this car; we will find them, I feel we are getting closer.'

'The phone call we got from the public about the sighting was true, we think it's Gary but he had his hoodie on. From the phone signal from his phone, and the CCTV image. Ellie has been in Watford the whole time.'

'Me and Damon have got a plan for the next few hours, can we come back here later and have a look at the cabin?' Nick asked, looking at DC Walker.

'I am not going to say no, you've both been great help to the case. Once this is all over, we will tell the press what we were doing, just ignore what they say. See you both soon, keep your watch on at all times.'

Parking outside his mother's old house looking better than Scotland, the houses seemed working class and looked after. Looking at each other when turning the engine off. 'So how are you going to ask to look out of the window? It's not a normal thing to do,' Damon asked Nick.

'The reason I want to look around is something I learnt in Scotland: Donald would only do business in one area. He would not leave it; his drug den was close by so he could see the police coming.'

'That does make sense in a way. Should we knock on the door?' Damon asked as they both stepped out and knocked on the door.

The door opened when an older lady in her late fifties opened it. 'How can I help you boys?' she asked with her chain still on.

'I am sorry to bother you but we need your help. I am Nick West and my friend is Damon Goldfield. My mother used to live in this house and we need to look out of your top window and see locations in the area.'

The old lady shut the door with Nick not knowing what to do next. 'That was expected. Let's go.'

The boys walked away when the door opened. 'I have seen your face in the newspaper. You're helping out the police. Come on in.' The boys followed the old lady in.

'That silly reporter this morning saying you're all trouble, you're only helping out your sister. What do you need from me, boys?' she asked, staring at them while smiling.

The house seemed cosy with flowered wallpaper, lots of cat pictures, glass doors and bright red carpet all around. 'We just need to look out the top window, we won't take much of your time.'

'That's fine, boys, go straight to the top, turn left and you'll be facing the fields and forest. I'll bring up a nice cup of tea for you,' she said as she went into the kitchen.

'She's nice. Let's go.' The boys made their way to the top of the stairs.

The red carpet went all though the house. When reaching the top, they opened the door to find an empty room. Walking across to the window and Watford in distance, the old lady's house was a three story where opposite was one story. This gave the view of the parks, forest and miles ahead. 'Looking right to left, there are a few parks with a few buildings but they seem to be used. The forest is huge but the police are doing that. What is that over there?'

Looking closely, Damon said, 'I think that is a golf course, Nick. It has a few outbuildings but they look run down, that's it really.' Then the door opened.

'Here is your tea, boys. I overheard you talking about the golf course. My husband used to play it before they built the new building, never was the same, he said.'

'What happened to it, it's still standing?'

'It's used as a hire hall now, lots of parties mainly. Have you spoken to next door yet, Nick?'

164

Nick was confused by the old lady. 'Why would I talk to next door?' he asked, sipping on his tea.

'Next door was Sarah's best friend Daisy, she never moved. She lives with her mum taking care of her. They might know some questions you're looking for. We were talking the other day about Sarah living here with her parents.'

'Are they in now? It'd be good to chat to her. You have been so helpful.'

'No, they both still work at the café. It's at the end of the road if you want to go now and catch her.'

They both cuddle and kiss the old lady on the cheek when running down the road to meet Daisy and her mum. Nick had a good feeling something was going to come out of this. Within a few minutes they arrive at the café. It was a typical café with standard wooden chairs, chalk boards and a fish tank along the edge. Opening the door when a lady was standing in front of him, hugging him and holding his hands to the table. 'You can come over, Damon. When I saw your face, I had to hug you. What you're doing is amazing. I forgot to say I am Lisa and this is my daughter Daisy.'

Nick took a few minutes before talking back. 'You must be the lady who looked after my mother and played with Daisy. It's nice to meet you. I am doing what any brother would do. How well did you know Gary and Donald when they lived next door? I am sorry if I'm asking straight away. We don't have much time, that's all.'

'No problem, Nick. I saw your mother earlier today. She is an amazing woman, four kids and great husband. My husband at the time knew they were trouble when they moved in, I didn't really know Gary much. He was in prison for most of it, Donald was a weird character. Also spent his time in the forest. My husband walked the dogs and saw Donald in there a lot.'

'Is that the part the police are searching now? My mother was in the café this morning?'

'Daisy, can you make us some coffees, please. Yes, she did. Sarah was driving past and saw I still had the café. It was nice seeing her. What she is going through breaks my heart. Her own family doing this to her. Sorry, back to the question. Yes, the police are now searching the forest, there were a few times Donald used to deal drugs at the golf club, at the old building not new one. My husband played golf there and caught him, he once threatened to hurt him if he said anything.'

Sipping his coffee, Damon spoke. 'When was the golf club last used? Who has keys to the building?'

'It was two weeks ago, big Irish party. Went on till four in the morning. I remember that day as all of them had full English breakfast. I tell you something, best day of making money. Since then, it's been empty, I can see it from my window. The building is so nice and belongs to the community. I am sorry again. I do go on when I chat,' she said, drinking her coffee.

Both smiled at her. 'That's fine. Have you seen any lights or movement in the night since yesterday?'

'I was looking last night when the police were in the forest, the only lights came from the police. The building is also secure and security guards walk around at night. I believe Gary is still in the area. Keeping it close to Sarah. Any more questions? I need to go soon for an appointment.'

Nick looked at Damon, shaking his head, 'No, Lisa. You've been more than helpful and I think we're going to check it out. I'll be here tomorrow for my breakfast, Lisa,' he said, smiling at her.

'If you come in, you both have it on the house,' she said

as they were leaving the café.

On the way out, a man grabbed his arm. 'Here, boy. The golf club is closed down due to roof leaking and rotten floor boards. If you take a look, be careful. We don't want you getting hurt when your sister is missing, she needs you. Well done and good luck.'

Chapter 14

25th March 2019

Driving back to the forest where the police had cornered it off, going to the cabin then the old golf house. Their plan was to search the cabin, even knowing the police had searched already. 'So, having little information on Gary's whereabouts, what are you expecting from the cabin, Nick?'

'I have no idea, to be honest. If the police have found nothing then I will not,' he said, finishing off his sandwich.

'You will, Nick, you find the smallest details and it leads to new places. I have faith in you, I am surprised your mother is here. That Lisa was nice giving us free lunch.'

'I think Mother is here for Ellie, the police must be confident to find her today. Look ahead, Nick, the press are here,' Damon said as they drove past the press.

There were four to five people with cameras behind the police. Driving up to the car park entrance when the policemen opened the gate, driving in when the press was taking pictures of them. Stepping out of the car, the press continued taking pictures when stepping into the tent. DC Walker was talking to three men in white suits. While they both waited for DC Walker, both boys stepped outside smoking a cigarette. 'Do you think the press will ever give up? I know it's their job to get a story but at least get it right,' Damon said, staring at them.

'Imagine if the police told them everything that was going on, the criminals would have an easy time. Do you think we will have to wear the white suits?'

'I am thinking we will. Always wanted to do that. Me and Natalie wanted to have sex with them on, you know, trying something new,' he said as Nick laughed at him.

'What is wrong with normal sex? Is that a crime scene how to find her special part?' he said, putting out his cigarette.

'Funny.' They both walked back into the tent.

DC Walker was sitting at the desk when he saw them both. 'Any luck, boys, this morning? We got a few roads where the car drove to but now at a dead end.'

'Same here, nothing new, might have a place to search later but will let you know. Can we go and have a look in the cabin?'

Looking at his paperwork then he looked up. 'Yes, that is fine. They have finished in the cabin so you can have a look. If you go searching, I would like you to take a policeman with you. It's more for your protection also the press think we are not doing much after what happened in Scotland.'

'We are both fine with that. Have there been any more letters or messages from them? Our time is running out,' Nick said, sitting on the chair.

'No, there has been nothing yet. I need to do a statement to the press about what's going on. I am going to mention about you two helping out with full protection wherever you went. Before I go, I can tell you that no blood was found in the cabin. We found DNA of Gary McDonald, Donald and Ellie, blonde hair was found on the floor. As there is no sign of blood, we are confident that Ellie is still alive. Walk into the forest, follow the police tape so you don't get lost. It's a one mile walk to the cabin; it was well hidden with trees and weeds growing around it.'

DC Walker walked out of the tent, going over to the press. The boys left the tent going into the forest. 'Wonder how long it will take us to walk one mile.'

'Well, Damon, how about we run to the cabin. We haven't done much running since we've been on the case.' The boys started to run into the dark forest.

Running closer to the cabin, the trees got closer together, the path got muddier with them running on the edge. Seeing another white tent when a policeman stopped them. 'You can't be running around here, this is a crime scene. I will get someone to walk you back,' said the policeman as he stepped out of the tent.

'We are not runners, I am Nick West and this is Damon. We are helping out on the case. DC Walker sent us to have a look in the cabin.'

The boys stared at him, as he went off to talk on his radio. 'What is his problem? The whole area is taped off so how could we be runners?'

'Remember he is doing his job, Damon. He is a bit of a prick giving us attitude.' The policeman came back.

'Walk this way boys. You will need to get changed into these white suits. The cabin is in front of you. Once finished, put the white suits in the bin,' he said, walking out the tent when another policeman joined him.

The boys were changing when overhearing the policemen. 'I tell you something, that DC Walker is mad. These two boys don't know a thing. We have years of experience and have found nothing. I tell you one thing, they're both lucky they survived Scotland. I would have done a better job.'

Damon saw red when he spoke to them. 'What is your problem? You think you could have done better? You got this far because of us. I trust DC Walker with my life. Is that why you're standing there doing nothing?' he said, walking back into the tent.

'Fucking twats. Let's go and see what we can find,' Nick said, leaving the tent.

The cabin door was hanging off with weeds growing everywhere on the outside, walking in, finding two broken beds and a bottle of whisky broken. The smell off piss was everywhere in the cabin. 'How the hell were four people sleeping here? Two beds, I bet you Ellie slept on the floor, poor thing. Maybe there is nothing here about where they have gone next.'

Nick was walking around, kicking the newspaper under the bed. Looking on the floor when stepping back, he heard a crack, with his hands moving the mud around. In his hands was a mobile phone. 'Call DC Walker, don't tell them idiots.'

Damon spoke to DC Walker as Nick pulled off some panels. Nothing. Under the bed was an old newspaper, pushing it to one side when Damon spoke. 'DC Walker is coming now. What date is that newspaper?'

Nick picked up the newspaper with the date showing twenty-fourth of March. 'The paper is only two days old. Nothing we can take from it,' he said, throwing it into the corner. Damon picked it up, skipping though the pages.

'It's not time to read the sports page. Remove some wood panels,' Nick said but Damon kept skipping the pages in the newspapers.

'Oh, Nick, this is a local paper. There is a page missing from the newspaper, you're missing a clue, Nick. On the front page is the building of the golf course, it says turn to page sixteen. The page is missing, why is it missing?'

Both in silence thinking when DC Walker walked in. 'This is great work, Nick. This is a modern phone, so must belong to Patrick, what else have you found?'

'Nothing really but something to do with the newspaper, it's missing a page. I think we need to check out the golf course near here.'

'That is fine, Damon, great work, both of you. I need to get the team back in here, you can take one of them policemen with you at the entrance of the tent. I need to get this checked out straight away,' he said, leaving the tent.

'DC Walker, we'd rather have different ones. They were rude and saying all sorts about us,' Nick said, staring at him.

'Yes, that is fine, come to the car park where I will find someone to go with you. I do understand what you mean by them two,' he said, leaving the tent.

Both boys got changed when leaving the tent and making their way to the car park when Damon turn around to the policemen. 'What did you say, we don't know a thing? We've been doing this for three days and have found more out than you standing there for thirty minutes.'

Waiting near their car for a policeman to watch them search the golf course when DC Walker saw them. 'Good news. The phone works perfectly and from one of the messages, it's Patrick's phone. He has made lots of phone calls and messages so the team can find out who the messages are from. PC Moon will be joining you on the search. Any signs or you see them, call me and we'll be straight over, do not enter the building. Good luck, boys,' he said as a policeman was walking over to them.

'Pass the keys, I'll drive for you.' Damon threw the keys to him.

The golf course was only a few streets away from the cabin when PC Moon spoke to them. 'When we get there, let's try and stay near each other. There is a possible chance Gary might be there.'

The boys agreed looking around when seeing the new golf house, double the size compared to the old one. Driving round the house, they were stopped by the guard. 'I am PC Moon, I need to search the old golf house,' he said, showing him his police badge.

'You will need these keys; they open the doors to it. I had a walk there less than two hours ago, it was all quiet down there.'

Driving down, passing the golf course where there were a few people playing golf. 'Once I get old, I want to play golf, it seems nice and quiet.'

'You playing golf, Nick? I've seen you play crazy golf and you're rubbish. You will need a few lessons,' Damon said, laughing at him.

'Crazy golf is different to this. I don't take it seriously with crazy golf. I see what the old man said in the café; the roof is in a bad state,' Nick said as PC Moon parked the car.

Stepping out of the car, looking at the old building. 'Let's all walk round the building, we are checking for broken doors or windows. You can tell the difference of break-in or old age.'

'Yes, PC Moon.' They all started to walk round the

173

building.

Starting with the main door, Nick tried to open it but it was locked. Staring in to find broken chairs and tables. Moving round to the next window finding the bar, an empty bar with dust and empty bottles of beer. Round the side was a fire exit when Damon pulled it, it was locked. The weeds were long round the back with empty gas bottles on the floor, four big red bins with a broken window. Nick looked in to find an empty room with muddy foot prints, they seemed fresh to him. Nick called PC Moon to have a look. 'They are fresh prints. They seem to come from here when they climbed in. Let's look some more.'

Damon went ahead when Nick found something covered up. He pulled the cover off to find a car. PC Moon looked at him. 'This is the car that they used last night. Keep calm, I've got a funny feeling that they are inside. Where is Damon? I will call it in. Move from here to somewhere in the forest,' he said when Nick heard a gunshot.

Standing still with his head thinking, *where is Damon?* he turned his head to find Damon at the end of the house standing. Turning his other way to find PC Moon on the floor bleeding from his stomach. 'Move one inch or try running, I will shoot you, Nick.'

Hearing footsteps from the forest, Gary McDonald walked out with the gun pointed at him. Feeling nervous about the situation, Nick just listened to him. 'Who else is here?' he asked, pointing the gun to his head.

'It's just me and the policeman, I promise you. Don't shoot me, please.' Gary laughed at him.

'Shoot you, boy? Nah, not yet. You can meet your sister first then I'll shoot you both.' Nick fell to the ground.

Opening his eyes with a sore head, touching his head with his hands feeling blood. Sitting up to find a small light on, the room was cold, broken chairs, kegs in a row and Ellie. Ellie was next to him tied up. His sister was alive! Her clothes were muddy all over, her wrists and face covered in bruises and her hair dark blonde. 'How you doing, Ellie? We've been looking for you all over. I am here now,' he said as Ellie cried on Nick's shoulder.

'This is the worst thing in the world to happen to me, they have been evil. Gary is the worst one, did you know Gary is our uncle? Our other family name is McDonald,' she said, leaning on Nick.

'Yes, Ellie, Mother told us all about them the other night. They are more than evil, they don't deserve to live. If you think they are evil, I met our grandad. Oh my god, he is worse than evil. I need to know one thing from you. Gary is known for having sex with young girls. Did he touch you or anything?'

Ellie looked away before answering Nick. 'No. They have tried to do stuff but I keep kicking them when they tried sexual acts. Patrick won't try any more after I kicked him in the privates, but Gary keeps trying. I was so scared, I want to go home and see my mother.' She was crying again on his shoulders.

'I am glad they didn't do anything. I heard things what they did to girls on Bedmoor estate.'

'Where is Mother? I want her now. I've been so hungry since they kidnapped me. They're feeding me less now. I feel so weak, when we moved last night, they had to carry me. I need to get home.'

'We will get out, Ellie. I need to think of a plan but at the

175

moment I don't have one,' Nick said with Gary and Donald looking at them.

'Ah, look at them, I did hear you were in our old town. I am surprised you made it out alive, working with the police as well. That is more of a disgrace to the family than Sarah reporting us,' Gary said, kicking Nick in the stomach.

The pain was bad with his head on the floor. 'I also heard my sister is in town. I would love to meet her and show her the pain I have been doing to her. We do have a little problem, because of your police friend we have the police coming so…' A young man ran towards them.

Nick looked up, seeing Patrick McDonald. 'I can see police coming towards the house. What are we going to do, Dad?' he asked, looking concerned.

'Why did you shoot him? You're an idiot. We were lucky last night and now the police are here.' Donald pushed Gary to the wall.

'What was I supposed to do? That pig saw me holding the gun. It's fine, relax. We are going to plan B, get these two on the ground level. I am going to show the police what I want,' Gary said with Nick looking at him.

Gary pulled up Nick by the ties which dug into his wrists, causing pain. Ellie cried as Patrick picked her up when walking up the stairs. When they reached the ground floor and standing near the doors leading to the golf course, Nick could see blue flashing lights coming closer to the house. He knew it wouldn't be long till the police raided the house. Ellie was placed on the other side of the room when Gary picked up Nick by the ties which this time caused more pain but he felt it was a bit loose. 'Come with me. Get out of line or run away I will shoot you. I am very skilled at shooting people. Do you understand, Nick?'

Nick agreed when Gary opened the door to find over fifteen police cars, fifty police offices looking at him. There was silence for a few minutes before Nick heard a voice he knew. 'Let the hostages go. Put your hands in the air and place the gun on the floor.'

Nick felt the gun pointed at his head. 'Nah, I don't like that idea. This is my idea: I want my fifty grand within one hour or I will shoot Nick or Ellie. Oh, yeah, I want Sarah West to bring the money to the house.'

Staring at the police, there was nothing Nick could do. 'Just let the hostages go and we will do what you want. I am throwing you a phone so we can talk about this.' One of the police officers walked over throwing the phone near them.

'Get the phone, Nick. Run away and I will shoot.'

Nick got the phone, bending over and picking up with his hands tied up. 'No, I want fifty grand from Sarah then I will let one of the kids go.'

Gary pulled him back with the gun at his head, walking up the steps when Nick saw Gary point the gun in the sky and shoot up. 'I will shoot him within the hour.'

There were thirty minutes left before Gary wanted fifty grand which Nick didn't know how he was going to get away with the money. Nick was placed next to Ellie, making her feel better, his ties were getting loose the more he moved his hands without them noticing. 'So, Nick, let's have a little chat. You have been really clever getting the police here which is not a great thing,' Gary said, pulling up a chair still holding the gun.

'I am not sorry about this, Gary. I want my little sister home within the hour and you back to prison,' Nick said, staring at him.

'You are a McDonald in there somewhere, brave. When I was your age, I was all about family but you're stupid. I hate the pigs. You brought them here so you will have to pay.' Donald and Patrick sat near him.

'Looking at you, Nick, is like looking at my sister, not a pretty sight. Should we tell him yet, Donald?'

'No, it's too early and we don't want to spoil the fun, we are waiting for Sarah.'

They laughed all together. 'How is your girlfriend, Nick? I was so close to getting her, pulling such a stunner. While you were in Scotland, I was watching her around university,' Gary said with his gun pointing at him.

'Why would you want to kidnap her? She has nothing to do with us. Doing my research, it's about my mother and betraying you. All because my mother handed in the knife, also the Lucy case.'

Kicking the chair across the room, waving his gun at Nick, Gary said, 'Yes, my sister did betray me in the worst possible way, yes, I did rape Lucy. That silly old man was reporting on my family, the only punishment was killing him. Lucy wanted me to have sex with her. The girls always wanted sex with me on the estate, then your mother saw me. Lucy bought drugs off me, and had no money, she knew she had to have sex with me.'

Nick knew Gary was lying. 'What a pack of lies. I have seen the case notes on Lucy, there were no drugs in her body at all. You pinned her down while she was crying, looking at my mother. You're disgusting doing that to girls, you do know there is a name for people like that?' Nick saw Gary's hand coming towards him.

Gary punch him in the face when hitting his head on the

floor, getting his head up after a few seconds. 'So brave, West, but stupid. When are you going to learn to shut up? As your cousin, Nick, I think I might need to teach you a few things,' he said, picking up Nick by his ties.

Patrick punched him in the stomach, falling back to the floor, standing Nick up again when he heard a phone ring. 'Patrick, I think you should talk to the pigs,' Gary said, chucking the phone to him.

Patrick answered the phone just listening. 'No, we don't, we want Sarah to bring the money over. What are you idiots out there? I will remind you I will shoot one of the kids if you don't listen.'

Patrick pulled up Nick from the floor, his hands were getting loose and he was able to get one hand out but waited. Walking towards the doors with the feeling of the gun to his head, Gary walked in front of them leaving Donald with Ellie. 'We want the money with Sarah, now. Or I will shoot Nick in the head.'

Within a few minutes Nick should see someone walking over to them. It was his mother. 'Patrick, take Nick near the door but not inside. I will deal with my sister,' Gary said, walking back to the house again.

Nick was watching his mother get closer with Gary, pointing the gun towards Nick. Was he going to watch his mother get shot? No, Mother was walking towards him to the house. Patrick pushed Nick to the floor again with his arm in pain. Nick saw his mother walking into the house with a bag when Gary slapped her across her face, making Sarah fall to the floor. 'You have been a very silly woman, now the party can start. Tell me, little sister, what one of your kids should I let go? Remember, make the right decision, the other one will

179

die. I am sorry but this is payback.'

'You can't make me choose what child I want to die, that is cruel, Gary. I will not choose.' Gary was walking around holding the gun at his mother.

'Sarah, Sarah, Sarah, it was such an easy choice. Do you want to save Nick or Ellie? If you want, I can help you. Nick is the oldest child, or Ellie but then you do have another twin at home.'

'No, I will not choose, Gary,' she said, losing his temper.

Mother was screaming in pain when Gary picked her up with her hair, putting Sarah in front of her kids. 'Choose or I will shoot one of them right now so you lose both kids.'

Nick looked at his mother, nodding his head slightly to say Ellie. 'Okay, Gary, let go of me, I save Ellie. Let her go.' She was crying when saying Ellie's name.

Gary picked up Ellie when cutting her ties. 'Run, little girl. It was nice seeing you, little niece.' Ellie ran out of the house.

'Now, let's have some fun and see your son die,' Gary said, smiling at him.

Chapter 15

25th March 2019

Gary tied up his sister next to Nick, with Patrick keeping watch. Donald was sitting in the chair watching Nick, his hands were loose now but still not sure what to do. If Gary was only using the knife, it would've been easy to get away but the gun was a little harder. 'You're not so little now, Sarah. How was your new life when you put us in prison?' Donald got up walking over to his niece.

'Of course, I am not little any more, Uncle, I have grown up and it's not my fault you were put into prison. Maybe next time don't commit the crime. I made a life for myself.' Nick saw his mother rolling her eyes at Donald.

'Don't roll your eyes at me. I always told your father every time you did that, he should hit you. John never did and look at you now, all this is your fault. Spoiled little brat, you were.'

'Don't talk to my mother like that. Hitting children doesn't get you anywhere. I am surprised you're doing this; you're old now. What is wrong with calming down and relaxing like a normal person?' Nick ignored the shaking in his leg.

Donald kicked Nick in the leg when holding in the pain. 'Not too old to be kicking you, boy. Respect your elders.

You're the same as Sarah. No control and mouth like a razor blade. I think I need to teach you a lesson,' Donald said when leaning over him.

'Stop, Donald, we still need him. Get back on your chair, I am leading this operation and do as your told. Right, next part of the plan, shut up and any movement I will stab you in the leg,' he said, pulling Nick up.

Gary walked over to the door, putting the gun next to Nick's head, walking to the top step. 'Who is your boss, Nick?'

'His name is DC Walker.'

'Where is DC Walker? I am prepared to make a deal for the release of both hostages.'

A man was walking towards them. 'I am DC Walker and in charge of this operation.'

'So, you're in charge, thank you. I am the one with the gun. I will end all this if you get me a car with no tracking devices on it. I need to get away with my cash, I don't want the police to follow me but Nick will be coming with me. Once I am far away, I will let Nick go and that's the end. Do we have a deal?' he said, smiling at him.

'What about your murder of the policeman early today? We can talk about this and reduce your sentence.'

Gary pointed the gun at DC Walker. 'What a funny man you are. There is no way I am going back to prison. You will have to find me first. I want a car, within two hours or I will shoot Nick. You know my criminal past; I killed more people than I have children. I am no idiot but if anyone goes in the golf house, another reason I have to shoot him. Do we have a deal?'

'Yes, we will find you a car. I will ring you once we have one.'

Nick was walking backwards with the gun at his head again. DC Walker looked at Nick before they entered the house. 'You are a good boy, Nick, I was thinking you were going to be trouble like your sister. Get back on the floor and shut up. Patrick, watch him while I go for a piss,' Gary said, leaving the room.

'So, cousin, it is weird for twenty-one years we never met. Imagine us being friends back in Scotland,' Patrick said, sitting next to him.

'You're dead, remember, you got killed in a shop that you burgled. You left a little detail in the photos. I don't have cousins on my mother's side and it won't work out.'

Standing up with the gun pointing at him, Patrick said 'The police don't know I am Patrick McDonald. There is nothing linking me here. They know it's Gary and Donald, the police need to work me out. What have you done?'

'I have done nothing wrong, Patrick, or your fake name, Finley. I have told the police it's Patrick McDonald, who the third person is. You were wearing a small earring but the dead man on the floor was not. Small details, Patrick. So, the police know you're here too.'

Walking around the room when Gary appeared. 'So, Patrick, how did you fake your death and get away with it?' Nick asked, looking at them and out-smarting them.

'Patrick, what is wrong?' Gary stopped him walking up and down.

'We can't get away with this, the police know who I am because Nick found a small detail. It was the job I did with Finley,' Patrick said, putting his gun on the table.

'You're going to tell me, Patrick, how you did it?'

'Well, I swapped wallets with him after the shop keeper

shot him. My mum made me move to Spain for my protection from the police. Only came back to help my dad get revenge on you lot.'

Gary and Patrick walked up and down while the gun was still on the table. 'Shit, this was one part which could not fail. How can you get away with the cash if the police know who you are? The forest behind us is covered, and the front. How the hell I am going to get you back to Spain?' Gary picked Nick up and threw him at the wall.

'That is it with you, snitching on your own family to the pigs. You need to be taught a lesson,' he said, picking up Nick again.

'Stop, Gary, this is about us, and your sister. Nick's just been a snitch to the pigs like his mother, put him down.' Donald was holding onto Gary.

Gary put Nick next to the table when punching Sarah in the stomach, looking to his left was the gun. On the floor was a gap, looking closer, it seemed to be rotten wood. Standing up when Patrick saw him, running towards him when Nick knocked the table over when the gun fell on the floor. Patrick went towards the gun when tripping on the broken chair when the gun fell down the hole. 'What you doing? You idiot, that was my gun. Now you're going to pay for this.'

Patrick punched Nick in the stomach over and over again till Gary pulled him off. Nick was with his mother holding his head. 'We'll both go and get your gun. Donald, watch them,' Gary said, passing Donald his gun.

Mother whispered to Nick. 'What are you doing, Nick? Wait for the police to raid the house. I don't want you getting killed,' she said, stroking his head.

'It's fine, Mother, all this pain will heal. Don't you see

what I am doing? If they can't find the gun, it's only one left. I am not scared of the knife that Donald is holding. I will wait till I know it's safe to get rid of the other gun.'

'I know you're trying to help but it kills me watching you get beat up. Relax for a while, promise me.'

Nick looked at his mother knowing he couldn't. 'I'll do my best but if I see an opportunity, I will risk it.' Then they heard footsteps coming.

Both of them walked up to Nick when Gary stopped Patrick attacking him. 'We have lost the gun now because of you. You will pay, there is no way you're getting out alive. I will make sure of it,' he said, walking away, kicking the chairs.

Gary was sitting at the table with Donald, with Patrick keeping watch again, Nick and his mother sitting on the floor when Gary was looking at them. 'You got a problem, Sarah? You keep looking at me,' Gary said, walking over pulling a chair up.

'I want to have a chat with my brother. Why do you hate me so much to kidnap my daughter? You knew I was leaving town to start a new life.'

'I don't hate you, Sarah, you were always my baby sister who helped the family out. What pissed me off was you running away and leaving us, when our dad needed you. You wanted to run away and started again with posh boy.' Gary was all calm and talking normally.

'I'd had enough of that life, criminals, drugs and the weapons. I wanted to start a family in a nice area and not around drugs,' she said, holding his hands.

Letting go of Sarah, Gary said, 'Is that why you grassed us to the pigs? You knew I had to have sex with Lucy, she

185

wanted to have sex with me anyway. John was different, he deserved to die. Dad told me to do it. Dad and John were friends and that is what he does to us.'

'You're sick in the head. Why did you get my mother-in-law attacked by Billy King?'

'There is something I've been looking for, my gold pocket watch which Mum left me. I knew you took it before you left, worth so much money. I sent Billy to search the house but the old lady got in the way. I will get it once I am out of here.'

Sarah laughed at him. 'Oh, Gary. I do have the pocket watch but there is no chance you're getting it, it belongs to me and then my children. You don't deserve it.'

Gary slapped his sister across the face when standing up. 'You got the pocket watch, John's money and what did I get? A prison cell for twenty years. I am due something. I've got this cash now so it's a start. Speaking about hating you, I changed my mind I do hate you. The worst thing you did was killing my daughter, Lily.' Nick looked shocked by what he was listening to.

'I didn't kill your daughter, I walked away when Lily was alive. I loved that girl, and she loved me. Julie was so unlucky meeting someone like you. What happened if I killed her then?'

Gary was getting angry with Sarah mentioning Lily. 'Julie was home playing with her when you wanted to stay goodbye to her. After you said goodbye to my daughter, Julie was walking back a different way when a car hit her. You have no idea what it means to lose a child, she was my little girl. If you hadn't made that call, she would be alive now. That's another reason why I've got to kill Nick: one child for another,' he said, pointing the gun at Nick's head.

'Don't shoot him. I didn't kill her. Just because I called her down doesn't mean I killed her. You got to say goodbye, didn't you?' He was still holding the gun to his head.

'No, I didn't go as I was dangerous to the public, was not told for three days then I couldn't grieve in prison, not a good look. That little girl meant the world to me, my first born.'

'It's not time yet, Gary, keep the boy alive for a little longer.' Donald spoke to him.

'Where is Julie now? You still in contact with her?'

'Julie helped out a lot on this, between her and Billy. She got all the information on your family, when you got married, any connections in the world. She wants revenge like me,' he said, smiling at Sarah.

'The police will get proof on Julie, trust me, Gary. So many people going down for this kidnapping. All three of you will be going down for this.'

Nick looked at them. 'I have some bad news for you, Patrick. The police found your phone, found earlier today in the cabin. Not long till they read the messages. They will find out where your mum is and that's all four of you in jail.'

Patrick left the door and stood next to his dad. 'If you don't shoot him I will. I want him dead, if you're telling the truth. My phone is in the bag.'

'In the mud of the cabin, tell you the truth I found it. Only a matter of time, before the police raid this house. Why did you try to grab Katie in the night club?'

Patrick went to search his bag when kicking his bag, walking back and kicking Nick in the stomach. 'My phone is not in the bag, you are so dead, Nick. The original plan was to kidnap Katie due to being connected to you, then you would have come to find us. After you found us, we'd kill you. As my auntie killed my older sister, child for a child. Unfortunately, it all went wrong so we thought we'd get Mickey which failed so Ellie got kidnapped.'

Walking back to the door, looking outside then coming back.

'Why are you waiting to kill me? I am here and you're waiting. I don't understand,' Nick said, moving his hands as the ties are loose.

Donald walked over. 'John wants it this way. He wants you to be in pain before we pull the trigger, we're not finished with you yet.'

Mother stood up and got into Gary's face. 'I get it now. This whole thing is connected to him. I walk out of the family home. Ruin his business while getting my brother and my uncle sent down, I apparently killed my niece by me saying goodbye. I go to London, get married, have four wonderful children and he is jealous of it. He wants me to pay for leaving. I remember the last words he said to me. *I will get you back one day, bring your life to sad and loneliness, time is the key.* Let me guess, he paid for the fancy lawyer who nearly got you off?'

Gary head-butted Sarah on the nose when falling back to the ground. 'Yes, Sarah. Finally, you get it. We all hate you. Our father planned it all, when I was in prison. He visited me saying once I am out payback will happen. Father planned to get Patrick dead on records so no one would know it was him. Then Julie helped out digging up information on you and your children, schools, friends. She found the cabin was empty so perfect for us to hide when we kidnapped Katie, we found this place in the paper as a back-up. When I got the phone call Nick was in Scotland, I was going to have him sent here but I knew the police would pick up James' phone so had to come here. This was twenty years of planning, all under your nose,' he said with a smug face.

'Oh, and it was not Father who paid for the lawyer, it was you. A few weeks after you had John's money, you gave Julie ten thousand pounds for the new baby. We were so close to getting not guilty with his fancy words. Try and get up again I will make sure your kids lose their mother,' he said, kicking Sarah in the stomach.

Time was ticking on when the sun was setting, making the room dark. Donald found some candles, placing them around the room, then lighting them. 'Are you okay, Mother?' Nick asked, staring at her.

'I will be, Nick. What is your plan? We need to get out soon before they shoot you. They are not joking and I'm not watching you get shot. Where is Damon, Nick? I thought you both searched the house together?'

'We did, last time I saw him he was searching the other side of the house. I thought when Gary shot the policeman, he went straight to DC Walker and told them.'

'No, when I was standing with DC Walker, he thought he was with you as a hostage. So, where is he?'

'No idea unless he is here waiting for the right moment. Damon promised he would never leave my side.'

Looking around the room, there were many doors leading to different directions. Stairs going up to the next level or the basement where Nick started. 'My plan is to get the other gun from Gary. My hands are loose so I can break free any moment. I need to wipe out one of them first, I'm going for Donald first. Gary will be the hard one, once the gun is gone.

Run straight to the police, Mother,' Nick was saying when a phone rang.

Gary answered the phone, watching him get annoyed at the police. 'If the car is not here in fifteen, you will be seeing a dead body. Time is ticking, you've got fifteen minutes or Nick will be dead.'

Chucking the phone across the room, searching within the tables when reaching to pick up the phone. 'Shit, now I don't know what time it is. Nick, give me your watch.' Taking it off, Nick passed it to Patrick.

'The plan is when the car gets here, you run into the car with the cash. If me and Donald are not with you in thirty seconds, drive off. I know this is not part of the plan, but two things are going to happen. I will be joining you or the pigs arresting me.'

'What will happen to me and my son?' Gary turned around.

Getting on his knees in front of Sarah's face, he said, 'I will be shooting your son so you can watch. I will let you live. I want you to moan and cry over your dead son.'

'Gary, the police are coming over with a car. I think we are nearly ready to go. Should we get the boy ready for his death?'

'No, not yet, Donald, we will wait five extra minutes. Patrick, grab the bag. Whatever happens, we will see each other again.' They hugged each other.

'I know, Dad. It's been nice doing this job with you. Should we finish the job, Dad?'

Gary grabbed Nick by his throat, kicking him in the stomach, falling to the floor laughing at him. Picking Nick up again when pulling him towards the door seeing bright blue lights. 'Time has come, Nick, to die. Any last words for Mother?'

Gary pushed him round to face his mother. 'I'll be fine, Mother,' he said, smiling at her when he thought he saw someone on the stairs.

Nick was facing the doorway again when falling to the floor and kicking Gary in the legs, they both fell to the ground when Gary dropped the gun. Kicking Gary in the stomach when Patrick was coming towards the gun on the floor, looking around when Nick kicked the gun down the stairs. The gun went at fast speed. 'Get the gun, Donald, quick.'

Nick took the ties off when catching up with Donald, pushing him. Grabbing the handle of the door when Donald fell down the stairs in darkness. Standing up with Gary and Patrick standing in the door way. 'What is next, Nick? Trying to be action man and save your family? You need to die. Pushing my uncle down the stairs. Patrick, go and find the gun, check on your great uncle. I'll make sure Nick won't escape.'

Patrick walked down the stairs with a candle. 'I am not scared of you, Gary. You might scare people in Scotland but this is England. What is your plan now? One gone two to go.'

Nick kept moving about to avoid getting caught by them with Mother moving to the corner of the room. Gary thought he was clever by running towards him but was too slow. 'Losing your sense, are we?' Patrick returned to the room.

'I can't find the gun. Someone is here with two guns. Are you going to tell us who it is, Nick?'

'You must be blind, Patrick, no one is here.'

'How is Donald, Patrick? He'd better be alive or you're paying for this, Nick.'

'I am sorry, Dad, Donald broke his neck falling down the

191

stairs. Donald is dead, Nick is now a murderer but I do have Donald's knife.'

Gary and Patrick got angry when they were getting closer to Nick but it was too late, Patrick had grabbed him by his arm. 'Get back here, Sarah.' Sarah ran out of the house with her hands still tied up.

Moving back to the bar area with Patrick holding Nick. 'Stab him now, Dad.' Nick saw the knife coming towards his stomach.

Feeling this was the end of his life, closing his eyes as Patrick was too strong for him when there was a gun shot. Falling to the ground slowly when opening his eyes to find Gary shot in the leg, Patrick running out of the house seeing police running toward the car grabbing the bag of money. The car sped off in the distance when Gary got hold of his leg, trying to kick him when Damon was standing over Gary with the gun. Relaxing his head on the floor when feeling a sharp pain in his stomach and then another sharp pain near his ribs with another gun shot, hearing loads of footsteps around him.

Chapter 16

25th March 2019

'Nick, Nick, wake up. You need to stay with us,' Damon said, moving Gary away from Nick and placing the knife on the bar.

'I said I would kill one of her children, I feel so much better knowing one part of the plan has come true,' Gary said, laughing away.

Damon was standing in front of him kicking Gary in the stomach when DC Walker walked in the room with five police officers. 'Stop, Damon. We need to save Nick as soon as possible. Use your shirt and hold the pressure on the knife wounds. DC Walker here, we need an air ambulance. We've got the ambulance team here but Nick needs to be rushed to hospital.' Two ambulance crews went to Gary with his legs bleeding from the gun wounds.

Two more ambulance crews were kneeling around Nick putting on an oxygen mask on him, placing pads around the knife wounds leaving Damon to watch. Damon sat on the chair when hearing DC Walker on his police radio. 'A red Ford with the suspect Patrick McDonald driving it. License plate is Mike, Zulu, ten, Papa, Charlie, Hotel. Going towards Bateman Road, off Bushley golf course.'

'We will find him, Damon. We've got three police cars chasing him at the moment. You've done a great job, Damon, hiding out, without you it could've been a lot worse.'

'Great job. You're a pig. like my nephew is; you lot deserve to die. Nick lied to me saying someone wasn't with him.'

DC Walker walked over to Gary. 'I am arresting you on suspicion of attempted murder. You do not have to say anything, but it may harm your defence if you do mention when questioned something you later rely on in court. Anything you do say may be given in evidence. A police officer will be with you till we can question you. Police officer Jackson, can you go to the hospital with Gary McDonald?'

Gary was wheeled away when Damon heard the air ambulance landing, going outside finding the helicopter landed and two more crew running towards them. One of the ambulance crew spoke to them. 'Nick has two deep wounds. One is in his stomach and other one near his heart. We are ready to put him in the helicopter.'

Running towards them was Ellie and her mother. 'How badly is Nick hurt? Please help him,' Sarah cried, putting her arms around Damon.

'Nick has two stab wounds, he will be taken to the Royal London Hospital. Sarah, Nick will be fine, he's tough as boots. Nick was amazing getting you and Ellie out, remember that,' Damon said, cuddling Ellie as well.

'I know, I know. DC Walker, can I go with them? I need to be with my boy.' DC Walker walked over to the air ambulance.

'How was he, Damon, when the ambulance crew got there? Was he talking to you?'

'I am sorry, Sarah, he was unconscious on the floor when the ambulance crew got there. Remember, Nick will be in hospital within ten minutes and they'll be saving his life. Nick was a great hero the last three days saving Ellie,' he said, giving Ellie a full hug when DC Walker walked back.

'Sarah, there is room for you and Ellie to go with Nick. They're leaving now. I know this is the wrong time, but I will need statements from you both as soon as possible.'

'Yes, that's fine but not now.'

DC Walker nodded with Sarah and Ellie getting on the helicopter when taking off from the ground, Damon looking in the sky at the helicopter, underneath his breath saying don't die Nick. Walking with DC Walker not knowing what was next for him. 'Can I get a lift back to London or can someone take me?'

'That is fine, I will organise a car for you. I will need a statement from you as well. Walk this way.'

Damon stopped looking at DC Walker. 'You said to me, don't use the gun. Because I used it on Gary what will happen to me? I shot someone,' he said, looking scared.

'Nothing, I will talk to DI Watson about the situation you were in and that you had no choice to protect Nick. We police officers only use guns when we have to. We shoot them in the legs so they drop the gun. Why did you shoot Gary?' They were sitting on the police car bonnet.

'Patrick was holding Nick in the bar area when Gary was about to stab him, I remembered DC Hill telling me how to disarm a man, shot him in the leg.'

'Well, to me, you saved Nick. Nothing will happen...' DC Walker's radio started talking.

'We have lost Patrick McDonald. He stopped at Aldenham Reservoir and ran on foot with a bag. We need back-up for a search.'

'I've got to go, Damon. I will sort out a car for you,' he said, leaving Damon on the police car.

Lying on the car when remembered something Gary had done, running towards to DC Walker. 'Let me help you, we can find him easy without the search.'

DC Walker turned around to Damon. 'How, Damon?'

'When Gary chucked the phone, Gary took the watch off Nick and passed it to Patrick for the time. Nick's watch still has the tracking device on it. Let me help you. I want to come with you.'

'Okay, you can come with me. Let's go to the car, I'll call them in the car about tracking the watch,' he said, running towards DC Walker's car.

Driving towards the reservoir with DC Walker's blue lights, weaving through the traffic, Damon was feeling what it was like to be in a speeding police car. 'Right, Damon. When we get there, you can work with me and search the forest. I will give you an ear piece so you can hear what is going on,' he said, swerving around cars.

Turning the corner when the forest was ahead of them, DC Walker's phone rang. 'DC Walker, it's PC Grant, we have picked up the tracking device at Elstree Aerodrome. Which is near the reservoir when Patrick went on foot. We are sending police cars there now to search the area.'

Turning the car around, stopping traffic both ways when speeding back the other way. 'PC Grant, can you get a team to surround the area. All exits, entrances and wait on my command. We don't want to scare him. Patrick has no idea the watch has a tracking device on it.'

He was hanging up when Damon saw the sign for Elstree

Aerodrome. DC Walker turned off his blue lights then parked up outside the building. Stepping out of the car when opening the boot, DC Walker gave him an ear piece to place in his ear. 'We're all on the same radio, you will be able to listen to where Patrick might be. This is a large place. Let's go,' he said, closing the boot and walking along the building to the small runway. There were around fifteen small planes on the ground with street lights next to them. Looking around to see police officers around the site waiting on DC Walker's call, bending down while walking slowly. PC Grant was talking in the ear piece. 'The suspect is one hundred yards from you, DC Walker.'

Damon looked around but didn't see him until a door opened on the plastic cabin. Patrick was walking out with a man holding keys. 'Team, stay down. Wait and see what happens. Hold back,' DC Walker told the team.

Patrick followed the man towards the plane when chucking his bag on the seat, Damon saw DC Walker walk forwards towards Patrick. 'Put your hands on the floor, any weapons to one side, Patrick. Let's do this the easy way, we have your dad in custody already,' he said, standing a few feet from him.

'Nah, I don't think so, pig, all alone out here. You're a very brave pig with me, how about you let me go before I stab you,' Patrick said, pulling out a knife.

DC Walker took a step back from Patrick. 'I have a team of officers behind me. Let's do this the correct way and drop the knife. We can talk about this like adults; weapons don't need to be used.'

'How many times have I heard that before? Same old rules. Why don't you back off so I can fly this plane, and you give me the keys? I know how to fly a plane,' he said, pointing his knife at the man, when throwing the keys.

Damon crawled round the back of the planes, slowly moving without Patrick knowing when DC Walker caught what he was doing. DC Walker moved his hands saying move around, while listening to Patrick. 'I am not going to prison with my dad, I am out of here. I will give you one more warning before I will make you another person dead today,' he said, waving his knife close to DC Walker.

Damon crawled towards Patrick when finding a metal bar on the floor, getting closer he swung his arms to hit Patrick in the back of his legs. Falling backwards and the knife falling next to him when Damon kicked the knife away from him. 'Go, go, go. Secure the area,' he yelled, standing over Patrick.

'Well done, Damon, great work. You should join the police force; you'd be a great police officer.'

'You got lucky this time, officer.'

Picking up Patrick, he handcuffed him. 'I am arresting you on suspicion of kidnapping Ellie West, attempted murder of Nick West and holding a dangerous weapon. You do not have to say anything, but it may harm your defence if you do not say something you later rely on in court. Anything you do say may be given in evidence,' he said, passing him to another police officer.

'How did you find me, pig?'

DC Walker walked over to him, taking off the watch. 'When Nick was doing police work for us, we gave him this watch for protection. It's a tracking device, Patrick. It was such a good idea your dad gave you this watch. You can now join him,' he said, walking away from Patrick with Damon.

'Jade, get your coat, we need to go to the hospital. Mother and Ellie are there. Mum, do you mind looking after Mickey for me? The police officer will be there till they find Patrick,' James said, putting his coat on.

'That is fine, James, you go to the hospital. I hope Ellie is okay. I am happy they found her alive. How comes you're going to the hospital anyway?' his mother asked, standing in the hallway.

Walking into the living room, he sat next to his mum. 'I was going to tell you when I got back, it's hard to tell. Nick was caught by Gary when searching the house with Damon, I am not sure what happened but Nick has been stabbed by Gary. Sarah is in the helicopter with Ellie now, they have stopped the bleeding by pressure. Ellie will need to be checked out by the doctors. I am sorry, Mum, about Nick. I will let you know what is going on,' he said, giving his mum a cuddle.

'You go and let me know when you can,' she said, kissing James on the cheek.

James left with Jade getting in his car when starting it up, driving down the road to the hospital. They both sat in silence when James' phone rang. 'Hi, Sarah. Are you at the hospital yet? We are twenty minutes away. How is Nick doing?'

'We have just arrived at the hospital, didn't take long to get here. Nick has gone to the operating room, the doctors have not said anything yet. Relax, don't rush to get her. Has anyone told Katie yet? I can't get hold of her. I don't want Katie to find out by the television,' Sarah said, panicking on the phone.

'Relax, Sarah, Jade spoke to her already. Katie is on her way up. She is upset and worried about Nick. I am not rushing, darling. How is Ellie doing? Did Gary or any of them touch her?' He had his worried face on.

199

'No, they both tried but Ellie managed to push them off her. Ellie is a tough cookie. Ellie is being checked by the nurse now. She's got a few bruises, black eyes but is just shaken up. Ellie keeps asking for you.'

'I can't wait to hold her. How do you feel? I was so scared when Gary took you in the house. Are you shaken up, honey?'

'I am fine, honey, and trust me, Nick looked after me. This was another side to him. Nick had plans for us to get out and even managed to dispose of a gun. I didn't see what happened but Damon saved the day by hiding in the house. I will tell you more when you get here. Love you, James.'

'Love you too, Sarah,' James said, hanging up the phone.

Driving along the road when they saw a sign for the hospital a few miles ahead. 'Nick sounds like he really helped out the police. I am proud of my big brother, and Damon.'

Father looked at Jade with a smile. 'You should be proud of them both. They both put their lives on the line to find Ellie. At first, I didn't agree but I knew it would pay off. Nick will pull though this, trust me, Jade.'

Jade had a little tear when Father put one of his arms across her shoulders. 'I do, Father. Is this the end of the McDonalds?'

'Nearly, Jade. We are waiting for DC Walker to ring me about Patrick McDonald. Once they have found him then this is all over. The whole family will be in prison. We can live again and start enjoying life. What is the first thing you want to do?' he asked, looking across at Jade.

'Me and Nick were talking about this. We'll go on a nice holiday. We can get a large villa between us all, including Katie's family. Hire some chefs, large pool and lots of sun. That is a holiday.'

'That sounds like a great holiday. I'll make a deal with you. You, Ellie and Nick can plan this holiday and whatever you want. Cost is nothing, family means more and us spending time together. We are here now.' Father entered the hospital car park.

Parking on the ground floor of the car park, staring at the hospital, Jade could see the helicopter on the roof. Feeling nervous not knowing what the doctors were going to say, and about seeing Ellie. Walking into the hospital with her father, they walked to the operation area. The walk was short then Ellie ran towards her father. James hugged her tightly, kissing her on the cheek. 'I am so happy you're fine. I have missed you so much, Ellie. Mickey made you something when we go home later,' he said, still hugging Ellie.

'Where is your mother, Ellie?' he asked, looking around.

'Mother is giving her statement to the police about what happened when she got captured by Gary. Mother wanted to do it straight away. After, I have to go on in and do mine.'

Sitting on the chairs holding Ellie's hand, he said, 'As you're under eighteen, you will need an adult with you, darling. Do you want me or your mother to come with you?'

'I want Mother with me. I feel more comfortable when I have to talk about what they did to me,' she said, holding onto her father's hand.

'That is fine with me, sweetheart. Any news from Nick yet?'

'No, not yet. It will be a few hours before we know what is going on.' Sarah was walking out with the police.

Sarah ran up to James with a big hug, hugging in silence. 'I am so glad you're here now. I was losing my mind. No news on Nick yet and Katie is not here yet.'

Sitting on the chairs, he said, 'You go with Ellie and the police while me and Jade get some coffee. After you finish with Ellie, we'll decide what to do.' He kissed her on the lips.

Ellie, her mother and the police officer sat in the office while the police officer found a pen. 'I am PC Hardy and I will be taking a statement from you about the kidnapping, also anything that they did to you. Take your time and give me as much detail as possible,' she said, looking at Ellie.

'Let's start from the night you were taken by Patrick and Billy. What do you remember?' She had her pen ready to write.

'I remembered getting grabbed by a masked man, his name was Patrick McDonald. They were talking about something when the bald man was talking to him. I was blindfolded in the van with one of them holding me down. I didn't know at this point what was going on.'

'Do you remember where they took you?'

Silence thinking about the event. 'I remember being in the van for few hours then a blue car. The car was a small journey then they let me walk through the forest. The cabin was covered in weeds, broken down with only two beds. I had to sleep on the floor and they were feeding me two meals a day. Gary kept saying if your mother doesn't pay then you will die. It was horrible being in the cabin. I was cold most of the time with only a thin blanket,' she said, holding onto her mother's hand.

'While you were with Gary, Patrick and Donald, did they try anything with you?'

'They didn't have sex with me but they did try to have sex with me. Patrick put his hands on my legs while kissing me, then tried to pull down my trousers but I kicked him. Patrick tried a few times but gave up, when punching me in the face. Gary did the same trying to pull my trousers down when he pulled his down, I kicked him. That was it, PC Hardy, it was horrible but I was not going to let them rape me.'

'I am sorry to ask more questions but did Donald touch you and did they expose themselves to you?'

Looking at her mother, she answered, 'No, he didn't touch me. Gary and Patrick showed me their penises when on top of me, with my trousers off but I had my knickers on. Gary tried to take them off but I stopped him.' She was crying into her mother's arm.

'Just a few more now, did they threaten you in any way during the time you were kidnapped?'

'Yes, they kept beating me up each time something didn't go right for them. Gary kept pointing the gun to my head saying he would shoot me. Donald didn't do anything just sat there looking.'

Looking through her notes, the police officer said, 'Do you remember where they took you after you left the cabin, Ellie?'

'Yes, they took me to a golf house where I was locked in the cellar. Most of the time they didn't talk to me. They just wanted the money so they could get away. After one day, Nick joined me and he protected me from them.'

'Good, Ellie, that's all we need for now. This matches the right places from our pictures. Gary and Patrick will be saying they didn't and this is the proof. One more thing, before I let you go, these are two pictures of the men who kidnapped you. Are these the men who kidnapped you?'

Ellie looked at the pictures. The first one was Gary McDonald then Donald McDonald. The third one was Patrick

McDonald and fourth one was Billy King. 'The first two and Patrick kept me hostage, with Billy King and Patrick kidnapping me in the hospital car park.'

'That is fine, Ellie, we will be charging them with your kidnap and attempted rape. Unfortunately, Donald died at the scene at the golf house. Also, the weapons they used on you. We will contact your mother if we need anything else. Thank you, Ellie, for all this information.' Ellie left the room with her mother.

'Sorry, Ellie, one more thing to tell you, when the case goes to court, we will need you to do this again but in front of the judge. You can do this on camera facing the court or stand in the box.'

'Don't worry, PC Hardy, I want to go to court and show the world how evil these guys are. I want to name and shame Gary and Patrick. You don't treat girls like this.'

Walking outside, Father was holding a coffee for Sarah. 'I am so proud of you, Ellie. That must have been scary for you. It's all over now,' he said, cuddling Ellie.

'I know from what Father said in the past that telling the whole story will put them behind bars and they can't hurt me any more. I want them to go down forever.'

'Anyone who is involved in this kidnap will go down, Ellie, and I will make sure they will. No one hurts my little girl,' he said, having a three-way cuddle.

Turning midnight with Jade and Ellie sleeping on the hospital chairs with their heads on each other, Katie walking up and down in the room. Father out getting coffees for them all with Mother staring out of the window. Still waiting for news on Nick's operation when Father returned with six coffees. 'Drink these. It will wake you up a bit,' he said, giving the coffees out.

Drinking the coffee when a young man walked in. It was Damon. Mother ran straight up to him. 'You've done so much work to help the family, you will always be a part of the family. Ellie is looking forward to seeing you. Have you got news on Patrick yet?' she asked when Father gave him Jade's coffee.

'Yes, me and DC Walker managed to catch him at some small airport. Patrick was trying to fly out of London. It's all over now. I have given my statement from the first day to the last few hours. I am glad we managed to catch them all. How is Nick?'

'We are still waiting for the doctor to come. I think he is still in the operating room,' she said when Ellie woke up.

'Thank you so much, Damon, you helped me so much. I saw you in the house but kept quiet also…' then an older man wearing a white jacket walked in.

'I am Doctor Khan. I was doing the operation on your son, the last few hours. Nick had two stab wounds, one in the stomach and another one in his lungs. We have been able to close the stab wound on the stomach and stitch it up. The one on the lung was a bit difficult, we tried to seal the lung but it was damaged so we had to remove it.'

Mother stood next to Father. 'Will Nick survive on one lung, doctor?'

'Yes, Nick can survive on one lung. When Nick entered our operation room, he had lost lots of blood already. At the moment Nick is on a breathing machine to help him, at the same time still unconscious. We can't say how long for. You can visit him one at a time.'

'Doctor, what are the chances of Nick surviving?' James asked, looking at the doctor.

Looking at James with a straight face, the doctor said, 'The next twenty hours will be critical to Nick's survival. I am really sorry, we are watching Nick all the time as infection can be high right now. I will be here all night.' He walked off out of the room.

'Can I see Nick first?' Katie asked, looking at Sarah and James.

They both nodded when walking out of the room following the doctor, feeling scared to see him. Within a few rooms from where Katie was waiting was Nick. Entering the room, seeing Nick lying on the bed with tubes coming out of his mouth and connected to a machine. Sitting next to him crying on his arm, holding his hand tightly. 'You get better, Nick, I need you in my life. I am telling you to come around and come back to your family, I need you,' she said, breaking down on the floor when James walked in.

'Come here, Katie. Nick will be fine. We are all here for you,' he said, cuddling Katie.

Chapter 17

26th March 2019

Katie was asleep holding Nick's hand with the support pipes coming out of Nick's month. The rest of the family went home to sleep. Katie was not leaving Nick, till he woke up, it was quiet in the hospital with the nurses walking into the room checking on him. The machine made a beeping noise each minute when Katie woke up still holding his hands. Looking at him but still holding his hands, her eyes were red from crying all night. 'Why are you not waking up, Nick? I know you can hear me. I am not leaving until you open your eyes and I get a kiss from you. I need to tell you something but only when you wake up,' she said, touching his skin with her hands.

'You've been a hero to your sister, she is fine now so it's time to be a hero to me. I'd be lost without in my life. We still need to go on our holiday to Italy. I need you to come with me.'

Holding onto his hands when the door opened. It was the nurse again, walking over to Katie with a cup of coffee and a sandwich. 'I thought you might need this. You must be hungry also a coffee to make you alert. I'll be checking Nick's oxygen and blood pressure. How're you doing?' she asked, smiling at her.

Looking around the room crying again when the nurse

cuddled her. 'It will be fine. I have seen this before where a young man has been stabbed, he recovered from it,' she said, walking back to do her checks.

'What happened to him after he was released from hospital? Was he the same person after?' The nurse was checking his blood pressure.

'Yes, it was a long recovery but good. How I know this is because I married him a few years later. He asked me out after he left hospital. Nick seems a good lad, it's a shame it happened at the last minute when it was all over. You've got a hero here,' she said when checking his oxygen levels.

'He is my hero. I want the next twenty-four hours to fly by so we know he will be all right. Are you allowed to date anyone when working on them?' she asked, drinking her coffee.

Writing down notes and checking his heartbeats on the machine. 'We can if I am not treating them and they have left the hospital. We went for a few drinks to thank me, best husband I could ever meet. A bit like you,' she said, smiling at her. 'I'll be back soon with the doctor' She put the notes back in the bed.

Looking concerned about her looks, she asked 'Is everything okay, nurse?'

'Nick's oxygen is a little low with his heartbeat, just want the doctors to look at him,' she said, leaving the room.

'You better not be dying, Nick. You got a family that loves you and me. You are my love of my life, soul mate and best friend. I promise you I am staying here till you kiss me,' she said, crying onto the bed.

Rubbing his hands when the door open, the nurse returned with a doctor. Picking up his notes then placing them back, he walked over to the machine then looked back at the nurse. 'Can we run some more blood test, CT scans on his organs? When they are back call me straight away.'

'Doctor, what is wrong with Nick. Did something go wrong last night in the operation?' she asked, wiping her tears.

The doctor walked over, sitting next to her. 'Sometimes infections can affect the body after a knife attack or it might be a little blood leak. As soon as we know what is going on, we will tell you.'

As he was leaving the room with the nurse, Katie decided to call Sarah on the latest news.

Sitting outside the hospital getting some fresh air while Nick went for his CT scans, looking across to the busy roads. There were a few people walking around Katie sitting on the steps. 'It's amazing how many people have different lives. People driving to work, appointments here at the hospital, rushing too much to notice anyone or just staring into space. I know you're here because someone stabbed that hero boy,' someone said when Katie looked up.

It was an old lady sitting next to her. 'Take it you've seen my photo in the newspapers and my family? Everyone knows everything about us right now, can't go anywhere without anyone staring.'

'Take no notice of them. So, what if they are talking about your family? No one is perfect out there and everyone has their own stories to be told. I was once in the paper for a few weeks for having an affair on my marriage. I was once a model in the late sixties and famous. I read past the negative news. Nick did something what every brother does. Saves his family,' she said holding onto her hands.

Crying into the old lady's arm, Katie said, 'I'd be lost if anything happens to him. I spent so long with Nick that we do everything together. I don't want it taken away from me.'

Cuddling her without talking when Sarah appeared holding two coffees. 'I knew I should have stayed with you last night. I am here now, Katie, thank you for supporting her,' she said, looking at the old lady.

'I have no idea what you're going through but at least it's all over now. You must have been so strong going in the house. Evil people doing that.' The old lady stood up, walking away.

Sitting next to her, when handing Katie, a coffee, Sarah asked, 'Any news yet on the CT scan?'

'No, they sent Nick down so I thought I'd come outside and get some air. Something is wrong with Nick, I can feel it,' she said, drinking some of her coffee.

'Let's go to the café and get some breakfast. James will be up later after sorting out a babysitter for Mickey,' Sarah said, walking into the hospital holding Katie's hand.

Leaving the cafeteria and walking back to Nick's room, passing doctors and nurses from different areas. Porters moving around patients, when entering Nick's room. The room was empty when a nurse walked in shutting the door. 'Nick is fine, don't worry. The CT scan's taking a bit longer due to his machine attached to him. I saw you walking in and didn't want to alarm you. How are you feeling, Katie? You need some sleep.'

'Thank you, I was scared that Nick had died. I have tried to tell Katie to go home for a while but she's not having any of it,' Sarah said, looking at Katie.

'I told you all I am not leaving Nick till he wakes up and

kisses me, then I will know that Nick will be fine. I am fine now after two cups of coffee,' she said, sitting in the chair.

The nurse left the room with Sarah sitting on the opposite chair. 'I am sorry if I sound bossy. You look tired and trying to care for you, Nick would have wanted me to look after you. In other news, your mum and dad are coming down today.'

'I can't wait to see them. Is my little sister coming? I can't remember if she has a dancing tournament this week.'

'No, she is coming down. She wants to give her big sister a cuddle.' Then the doors opened and Nick was wheeled back in.

Sarah looked happy to see Nick but still a little upset seeing him in this way. The porter placed the bed back, making sure the bed brakes were on. Leaving the room when Sarah sat next to him. 'I remember the last time Nick was in hospital. He was around fourteen years old and James let him ride his bike at the park. Nick thought it be funny to go down the big hill, when just learning how to ride it. James ran after him but it was too late, Nick fell into the water and broke his arm,' she said, smiling a little.

Katie smiled with a small laugh. 'Nick said you were mad at him for weeks. Missing weeks of school because he broke his right arm and could not do any work,' she said, sitting next to Sarah.

'I was mad at him. He thought it was funny not doing any work but I gave him a laptop which he didn't like. I remember when Nick brought you home for the first time, first time he brought a girl home. He didn't take his eyes off you, he loves you so much.'

'I was scared meeting you all. Nick was my first boyfriend and meeting parents. I was happy after I made a great impression, Nan liked me so much. Nick said Nan likes me more than him.' They were laughing away.

The door opened when the nurse from earlier walked in. 'Don't worry about me. Keep talking, I am just doing checks again,' she said, picking up the notes and writing things down.

'Nan this morning was in bits. She's not coping at all. James has taken her out for a coffee. I give it a few days and she will be fine. All good, nurse, on the blood pressure and oxygen levels?'

'I am not sure, I need a doctor to see Nick. His blood pressure is lower than this morning and his heart rate is lower. Don't worry, I'll get the doctor,' she said, leaving the room.

'I don't like the sound of this, Sarah. Nick is not getting better.' Katie was standing up and stressing out.

Sarah got hold of Katie, calming her down. 'Nick is in the best place possible. The doctor will know what is going on. Relax, Katie,' she said, cuddling her.

The nurse walked in with the doctor looking at the notes. 'I will ring for the results of the blood and CT scan. Every fifteen minutes do checks on Nick. Sarah, Nick might have an infection which might be causing his low blood pressure. I will get the results fast then return with some news.' He left the room.

'If Nick does have an infection, we will put Nick on antibiotics and his blood pressure will go back to normal. I'll be back soon,' the nurse said, leaving the room, rubbing Katie's back.

'I am scared, Sarah, I don't know what to do with myself. Nick was fine all night and now getting worse. What if he dies, Sarah?' she says, staring at Nick.

'Stop this now, Katie, you need to relax and calm down.

Sit with me on the sofa, close your eyes and breathe through your nose. Nick will be fine, and the doctors are looking at the results now. It only changed this morning so they have caught it fast if it is an infection.'

Katie was calming down, breathing through her nose when they heard a noise, looking at the machine seeing a flat line. Sarah ran out of the room, shouting for doctors to come. Within a few seconds two doctors and the nurse were running towards their room. The doctor looked at the machine, asking for the defibrillator, the nurse passed it to the doctor when asking Sarah and Katie to wait outside. With the nurse shutting the door, they both looked through the window. Pulling down Nick's bedding when placing two pads on his chest, standing back when Nick's body jumped on the bed. The nurse put her hands together pushing onto Nick's heart for a few seconds, the nurse cleared the way when the doctor pushed the button making Nick jump again. After a few minutes the doctors stopped looking at his watch. The doctor saw them both looking in the window when walking toward them. 'Come this way, ladies,' he said when walking to the next room.

'I am sorry to say this, but Nick has passed away. We tried to restart his heart but nothing was working. I am extremely sorry for your loss.' Katie fell to the floor crying with Sarah cuddling crying Katie.

'Do you want me to call your husband, Sarah?' the doctor asked, looking on.

Sarah nodded with the nurse walking in 'Stay with them, nurse. I will ring her husband to come up,' he said, leaving the room with both women kneeling on the floor.

Arriving back home, with James driving, Sarah and Katie sat

in the back. The car was silent on the way back with Katie staring into the streets, James turned off the engine leaving the women in the car. Opening the house door when Colin walked out, opening the door and grabbing Katie. 'Let's go inside, the press are here.' He took Katie into the house, with James, walking in with Sarah.

The house was quiet with the family sitting in the kitchen waiting for news, James walked Sarah to the living room when looking at his mother. Katie sat next to her mum and dad. 'I don't know how to say this but Nick passed away less than an hour ago. The doctors think Nick had an infection which caused his heart to stop. I am so sorry, everyone,' James said when sitting next to Sarah.

Jade cried on Ellie's shoulder, when Colin got up and sat next to James' mother. 'Who is going to tell Mickey?' Colin spoke to James.

'I will go, Colin. How I am going to tell a six-year-old that his brother has died? Colin, can you make us all a coffee, please?' he asked, leaving the room to find Mickey.

James left the room with Colin making coffee watching Sarah. Sarah walked over to the pictures on the wall. Pulling one of them when collapsing to the floor, Colin ran over to her. 'Come here, Sarah, I am here. I don't know what you're going through but I can tell you're in pain. Nick was such a nice boy, never had a problem with him, only that he supported Queens Park Rangers,' he said, making Sarah laugh.

'That is true, Colin, his father tried to make him support Chelsea but it never worked. I'll finish off the coffee,' she said, then both walked to the kitchen.

Pouring out seven coffees when Nan went for a cigarette closing the door behind her. 'It must be hard for her, watching a grandson die. My dad always told me you should never bury your kids. Wonder how Mickey is taking the news?' Colin said, sitting opposite Sarah.

'I have no idea, Mickey has never experienced death before. When James' dad died, it was when Mickey was one, so didn't it affect him. I might go up and see him,' she said, leaving the table.

Judy came into the kitchen sitting next to Colin. 'Should we go and find a hotel? Maybe give the family a bit of space?' she asked, looking at Colin.

'I'll speak to James about that. I see what you mean by getting in the way. We didn't expect this to happen to Nick. How is Katie doing?' She was lying across the sofa looking at her phone.

'Not good, Katie is looking at photos of her and Nick. I am going to leave her today and see how she gets on tomorrow. I feel I want to cry but need to be strong for everyone.'

Cuddling her when drinking his coffee. 'Let it out, Judy. Nick was a son-in-law to us and made our Katie happy.'

James walked in the kitchen cuddling Judy. 'Colin is right, Judy. Nick was your son-in-law and you need to grieve over him. I am going to miss him so much like the little things he did. I overheard you saying about a hotel, but you are welcome to stay here as long as you want. We are all family and need to support each other. Emily can share with Mickey. We can pull out the sofa for you both.'

'Thank you, James. We don't want to be in the way. Any time you want us gone let us know. I will get a takeaway if anyone fancies eating later,' she said, looking at them all.

Morning after Nick's death, James was in the kitchen with

Colin looking at old photos. Keeping strong for the family, looking after everyone in the house. There was a knock on the door when James went to answer it. Colin picked up a photo of Nick playing football in the garden with Mickey, making him cry a little. DC Walker walked in with a bag. 'I am sorry to call this early. I thought I left it till today after yesterday events. I am sorry for your loss. Nick was so brave. I feel a little guilty for letting Nick help out. Do you want Sarah down here for an update?' he asked, putting the bag on the table.

'Don't blame yourself, DC Walker, Nick knew it was dangerous and you didn't know Gary was going to stab him at the last minute. Damon was here last night upset and emotional; he blames himself for the death of Nick. Damon wishes he'd seen the knife in his hand, he would have kicked it off him. What's in the bag, DC Walker?'

'I've got bacon sandwiches for everyone in case you didn't want to cook, I don't mind one of your coffees. You make them really good,' he said with James laughing at him.

'Of course, I don't mind and thanks for the breakfast. What news do you have for me? Damon told us you caught Patrick trying to fly out of Watford,' he said, pouring him a coffee.

'Damon did a good job. I said I'd offer him a job in the force if he was interested. I spoke to him about Nick getting stabbed and that it was not his fault, no one knew Gary was holding the knife. Before Nick died, Gary was charged with attempted murder. Gary now has been charged with the murder of Nick West. Both of them are in custody till the court date, bail was not given and they will remain in jail,' DC Walker said, drinking his coffee.

'Can I attend the hearing of the plead? It is something I

216

need to do and look at them. I know the rules about keeping quiet, been so many times now,' he said, looking at DC Walker.

'Yes, that is fine, most families want to attend to see what they say. At the moment they are saying no comment to all our questions but with the proof, they will be sent down. Will Sarah be attending the court?'

'I am not sure at the moment, I will leave it till the day. Sarah had a bad night's sleep so I'm leaving her at moment.' He opened the bag of bacon sandwiches.

Passing them one each when Mickey walked in the kitchen. 'I am hungry, Dad. Can I have breakfast?' he asked, staring at him.

Father passed him a sandwich, walking in the living room turning on the television. 'How has the youngest one taken it? Must be hard for him.'

'He doesn't understand why someone would want to hurt his big brother. Last night he slept with Katie in his room. I don't know what to do,' he said, staring at him.

'Young kids find it hard. When Nick was in Watford, he found a phone which belonged to Patrick. We looked at all the messages when a new name came into the case. Do you know anyone called Julie King?'

He thought about it but nothing came into his mind. 'Not really, DC Walker. I take it that is Billy King's mum by the surname,' he guessed, finishing off his sandwich.

'You're on the right tracks but it's Patrick's mum. We found out she married Harry King two years after Gary was put into prison. So, Billy and Patrick who kidnapped Ellie are step-brothers, Julie had Gary McDonald's number with a few messages discussing the kidnap of Katie. Which we know went wrong so went for Ellie instead, they had a meeting last year when Gary got out of prison, so planned from day one.'

Looking shocked by what DC Walker was saying, James felt sick to the stomach knowing this was planned out last year. 'I don't know what to say, I am shocked by what I am hearing. Is John McDonald involved in this kidnap?'

'There are a few messages, but nothing mentioning about the kidnap, we are still looking into it. We managed to track down Julie in Spain, we got a special team getting her back to England to arrest her. So far nine people are involved in the kidnap with John McDonald being number ten. I've never seen a case this big before. By the end of this, Sarah's family will all be in prison for a while,' he said, finishing off his coffee.

'I am grateful for what you have done and for this family. Sarah will be happy knowing it has come to the end. Did Julie have kids with Harry king linking this to the case?'

'Yes, Julie had a little girl in 2003. The girl is fifteen years old but no connection to the case, her name is Emma King. She is no threat to your family. Once Julie is arrested the case is over. All I need to do is go to court and make sure they get sent down for life.'

'One more thing, DC Walker, about Nick's death, how much proof is there so they can't get away with it?'

'We have the knife what Gary used on Nick with his fingerprints on it, and his blood. Damon saw the whole thing so we've got a witness to the stabbing. Even if Gary pleaded not guilty to murder, we've got the proof so he will get sent down,' he said, standing up putting his coat on.

James stood up shaking DC Walker's hand, giving him a cuddle as well thanking him for all the hard work. Showing him the door when sitting on the sofa. 'I feel happy this is all over but at my son's life. I don't know how to grieve or what to do,' he said, crying into Colin's shoulder.

'Mickey, can you go upstairs and play with Emily. No one knows how to grieve or when to do it, you need to let it out, James. I understand you can't in front of Sarah but working as a team will help you.'

'I can't, Colin, Sarah is so weak. I feel I need to be there for her before I can grieve for Nick,' he said, sitting up and looking around.

Colin walked up from this seat pouring James another coffee. 'I don't know much about grieving but I know one thing. It's a marriage, you need to work together and let Sarah see you upset. Losing a son must be hard, James, but don't let it break you, because it will. Talk to Sarah but if you can't at the moment, we can go for walks and talk about how you feel. Judy is here to look after Katie so if you want to grieve with me, we can,' he said, giving James a tissue.

'Thank you, Colin, maybe later we can go for a drive. I will talk to Sarah,' James said, leaving Colin going outside for a smoke.

Chapter 18

29th March 2019

Standing outside the court, DC Walker was standing in the doorway waiting for James and Sarah. Waiting at the bottom of the steps was the press, about ten of them holding their cameras. Checking his watch when a car pulled up at the court, James walked out opening the door for Sarah. The press were taking pictures of them, with a police officer walking with them and trying to block them. DC Walker opened the door for them walking into the court foyer, with brown walls, blue chairs in a row and posters of crime numbers. 'Nice to see you, James, again. I am glad you're here, Sarah. I know it's going to be hard for you watching them, but I have been told something. Gary and Patrick are not taking this seriously, the judge sent them a warning about any talking or making you feel uncomfortable,' DC Walker said, passing James a folder.

'Thank you for this, this will help me with the case. Do we know if they are going to plead guilty?' James asked, placing the folder in his briefcase.

'We are not sure. They have a duty solicitor from the police station as they can't afford one. We start in five minutes, should we start walking?' DC Walker led the way.

Walking up the stairs, passing young men in suits talking about their cases. James saw Gary McDonald's name on the board saying court room five. Walking past court room two, then passing a guy nodding at James, it was one of his colleagues from work. 'Good luck with today, James, hope they get what they deserve,' he said, shaking James' hand.

'Thank you, Robert, hope your case goes well,' James replied, walking ahead to court room five.

'You know the rules, sit in the public area and no reaction to them. I know it's going to be hard but we will win this. I have to go in this way,' DC Walker said, leaving James and Sarah to enter the court.

Pushing the door to find ten seats, three people already sitting at the end. James and Sarah sat in the middle looking across to find DC Walker sitting behind his table. They both felt nervous waiting for the court to start when they saw Gary and Patrick been brought up into their box with two prison guards. Both of them were wearing handcuffs looking at Sarah. James held Sarah's hands, looking away. 'It'll be fine, honey, I am here at all times. They can look but can't hurt us any more,' James whispered.

Sarah looked at Gary with him staring back at her smiling. Sarah felt uncomfortable but looked at DC Walker when a guard said 'All rise' when they all stood up.

As soon as the judge sat down, they all sat down except Gary and Patrick McDonald.

'I am judge Tom Hilldon, we are here today for the plea hearing for Gary McDonald and Patrick McDonald,' the judge said, looking through his notes

The court clerk started talking. 'Thank you, your honour. Gary McDonald, do you plead guilty or not guilty to murder on the twenty-fifth of March of Nick West and PC Ben Moon?'

'Not guilty.' He was smiling when saying it.

'Gary McDonald, do you plead guilty or not guilty to kidnapping on Ellie West on the eighteenth of March of this year?'

'Not guilty.'

'Gary McDonald, you do plead guilty or not guilty to keeping hostage Nick West and Sarah West on the twenty-fifth of March of this year?'

'Not guilty.' He was smiling more this time.

'Gary McDonald, do you plead guilty or not guilty to attempted rape of Ellie West between the eighteenth of March and the twenty-fifth of March?'

'Not guilty.'

'Gary McDonald, do you plead guilty or not guilty to holding possession of a gun and a knife?'

'Not guilty.'

James looked at Sarah feeling angry at them. 'It will be fine, Sarah.'

'Patrick McDonald, do you plead guilty or not guilty to murder on the twenty-fifth of July 2014 of Jack Tate?'

'Not guilty.'

'Patrick McDonald, do you plead guilty or not guilty to kidnapping Ellie West on the eighteenth on March this year?'

'Not guilty.'

'Patrick McDonald, do you plead guilty or not guilty to attempting kidnap on Katie Turner on the first of March of this year?'

'Not guilty.'

'Patrick McDonald, do you plead guilty or not guilty to keeping hostage Nick West and Sarah West on the twenty-fifth of March of this year?'

'Not guilty.'

'Patrick McDonald, do you plead guilty or not guilty to the attempted rape of Ellie West between the eighteenth of March and the twenty-fifth of March this year?'

'Not guilty.'

'Patrick McDonald, do you plead guilty or not guilty to holding possession of a gun and a knife?'

'Not guilty.'

The court room went quiet with the judge putting his notes down and looking at them. 'You both will be kept in custody till your court date. You are too dangerous to be released on the streets, also no fixed address for you both. Anything to say?' he asked, looking down on their solicitor.

Standing up looking at the judge, he said, 'No, your honour.'

Sitting back down, the judge said, 'Court is over. Send them both back to prison till their court date.' The prison guard walked them back down to the dock.

On the way down hearing Gary's voice. 'How is your son doing?' Hearing him laugh.

Sarah cried on James with people leaving the court. 'Why did they plead not guilty when all the proof is there? I don't want to do this again, James.' He was cuddling her not knowing what to say.

Walking out of the public gallery meeting DC Walker. 'You okay, Sarah? That was not necessary, what Gary said, and that will be used against him in court later on. We will set a new date for them, we've got everything covered with fingerprints to pictures.'

Walking over to the chairs letting Sarah rest, James asked 'Do we have to come back and stand in the box to give evidence? What about the attempted rape charge?'

DC Walker touched Sarah's hands. 'I am sorry but you need to come back to court. Ellie has to stand as well to give her evidence. They want you both to crack so they get off, that is their plan. We will make sure that does not happen. We need to go outside as we planned. Are you ready?'

Sarah nodded when DC Walker walked through the court room corridors when James saw the press, there were more cameras linking it to the television. Walking down the stairs when near the exit, he said, 'Remember we don't have to say anything. Just hold my hand and let DC Walker do the talking.'

Walking though the exit doors with flashing cameras going off when standing behind DC Walker. 'Today in court, Gary McDonald and Patrick McDonald pleaded not guilty to murder, kidnapping, hostages, attempted rape and possession of weapons. They may have pleaded not guilty but we have proof they were involved in this from the start to the end. We will wait till the next court date to send them down for life. The West family will get what they deserve, life prison sentences for Patrick and Gary McDonald. We ask for respect to the family, let them grieve for their son Nick West. This morning a ninth person has been arrested for the involvement of the kidnapping; her name is Julie King. Mother to Patrick McDonald and ex-wife of Gary McDonald. Thank you.'

'Come this way, guys.' Two plain officers walked all three of them to the car with the press taking more photos of them.

Mother's Day

Jade, Ellie, Mickey and Katie were in the kitchen preparing for Mother's Day for Sarah and Judy. Jade was preparing the breakfast cooking the sausages, fried eggs and tomatoes. Ellie was setting up the table with plates and cutlery with Katie looking out the window. Mickey was sitting in the living room watching television holding Nick's favourite teddy. Jade and Ellie sat next to Katie cuddling her, looking down holding a photo of Nick. 'This is a weird day. Should we be doing this? Mother might not want a Mother's Day breakfast. Mother didn't get out of bed yesterday. What are we going to do if Mother doesn't like this idea?'

'It's the right thing to do, Ellie. We are here to make her feel special. Father agreed, we need to show Mother we love her and are here for her. Father said he will bring her down after nine. Is there anything left to do?'

'Just need to finish off the continental breakfast. Katie, want to help us?' she asked, holding her hand.

'I am not in the mood, girls, I am sorry. I just want Nick back in my arms; the bed is so lonely without him. You think I will have to move out?' she said, crying a little.

'Don't be silly, Katie, you're a part of this family. You're still the older sister to us, we need you to teach us life skills,' they said, laughing a little.

'Jade is right about that; this has made us stronger as a family. We all need to be strong. Father said the funeral is next week. No matter what, we will always be in contact. Nick wanted to marry you and be his future wife. Let's finish off the breakfast, it's nearly nine,' she said, getting up leaving Katie looking out the window.

Jade placed the continental breakfast when Nan, Judy and Colin walked in. 'Happy Mother's Day, Nan, we got you presents but are waiting on mother. Relax and put your feet up.' Nan kissed Jade and Ellie on the head, smiling.

'This is so sweet, girls, this is what we need a good day as a family. I heard your mother so she'll be down soon. Katie, how're you doing?'

Katie didn't say anything just kept looking out the window. Katie got up to open the garden doors to go out. 'I'll go and see her.' Judy followed her closing the door.

Katie was sitting on the swinging chair as her mum sat next to her. 'I know this is hard, Katie, but the girls are trying their best to put a smile on Sarah. When was the last time you slept, darling?' she asked, cuddling her.

Busting into tears still holding the picture of Nick, Katie said, 'I can't do this, Mum. I am so lost and don't know what to do. I get pains in my chest knowing Nick can't help me.'

'This is going to take time. You lost the love of your life. The best thing is time, you can take as much time as you want to grieve for Nick. Nick loved you so much, you know that, don't you?' she said, cuddling her still.

'Yes, and I love him too, I am so sorry I forgot to get you a card and present for Mother's Day. I let you down, Mum,' Katie said, wiping her tears on her tissue.

'Don't be silly, Katie, it's only one day. I don't expect a card this year, times are different. I am here for you today and whatever you want to do, if you don't want to do breakfast then we'll go out for a walk. Do you fancy this?' She was staring at Katie.

Katie nodded when walking back inside. 'Go and get dressed, then we'll go out.' Katie walked past everyone in the kitchen.

'Morning, Sarah and James, Katie is feeling she can't sit here this morning. I am taking her out for a while, girls. Katie doesn't mean to rude.' She was pouring herself a coffee while waiting for Katie.

226

'It's fine, Judy, Nick meant a lot to Katie and she doesn't know what to do. Tell Katie, she is welcome to stay here as long as she wants. She feels we will kick her out, tell her we will never do that. My friend spoke to me yesterday with some words; as much as we have lost Nick, I still need to provide for the rest of the family and support them. Nick will always be in my heart.' Judy hugged Sarah.

'You are stronger than I thought; they are wise words. Believe it or not, this plan was originally planned by Nick. My girls wanted to do this for him, he's watching us now having a nice breakfast,' she said when Katie walked back into the kitchen.

'I wish I had what you had, but I can't be brave, Sarah. This is what Nick ordered last month for Mother's Day and a card, I didn't know what to do with it,' she said, handing Sarah the present and card.

Sitting back in her chair holding the present. 'I don't know what to say. This is something I was not expecting but Nick does like to order presents early. Thank you, Katie. I am here for you if you want to talk about Nick. No matter what you're still like a daughter to me.' Sarah was hugging her with tears coming down her face.

Katie left with her mum with Sarah holding the present, looking at it not knowing whether to open it or not. 'Sarah, do you want to open it?' James poured a coffee for her.

Sarah nodded, leaving the kitchen to go into the garden. James followed her with two cups of coffee. Sitting on the bench still looking at the present, drinking her coffee.

'You don't have to open it now, we can wait till you're ready,' he said, placing his hands on Sarah.

'I want to open it. Nick is not here but still thought of his mother.'

Opening the card to see a woman in a business suit, with words around the clouds. *You might be a bit bossy, you might shout at me when angry, you might hug me too tight but that means you're the best mother in the world.* Opening the card to find Nick's handwriting, *to the best mother in the world. I am grateful for all the things you do for me, and of course my siblings. I need you no matter what, love from Nick,* as Sarah fell into James' arms crying. 'I will keep this card forever, a bit cheeky but I love it.'

Placing the card to the side when opening the present, a black box. Opening the box to find a gold heart necklace with the word *mother* on it. Sarah opened the gold necklace to find a picture of Nick and his mother on the beach when they were younger. 'This is best present I could ever get from Nick. What am I going to do now, James, without Nick?'

'Nick is in our hearts. This is a sign from him. Nick will always be in that heart.' James placed Sarah's hands on the gold heart.

Holding it close to her hands, she said, 'You're right, James. This is a piece of Nick with me at all times. I am so proud of the girls doing this breakfast for me. Let's join them and open their presents but before we go in, can you put the necklace on please.'

James took the necklace from Sarah and placed it around her neck when walking back inside.

Friday 5th April 2019

The house was quiet with James sitting at the kitchen table alone wearing his black suit and white shirt. His tie unfolded on the table looking at the pictures, the picture was of Nick sitting in a restaurant a few years ago. Staring at the picture with a small glass of whisky next to it, with a few tears coming from his eyes. Drinking the whisky then pouring himself another one when Colin walked in the kitchen. 'Better pour me one, James. Not good drinking alone.' Colin got another glass from the cupboard.

Colin poured himself a small measure of whisky. 'I know this is a silly question but how're you doing? I know you're feeling like shit right now,' he said, drinking his whisky in one.

'I know what you mean, how can you ask someone how they're feeling on a day like this? I've been up since six sitting here and looking at pictures. How can he be gone? I should never be burying my son. My mum is getting Sarah ready while I sit here being useless,' he said, picking up the bottle.

Colin stopped him when taking the bottle away. 'You need to stop drinking this much in the morning. You will regret it if you're drunk at your son's funeral. It's going to be hard for everyone and we are all here to support each other. Have you found the sixth person to carry the coffin?' he asked, putting the whisky in the cupboard and passing James the mints.

'It's me, you, Damon, DC Walker, my brother and Matt. Matt offered last night to help out. It's our Nick and we should be carrying him. You're right, I need to stop drinking. I don't know what I would do if you weren't staying here. You save me from making wrong decisions,' he said, looking at Colin.

'Yes, I have supported you through this. Go and see Sarah. Sarah needs more support at the moment.' Then James left the kitchen.

Colin made some toast, buttering it when Katie walked in the kitchen with red eyes. 'Come here, darling, eat this toast

I'll make more in a minute. I am worried about you, Katie, you're not eating much nowadays and you're not putting the picture down since Nick died. Talk to me, Katie,' he said sitting next to her.

'Nothing is wrong, Dad, I feel so weak without Nick and I don't know what to do. I am not hungry.' Then Nan walked in the room.

'Katie, you need to eat, you look all pale and white. We are only concerned for you, darling, and it's going to be a long day without food,' she said, holding Katie's hand.

'I am going to be sick,' Katie said, leaving the room running to the toilet.

'I'll go after her.' Nan left as Colin worried about this daughter state of mind.

Standing in the street, Sarah was talking to Judy, with the twins standing next to Katie. Damon, Matt, Natalie talking to James. Katie's uncle with his wife, DC Walker talking to two undercover policemen. Around fifteen young boys from Nick's university attending the funeral, Katie's friends standing near her with Nan shutting the front door coming out. Nan walked over to Sarah, cuddling her. Mickey and Emily watching from the window with the baby sitter arranged for them, when a car pulled up. James smiled when walking up to the man. 'Brother, I am so sorry for your loss. I completely understand what you're going through. I had to come to support you though this,' Henry said, hugging it out.

'I was devastated when you lost your little boy. How are the other two kids?' James asked, walking over to Sarah.

'They are all good, one just started his business and the other one just finished university. I am glad I made it on time,

230

the plane was delayed for two hours. Do you want help carrying the coffin?'

'That would be lovely, Henry. I am glad you made it. Nick loved his uncle Henry. Do you remember when Nick was little, you were the green train from Thomas?' he said, hugging Henry.

'Yes, for years I had to act as a train. How are you doing, Sarah?'

'I've been good but have had bad days. Still blaming myself for letting Nick go on the police hunt. I've been dreading this day,' she said when James cuddled her.

'Don't blame yourself; Nick wanted to do this from the start. His sisters will always know he was the hero who saved Ellie also…' Everyone went quiet.

The street went quiet with family and friends looking at the hearse slowing coming up the road, with neighbours closing their curtains. Sarah was holding onto James with her tissue in her hand, Katie was crying into her dad's arms. The hearse stopped outside the house with James looking at the coffin, breathing in and out trying to hold his tears. The man stepped out of the hearse walking over to James. 'I am sorry for your loss. My name is Keith. We will put the flowers on the back, take your time to get into the cars,' he said with the man placing flowers at the back of the hearse.

James and Sarah walked to the car seeing white flowers saying son and brother. All the flowers were blue and white for his football team. DC Walker walked over with some flowers. 'These are the from the team,' he said, giving them to Keith.

Feeling his eyes were going to cry, he got a tissue to wipe away the tears. 'How I am seeing this, I am attending my son's funeral. This is not right, they should have died,' Sarah said, crying into James' arms.

James saw Colin go over to the girls knowing he couldn't leave Sarah, but wanting to cuddle his girls. 'Mum, can you look after Sarah,' he said when walking over to his daughters.

'Come here, girls, remember Nick knew we all loved him. Think of positive images of Nick and what he meant to you,' he said, cuddling them both.

'I know, Father, I didn't know it was going to be this hard seeing Nick in a coffin when he should be with us alive.'

James looked over when Keith nodded to him. 'Jade, Ellie, you're with me and Mother. Nan, Henry, in the first car. Katie, you're with Colin, Judy, Damon and your uncle in the second car,' he said, kissing Katie on the head.

They all got into the cars when seeing Keith walking slowly towards the end of the road. As they got closer to the end of the road they saw two policemen holding back the press, driving past them taking pictures. Watching his mum breaking down, holding her hand. Henry cuddling Jade and Ellie when hitting the main road. Was this real, James was thinking, was his son in front of him in the wooden box? Not holding it in, James let out a little cry with Sarah kissing him on the cheek. The pain in his chest hurt seeing his son in front of him. Arriving at the church Keith opened the door, one by one they all got out of the car. Keith and his guys were getting the flowers out of the hearse. Behind them were around ten cars parking up and walking over to them. 'You can cry, son. You are doing the worst job in your life, watching your son and my grandchild getting buried. No one will care, son.' His mum was hugging him.

'I know, Mum, I am trying to support Sarah, Ellie, Jade and you. Nick was the other man who helped me looked after them, I am alone now. Mickey doesn't know what is going on, and Katie is grieving at the same time.' He let go of his mum.

'That is why Colin is here helping us, Henry is here as well. You're not doing this alone. Are you ready to carry Nick? Make him proud.' He kissed his mum on the cheek.

Keith was telling them how to carry the coffin when James was ready, James and Henry took the front. Matt and DC Walker took the middle, with Colin and Damon at the back. Slowly they walked into the church walking past friends and family. Resting Nick on the stands when Sarah passed the photo to James, placing it on top. Sitting down next to Sarah when the vicar spoke. 'We are here today for Nick West, a loving brother to Ellie, Jade and Mickey. A wonderful bright son to James and Sarah, and his girlfriend Katie. Nick had so much love and time for his girlfriend, and lastly, his Nan. Nick was her first grandson to be born, a moment that will never go. Nick was taken from us before his time. Nick had his life ahead of him with a wonderful career in being a lawyer like his father, James. Life is cruel to some people and this is one of them, but we all know Nick was a hero to his sister. You don't hear about brothers protecting their sisters much but this story will be in the family for ever. Putting his own life at risk to rescue Ellie; a moment with happiness. But remember this, his memories will live for ever. Before we go to our first hymn, we've got a reading from Damon.'

The vicar stood aside when Damon was walking to the front, with a letter and a tissue. 'Nick was more than a friend to me. We met in school, same university also same group of friends. We grew up together with both sets of parents treating us like brothers. Sarah always thought we were trouble when we hung out, which I need to tell her, I was the trouble one. I remember one day in her garden when we were playing football, the ball broke her favourite rose pot but Nick took the blame for me. It was me, Sarah, I am so sorry.' Damon took a break to look around.

Sarah had a little smile when wiping her tears about Nick. 'When we reached university, Katie joined us and the best thing to happen to Nick. We were the fabulous six on nights out, watching movies in Nick's room or even causing trouble. I will remember Nick so much, he was my hero and watching him saving his sister and mother, you will never be forgotten, Nick Henry West.' He rubbed the coffin before sitting next to Natalie.

'That was wonderful, Damon, about your childhood. Kids are kids at the end of day causing problems for their parents. Let's turn to the first hymn, Amazing Grace.'

James, Colin, Henry, DC Walker, Damon and Matt carried Nick out of the church, walking up the path to find an empty burial plot. All the friends and family walked behind, when gathering around the plot. 'This is our last journey of Nick's life where family and friends can come here and speak to him. Nick will remain here for the rest of time, watching over his family growing up or you coming here to have a little chat. As we lower the coffin, we will wait in silence.'

The four guys lowered Nick into the ground with Katie shaking and tearing up. Colin cuddled her with Nan holding Jade and Ellie, James, comforting Sarah. The babysitter brought the two young ones holding a toy. 'We are here for the closing stages. One by one you all will throw an item down of your favourite memories of Nick with a handful of soil. You can say a few words or say it in your head.'

James stepped forward, throwing down a Queens Park Rangers hat when picking up a handful of soil. 'Look after yourself, son. Love you loads.' He was crying when stepping back.

Sarah stepped forward with a photo doing the same as James. 'You were my first-born child. You still are and I love you so much.'

Then Katie stepped forward. 'This is a photo of us on our first date. You were the one for me,' she said, throwing soil with the photo then walking off crying.

'I'll go after her. I will go last, James.' Nan went chasing after Katie.

Finding Katie on the bench then sitting next to her. 'It's done now, Katie. Nick is rested with peace; he will always be here at the graveyard. Tell me what you're thinking,' she asked, holding onto her hands.

'I can't do it. I need Nick to help me and I can't do this alone,' she said, crying into Nan's arms.

'You can do it, Katie, you're as strong as Nick was. That is why you two were perfect for each other. The first time I saw you, I knew you were the one for him. My husband was the only person I had in my life; I miss him so much. Tell me what is going on. I can tell there is something more on your mind.'

Katie wiped her tears with a tissue when looking at Nan. 'At first, I was going to tell Nick and then decided to wait, but I can't keep the baby. I can't do it alone, it was a mistake which I'd never done before and now it's happened,' she cried, holding her hands.

'I knew anyway, you were sick this morning. Off your food but that could be Nick's death affecting you but that is your choice, Katie, about the baby.'

Breaking down in tears when looking back. 'I don't know what to do, it was in Leeds and I was supposed to put the patch back on but forgot due to the kidnapping. I can't raise the child alone, I don't know what to do.'

'It's your choice but we are all here. You have five grandparents to help, Nick's brother and sisters to help. A child is a blessing from God, maybe this was supposed to be. The child will know about Nick and be able to see him here,' she said, hugging Katie.

Chapter 19

1st July 2019

Waiting for the car to turn up outside the hotel, James and Sarah waited patiently looking over at Glasgow train station. Sitting on the chairs outside with a gusty wind blowing at them, looking at each other. Waiting near them was an undercover policeman looking around for anything suspicious when the car turned up. Stepping into the car with the other man sitting in the front seat as James was holding Sarah's hand. 'Do you think Ellie will be fine in the hotel? I am worried about her. Ellie says she's strong but I know deep down she is scared.'

'Yes, Ellie will be fine, but she's got Damon and Hazel if she needs them, Sarah. Also, she's facetiming Katie later this afternoon. Ellie is strong and wants to stand in court. The lawyer said it will show the jury that what they did was true. Remember they have a duty solicitor so this won't take long,' he said, kissing Sarah on the lips.

'I know I am too overprotective since Nick died, but I am letting go slowly and getting back to normal. I have contacted work yesterday about returning to my job, they are happy and my post is still there. It's weird being back in Scotland; twenty-one years and nothing has changed much.'

'I know, Sarah, I had a good few years when I was in

university, also best thing to happen to me. Meeting you in the High Street, looking sexy, you were wearing your Scottish shirt and showing them legs. Having our kids and I still love you from the first day I saw you. I think we are here now,' he said, looking at the High Court.

The car slowed down when they arrived at High Court of Justiciary, with its grey pillars looking grimy. Watching around was the press taking pictures as the man opened the door for them, not looking at them and walking straight into the building. The hallway was quiet and empty, looking around when DC Walker walked from around the corner, smiling at them both. 'Let's walk this way to the office we have been assigned.' They followed him to the room.

The room was plain with a desk, four chairs, plain white walls and grey carpet. Sitting on the chairs with DC Walker pulling out paperwork from his briefcase. 'We have news which we didn't know about. Gary and Patrick have got a new lawyer from last night who unfortunately is a top class one. We don't know how they afforded him but it was the same firm they used last time they were in court. But I have faith in the information we have and proof.'

Looking angry but keeping a smile on, Sarah said, 'I can guess who paid for this fancy lawyer. My father paid for it, I know it. Is there any way of finding out, DC Walker, how they paid for him?' She was calming down.

'I am sorry but it's not police business. John has been a pain in getting him charged by the police. We've got no proof he was involved in the kidnapping. We'll be leaving in a minute to the court room. Sarah, you're not allowed in the public gallery until you've given your evidence. You're going first today James, as you're not giving evidence, you can sit in the gallery. Are we ready?' he asked, putting his paperwork back in his briefcase.

All three left the room, walking towards the court room with Sarah sitting outside with DC Walker. DC Hill and James walked into the court room seeing different people in areas of the court. Gary and Patrick were sitting in the dock with two guards behind them. Sitting on the chairs when the court clerk speaks, 'All rise' when they all stood up.

James saw the judge from the doors then sat back down. The judge opened his briefcase taking out paperwork and placing them on his desk. Picking up his glass of water, drinking it then placing it back down. 'I am Judge John Jackson. We are here today for the trial of Gary McDonald and Patrick McDonald. Gary McDonald is charged with the murder of Nick West and PC Ben Moon. Kidnapping Ellie West, hostages of Ellie West, Nick West and Sarah West. Attempted rape of Ellie West and possession of weapons. Patrick McDonald is charged with the murder of John Tate, kidnapping of Ellie West, hostages of Ellie West, Nick West and Sarah West. Attempted rape of Ellie West and possession of weapons. They all will be given a fair trial to prove if they are not guilty. The jury will decide if they are found guilty or not guilty by hearing witnesses to the case. We will hear opening statements from the prosecution and defendant.' Having a glass of water, clearing his throat.

One of the men stood up with his paper in his hand. 'Your honour, my clients have been charged with a few charges which they didn't commit. My clients were at the scene but when they told the police during the investigation, they didn't listen to the them. This is unfair to them and why are we here today? They put two and two together and didn't look at the facts. I am here to prove my clients are innocent and to be proven not guilty,' he said, sitting down.

James looking at them, thinking how it was fair with all the proof they had on them. The court clerk stood up, calling the police lawyer to stand up. 'Your honour, these suspects were fully involved in the charges against them. We're here today to prove they were involved in the kidnap, murder and attempted rape of Ellie West. There is no question these people were involved and using gaps in the system to prove they are not guilty but with our evidence, these guys are guilty of all charges,' he said, sitting back in the chair.

There was silence in the court room with the court clerk standing up. 'Can we call the first witness to the stand.' Another guard walked out of the court.

Walking in the room Sarah followed the man when standing in the box, Gary looked at her smiling. A man walked up to Sarah with the red Bible. 'Repeat after me.'

Sarah placed her hand on the bible then spoke. 'I do solemnly swear, sincerely and truly declare and affirm, that the evidence I shall give shall be the truth, the whole truth and nothing but the truth.' Then the man walked away from her.

The defendant lawyer stood up looking at her. 'Sarah, let's start at the beginning. The first time you saw one of my clients was in the hospital car park. Did you see their faces?'

'No, at first, they were wearing mask over their heads. I didn't see their faces till I pulled off their masks, when trying to get my children.'

'You said you saw one of my clients' faces, may you tell the jury is the person sitting in the court dock?' he asked, keeping a straight face.

'Yes, Patrick McDonald'.

'Are you sure, the CCTV from the hospital is a bit blurry so it's your word versus my client. Sometimes when you're rushing around to stop it, a quick look at the suspect is not clear. From the CCTV, you had less than two seconds and to me that is not enough time. Is this true?' he continued, walking backwards and forwards.

'No, it's not enough time but I remembered his face when being held by them in the golf house. You never forget a face; it's a younger version of my brother Gary.'

'From past history, your mind can think it's the same person from the hospital to the golf house. I don't believe Patrick took your daughter at the hospital and you're blaming him due to being family.' He raised his eye brows at Sarah.

'No, Patrick McDonald is the guy who kidnapped my daughter from the hospital, I swear on my daughter's life,' she said, calmly talking to him.

'At the golf house, the police told you to go over to the house with fifty grand. You say Gary pointed the gun at you to enter the house. My client didn't raise the gun to you to make you his hostage?'

'No, he didn't, but he said he would shoot Nick if I didn't come into the golf house; I didn't have much choice. I was been threatened by the gun so I walked in the house. Gary was pointing the gun at Nick.'

'So, it's your word versus my client on this again. No further questions, your honour.' He walked back to his deck.

The prosecution stood up, walking over to Sarah. 'Sarah, how confident are you that Patrick McDonald is the person who took your daughter from the hospital car park?'

'I am one hundred percent sure that Patrick is the man

who took my daughter. I work with lots of people and see faces, every day. I never forget a face.'

'Was Patrick McDonald the same guy who kept you hostage, same guy who kidnapped your daughter?' he asked, looking at Sarah.

'Yes, same guy, your honour.'

'From the pictures I am showing you all, the CCTV might be a bit blurry but clearly shows this is Patrick McDonald.'

The jury looked at the picture then Patrick McDonald in the dock with some of them raising eyebrows. 'At the golf house, would you have walked in if Gary McDonald hadn't threatened you with the gun pointing at Nick?'

'No, I would have walked away and back to DC Walker.'

'No more questions, your honour.'

The court clerk stood up. 'Can we have the next witness to the stand, Damon Goldfield.'

Damon's hand was on the Bible when reading out the words from the man. The defendant walked up to Damon looking at him. 'Did you touch any weapons you found in the golf house?'

'Yes, I did, but at the end before the police raided the golf house. I didn't touch the gun before that,' he said, staring at the lawyer.

'Are you sure? You shot my client in the leg, didn't you, before the police raided the house?'

'Yes, I was told I was allowed to use it for my protection or anyone in the house. Nick kicked the gun down the stairs when disarming Gary.'

'So, if you knew how to shot, my client is saying you killed PC Moon. Is this correct?'

'No, Nick and PC Moon were searching the building when I went around the corner. I knew I'd gone too far so I went back when I saw Gary McDonald walking out of the forest shooting PC Moon. I didn't shoot PC Moon. At this point I went through a window to get inside the golf house. The first time I touched the gun was before the police raided the house,' he said, looking stunned and straight at the defendant lawyer.

'That is for the jury to decide. I do recommend that Gary didn't shot PC Moon,' the lawyer said, looking at the jury.

'On the same night, your fingerprints were on the knife. My client is saying you struggled with him to get the knife, which lead to accidentally stabbing Nick West twice. You killed one man, why not another?'

'No, after I shot Gary in the leg, I thought it was over. Within a second, I saw Gary stabbed Nick twice when kicking the knife away from him. I picked up the knife, that is why my fingerprints are on it. Nick is my best friend, we worked as a team to capture Gary, Patrick and Donald.' He looked at the jury.

'I believe you wanted to be the hero in the situation which led you to killing PC Moon and Nick West. Gary didn't kill them. I believe you knew you would get away with murder, is this correct, Damon?' he asked, staring at him in the eyes.

'No, I am not a murderer. I was helping the police in their work.'

'No more questions, your honour.' The lawyer walked back to his desk.

The prosecution walked to him. 'Damon. Did you see any time Gary, Patrick or Donald holding them hostage and not able to leave?'

'Yes, I did, I was hiding in the cellar in darkness so they couldn't see me. Gary and Patrick held the gun to Nick, Sarah and Ellie a number of times. His plan was not to let them go, he wanted to kill one of them for revenge for his daughter Lily McDonald.'

'At the time of PC Moon being shot, how far away were you to seeing Gary?'

'I was a few yards away, I saw his photo before me and Nick went to Scotland so I knew what he looked like.'

'When was the first time you use the gun to protect yourself or others?'

'The first time I used the gun was shooting Gary in the leg then I didn't use it after. That was the first time I ever used it, your honour,' he insisted, staring at the jury.

'Can you explain how Nick was stabbed, please?'

'Patrick was holding Nick on the bar with Gary holding the knife when I shot him in the leg, after that Patrick ran out of the house towards the car. Nick fell to the ground with Gary, looking away when I saw the knife coming towards Nick. After he stabbed him twice, I kicked the knife, picking it up to one side,' he said, sounding confident.

'No more questions, your honour.'

Damon walked out of the court looking at Sarah and James when opening the door. Looking at the judge when putting his papers to the side. 'Time to take a break. Back here at half past one,' the court clerk said.

'All rise.'

Sitting in the cafeteria in the court house were DC Walker, James, Sarah and Damon having their lunch. Having finished their food with James reading the paper with the McDonalds on the front page, saying guilty or not guilty. 'How do you think the case is going so far, DC Walker?' he asked, drinking his coffee.

'Good so far even with their lawyer twisting what happened on the night, with their criminal past it should leave them leaning towards guilty. The Scottish police dealt with these lawyers before, they are the best getting criminals off but when I go ahead on stand in two days it should seal it, Damon.'

'Do you think they believe I killed PC Moon? The only witness is me who saw it with my fingerprints on the gun,' asked, looking worried.

'If we thought you killed him, you would be in the dock. We see this all the time where they blame someone else if there are fewer witnesses and going on fingerprints, Damon, I have faith they will get sent down. You were great, Sarah, on stand, I heard.'

'It was like last time I was on the stand with them on trial, they seem all cocky and think they will get away with it. I don't know how I would feel if they got away with it, they killed my son in cold blood,' she said with a few tears in her eyes.

'Trust us, Sarah, we will make sure they will get sent down. Their lawyers will twist my words but I will do my best,' he said, holding Sarah's hands.

'I am concerned about Ellie doing her time on the stand, they will make her crack and ask awkward questions which might make her freeze.'

'Ellie will be the hard one, their lawyer will break her down. Being an attempted rape with only her word against them, Ellie will need to do details. I have spoken to her and she is ready, she is brave. She reminds me of Nick helping us out,' he said, smiling at them all.

'I think it's time to get back.' James pointed at his watch with them leaving the cafeteria.

Holding Sarah's hand, smiling at her, making her feel comfortable, arriving at the gallery door when he saw Ellie in the waiting area. Waving at her when smiling back at her family, entering the door with Sarah and Damon taking their seats. Gary and Patrick were looking at them, Sarah saw them pointing at her when the guard put Gary's hand down. Sarah didn't feel threatened by them any more. The court clerk stood up when spoke 'All rise' when standing up. The judge sat down when the rest did. 'Hope we all had a nice lunch. Time to continue with the next witness.'

The court clerk stood up. 'Can we call the next witness, Ellie West.'

Sarah felt nervous about Ellie taking the stand. Was her daughter strong enough for their lawyers? Within a few minutes of waiting, Ellie walked in, passing the McDonalds, taking the stand. Gary and Patrick looked at her smiling and nodding their heads. Ellie placed her hand on the oath, reading out the card. The defendant lawyer walked over to her. 'I would like to start off with the attempted rape charge on my clients. That is a serious crime to tell the police. Did Gary and Patrick do any sexual acts on you, Ellie?'

Looking nervous with her hands shaking, she said, 'No. They didn't do any sexual act on me.'

'So, can you tell the court what the guys did to you, Ellie?' he asked, looking across to her.

'Patrick tried to kiss me a lot and was touching my body, I felt uncomfortable with Patrick doing this so I kicked him in his private area. I am only a kid and it's wrong'. She was feeling less nervous now.

'So that was it, he tried to kiss and touch you? So attempted rape didn't happen, Ellie, or are you making this all up?'

Ellie was silent for a few minutes looking across to Gary and Patrick. 'They did more than that. Both of them touch my legs getting closer to my private area. Patrick tried to pull down my trousers which he did, seeing my knickers, with his trousers and boxers off. Patrick showed me his penis, he got excited when I kicked him again. I felt sick I was been sexually abused. Patrick let me pull up my trousers. Gary was the worst one, the second day Gary tried again to pull my trousers off which he did. I tried to fight him but he was too strong, he pulled his trousers down with his pants when feeling his penis. Gary pulled down my knickers when I kicked him in the privates. That was the last time they tried to have sex with me.' She was crying in the box.

James wanted to cuddle his daughter but knew he couldn't; a guard gave her some tissues. After a few minutes the lawyer spoke again, 'So, you're telling the court, under oath, that my clients tried to have sex with you,' he said, upping his voice a bit.

'Yes.' She wiped her tears away.

'I believe you're lying to the court, telling lies and making my clients out to be paedophiles, miss Ellie West,' he said with his voice a little higher.

The prosecution stood up. 'Your honour.'

'Agreed, we'll have less of your voice talking to the minor. Move on,' spoke the judge.

'Sorry, your honour. At the time of your kidnap, did the guys show you their faces any time?'

'No, not straight away. I was tied up in the van till they

pushed me into another vehicle. I didn't see their faces until walking with them to a cabin somewhere.'

'Do you know who kidnapped you, Ellie West, from the hospital car park?'

'No, I didn't see their faces who kidnapped me.'

'When you got to the cabin, how many people were there? Are they in the court today?'

'On the first day there were four of them, Gary McDonald, Patrick McDonald and Donald McDonald. The fourth man I didn't know his name.'

'Were you able to leave the cabin at any chance, Miss West?'

'No, they all had weapons. Gary and Patrick had the guns with Donald holding the knife. They threatened to kill me if I tried to escape. I was scared for my life. I was never allowed to leave,' she said, shaking in the box.

'Are you sure they were real weapons? My clients didn't have weapons. They found them in the golf house. Is this another lie with the sexual act, Miss West?'

The prosecution stood up again. 'Your honour.'

'Last warning about you mentioning anything out of line.' The judge raised his voice.

'Sorry, your honour. At the golf house, you were allowed to leave so they didn't hold a gun to your head. This story doesn't make sense, Miss West, it's all confusing like you're making this all up.'

'I was allowed to leave after I was told to, that was the deal Gary made with the police. I am telling the truth,' she said, with a strong tone in her voice.

'Lying again, Miss West, this is the third time you've lied to the court.'

'Your honour.'

'I agree with the prosecution. Sit down.' The lawyer walked back to his seat.

The prosecution lawyer walked over to Ellie 'On the times Gary and Patrick tried to rape you. Do you remember what underwear they were wearing?'

'Yes, I do, when Gary was taking his underwear off. They were red with white stripes on them. Patrick's, were jet-black with white edging.'

'I am showing Ellie West two photos of boxers which the men wore when we arrested the guys. Are these the boxers the guys were wearing, Miss West?'

'Yes, it was, that was the underwear Gary and Patrick were wearing.'

'When you were kidnapped, was this the gun and knife they used in the cabin? Did they have these weapons at the cabin but took them to the golf house?'

Ellie was shown three pictures of the weapons, then the jury. 'Yes, from the moment I was in the cabin to the golf house.'

'I have no more questions, your honour.'

Ellie left the stand, looking at her parents with red eyes when leaving through the doors. Sarah got up and walked out, leaving James in the court room. The judge took a sip of water when looking around. 'I think we will call that a day, resuming tomorrow at ten.' Then he placed his paperwork back in his briefcase.

The court clerk stood up. 'All rise.' Then they all stood up with the judge leaving the court.

Chapter 20

2nd July 2019

The family were in the business room having breakfast away from the public eye, with James in his room. Ellie was sitting at table slowly eating her breakfast, with Mother watching her, holding her hand when Ellie smiled at her. Pushing her breakfast to the side when walking over to the window, Mother followed her. 'How are you feeling, Ellie? You still shaken up from standing in the box?' she asked, cuddling Ellie from behind.

'I am okay, Mother. That was horrible being in the stand. They made out I was lying about what happened. I would never tell lies. I want this to be over and go back to normal life. I want to go home,' she said, crying into her mother's shoulder.

'I know, honey, that's what some horrible lawyers do. They get paid to defend people who are guilty. Remember, the judge did give him his first warning. You were amazing, what you did, I am so proud of you and Nick would say the same.'

'I did it for Nick, every time I spoke, Nick would say be strong and do your best. I was feeling sick seeing them again sitting in court. Can I go home, Mother? I don't want to be here anymore,' she pleaded, looking at her mother.

'I can't send you home as no one is there. Mickey and Jade are with Katie. If you want, I will ask DC Walker to arrange a police car to take you to Leeds. You need your sister, don't you?'

'Yes, please, Mother. I can't be here any longer and don't want to go to court and watch them.' They walked over to the coffee machine.

Walking out of the room when James turned up. 'You okay, Sarah?'

'No, it's Ellie, she wants to leave. I said I'd talk to DC Walker and see if he can arrange a car to Colin's house. I'll see you soon,' she said, kissing him on the lips.

Walking past the rooms when knocking on his door, the door opened then she walked in. 'How can I help you, Sarah?' he asked, sitting on his sofa.

'Can you arrange for a car to take Ellie to Colin's house in Leeds? She wants to leave after what happened in court. She wasn't as brave as we thought. Can you do that for her?'

'Of course, I can, Sarah. I will arrange something for this afternoon. After you left court, the lawyer got spoken to and has been warned about raising his voice to a minor. That was uncalled for,' he said, putting his paperwork in his briefcase.

'Do you think they believe her about the attempted rape?'

'Yes, with the proof about what he was wearing and Ellie matching it. We've got a few more days left on the case. Next is Hazel. After that, our lawyer will be showing all the proof we've got on them. Nothing to worry about, Sarah.' He was clearly feeling happy about the case.

'I will make the phone call and meet you in the court, no need for a chat there,' she said, leaving his room.

Back in the gallery with James, Sarah and Damon, behind them was DC Hill. They seemed to have been waiting a while

251

when appearing were Gary and Patrick. Laughing and joking when sitting down, waving at Sarah. 'Ignore them, Sarah, this is the sort of behaviour that will see them being sent down.'

'Thank you, DC Hill.' Then they got told to all rise by the court clerk.

The judge sat down looking across to the lawyers. 'Good morning, everyone. Let's get today started with no raising voices and keeping it a good tone.'

The court clerk stepped up. 'Can we call the last witness. Hazel Rightworth.'

Within a few minutes Hazel went into the stand, spoke on the Bible when the defendant lawyer spoke to her. 'Ms Rightworth, can you tell the court how long you've been living on Bedmoor estate.'

'I've been living on the estate since 1971,' she said, with her neck stood straight.

'So, you've known Gary and his family from a young age then?'

'Yes, I know the family very well and what they do.'

'Can you explain what you mean by that?'

'They are known to sell drugs, weapons and young girls.'

'They are pretty strong words. Is that hearsay or have you witnessed any of this? Remember, you're under oath.'

'Mostly hearsay but I have seen Gary hang around young girls on the estate.'

'Well, young girls live all over Scotland, you're saying you can't be friends with them? If you're saying that, then what world do we live in?' he asked, getting closer to Hazel.

'I am not saying that, when young girls needed drugs and had no money, he would have sex with them. I knew one who was fourteen years old,' she said, looking into his eyes.

'So, you're saying my client abused underage girls and gave them drugs. We need proof or this is a made-up story,' he said, walking around.

'One of the girls was living with me, my daughter's friend. I was helping her get off drugs but one day she came back crying. She'd had sex with him for cocaine. We didn't report this as Gary was known for hurting people who grassed on him.'

'Only one problem, where is this girl to confirm this story? This is another hearsay around the estate, as far as I see it, this is nothing. Another pack of lies saying my clients are paedophiles. I believe this is fake, no more questions your honour.'

The prosecution stood up. 'Ms Rightworth, what happened to the young girl, may I ask?'

'The girl died on the estate near Gary's flat on the estate. The police questioned Gary but there was no evidence.'

'We have a report on this, a witness says Gary was with the girl on the day. She went back to his flat where they found hair on his bed but Gary had a reason for this. She slept there as her mother kicked her out. Nothing happened, he said. They were being nice to the young girl. Due to death on drugs, the case could not be taken to court. I will leave that up to the jury on whether Gary McDonald is capable of sleeping with underage girls.'

'No more questions, your honour.' He sat back in his seat.

Hazel left the stand without looking around when the court clerk called for the defendant Gary McDonald. The guard walked with him, standing near him at the stand. Gary placed his hand on the Bible then said the oath, the defendant lawyer walked over to him. 'Gary, on the day on the kidnap, did you kidnap Ellie West?'

Staring at Sarah when talking, he said, 'No. I didn't kidnap Ellie West.'

'How did Ellie West end up being in your cabin?'

'Ellie West was walking in town when I spotted her. I told her I could look after her. Ellie was able to leave at any time. She wanted to stay with me, I didn't hold her or keep her hostage at any stage.'

'What about hostages of Sarah West and Nick West? Did you hold them with any weapons?'

'Nope, I didn't keep them as hostages, Nick found me and wanted to see his sister. I let him in and said they could go at any stage, same with my sister. I would never want to hurt my family. I get out of jail and can't see my family without the police thinking I am up to no good.'

'What about weapons, Mr McDonald?'

'While we were sleeping in the golf house, there was a box. Me and Patrick opened it and found two guns and a knife. We didn't think at the time to call the police, knowing my track record. We touched it then placed it back in the box.' He was talking calmly and staring at Sarah still.

'Can you explain how PC Moon got killed with one of the guns?'

'Yes, I saw Nick's friend holding the gun outside. I was a bit scared when walking inside when I heard it go off. Damon had shot the policemen. I was shocked he'd killed a copper.'

'How was Damon when he killed the policeman?'

'Damon was happy, that's when I ran back inside and was scared for my life. He didn't seem normal, my nephew hanging out with a murderer. Damon kept me hostage when I wanted to leave then he shot me in the leg.'

'What did he do, after he shot you in the leg?'

'I got the knife to protect me when Damon was fighting to get the knife off me then accidentally stabbing Nick. First a policeman and now my nephew. I was happy when the police turned up.'

'What did the police do to you, Mr McDonald?' The lawyer sounded different with Gary.

'I told them what happened and then I am being charged with double murder. I just wanted a quiet life.'

'When Ellie West was in your care, why is she saying you tried to rape her?'

'I was giving her cuddles as Ellie was upset, my hand slipped onto her breast then she jumped. When Ellie jumped my hand rubbed her leg by accident. I would never try it with my niece or anyone underage,' he said, shaking his head with a sad smile.

'How did Ellie know what underwear you were wearing, Gary?'

'I was changing my trousers one day when she must have seen my underwear. I didn't show her my penis. It was a small cabin with us all sleeping there. It was nice getting to know her but not in a sexual way.'

'No more questions, your honour.' He sat down behind his desk, looking at Gary smiling at him.

The prosecution lawyer stepped forward. 'Gary, Ellie said the gun was in the cabin when she was kidnapped by Patrick, sent by you. How can this be when you said you found it in the golf house?'

'I am not sure why Ellie would say that. We never had the gun in the cabin. Maybe Ellie is confused about where she saw the gun first. I didn't kidnap her, Ellie found me in Watford.

Ellie wanted to stay with me, so I said yes to her, that's it, really. Maybe other people tried to kidnap Ellie.'

'So, when PC Moon got shot, Damon was hiding from you. Your fingerprints are on the gun, you've got form to handling guns in the past in Scotland. Damon touched the gun in the last five minutes before the police entered the golf house. We know that Damon didn't kill PC Moon. Did you Kill PC Moon?'

'No. This is simple; Damon knew the police would be on his side so setting me up would be easy. Have you got any proof I killed the man?' he asked, looking at the lawyer.

'Yes. PC Moon was shot in the afternoon. You took Nick inside the building when keeping them hostage. You didn't know Damon was in the house till he shot you, with your gun. Your timings don't make sense. You killed him like you killed Nick with the knife, yes, or no?'

'No.' He was talking calmly still.

'When you told the police about where the gun was in the house, there was no box.'

Silence for a few minutes then he answered back, 'Don't know, but there was a box.'

'How did Nick die?'

'Damon killed him by accident. He pulled the knife down on him. That's why my finger prints are on it.'

'Funny all this, you seem to be the good one. Didn't kill anyone, keep them hostage, or attempt rape on a minor. Why do we have letters saying you want money or Ellie will be killed? Your fingerprints are on the letters.'

'I don't know nothing about the letters and I am being set up here. I didn't kill anyone, try to rape a silly girl, or anything. This is the problem with the police, useless scum bags, I am being set up for all this.' He was shouting in the court.

'Order, order in my court. Calm down, Mr McDonald, or you will be taken downstairs. Do you understand?'

'You think I am scared by you, with that small hammer?' he yelled as the guard was holding him down.

'Take him down, court to resume at midday.' With Gary pushing him away, another guard went to help.

'I think Gary has cracked under pressure with the mixed-up questions. This is good, Sarah and James. This is what we want from them.' Sarah was feeling happy and staring at DC Hill.

3rd July 2019

James and Sarah were sitting in the office at the court room waiting for DC Walker to enter after an early finish in court yesterday. The judge didn't carry on with the court case due to Gary not calming down in the dock prison. The door opened with DC Walker walking in. 'Sorry I am late. Had a meeting with the lawyers about if Gary will go back on the stand or not,' he said, sitting at the table.

'How will this affect him now? I know from cases that it doesn't look good when you kick off in court.'

'Yes, it looks bad on him now. His lawyers made the question look easy when answering them. We just twisted it up, we knew he had a bad temper which we knew would come out sometime. The judge doesn't think putting Gary back on stand will help much so Patrick is next. I am on this afternoon then the jury will decide what the outcome will be,' he said, smiling at them.

'How will Patrick do on the stand after Gary's outburst?'

'I think their lawyers will be saying keep it simple as it's turning more guilty, James. Should we go?' he said, leaving the room.

Entering the gallery with Damon, Gary and Patrick sitting down giving Sarah dirty looks. Ignoring Gary when standing as the judge walked in, sitting down with the judge looking around. 'Good morning, everyone. Today should be last day before I hand it to the jury to decide guilty or not guilty. I expect a good day after yesterday's actions,' the judge said, looking at the court clerk.

'I will call Patrick McDonald to the stand.'

Patrick left the dock with the guard when placing his hand on the Bible and reading from the card.

'Patrick McDonald, I will keep this plain and simple. Did you kidnap Ellie West back in March?'

'No, I didn't kidnap Ellie. I was with my dad, Gary, in Watford,' Patrick said, looking straight at his lawyer.

'Do you know any reason why Ellie might say it was you?'

'No, maybe the guy who kidnapped her might have the same hairstyle or she thought I was the same person.'

'Did you ever hold Sarah, Ellie or Nick hostage at any time?' He was saying his words a bit slower than normal.

'Nope, like my dad. They were free to go at any time. Why would I keep my cousins when we are family? I don't know why they would do this and tell the police.' He was talking calmly and looked to be thinking before talking.

'Do you like girls, Patrick McDonald?'

'No, I am not into girls, your honour. I didn't touch Ellie at all. I am gay. I don't fancy girls. Ellie tried to kiss me when we were at the cabin when I turned her down. First thing I

258

don't do is underage and it's a girl.' He was shaking his head.

'Why would Ellie West say you took your trousers off when coming onto her?'

'I got changed a lot in the cabin so she might have seen my underwear. I never touched or went near Ellie West at any time.'

'Fair enough, Patrick. Your fingerprints were only found on the gun and the knife, not on the other gun. Can you explain how that happened?'

'Like my dad said, we found the box on the bar. Picking it up then placing it back on the bar. I have never fired a gun before, that is the truth,' he said with his hands down at his sides.

'Back in Scotland, did you kill a man with a gun? The police say you were a part of a robbery.'

'No, my mate shot the keeper. I did a runner from the shop. A few hours later the police were looking for Finley Holland. Apparently, I was dead so I left the country, but I didn't kill anyone. I do want to plead guilty for robbing the shop but not shooting him, your honour.'

'No more questions, your honour,' the lawyer said, sitting at his desk.

The prosecution stood up, walking over to Patrick McDonald. 'Sarah West confirmed you kidnapped her daughter but you said you were in Watford. Is this correct?'

'Yes, your honour.'

'The car Ellie was pushed into from Watford has your DNA in the car, also the van used in the kidnap. How can you be in two places at once? I will ask you again. Did you kidnap Ellie West? Remember you're under oath.'

Patrick looked round, seen his dad looking at him. 'Yes, I

lied to the police about where I was. Billy King was the ring leader pushing me into doing the kidnapping. Billy would hurt me if I didn't help him,' he said with a worried look on his face.

'So, you kidnapped Ellie West but lied to the police. What else are you lying about? Are you really gay? Are you using that as a getaway clause? What about keeping them hostages at the golf house? I believe everything you say is a lie.'

'I never touched Ellie West. I've been gay since I was young.'

'How do we know you're gay? We have no witnesses or boyfriends who can come forward. Do you have an earring, may I ask?'

'No, never had it done,' he said, holding his hands.

'That is weird, on the job there were two guys. You and Finley. Finley got killed by the shop keeper when you killed the shop keeper with a gun. Your mate Finley showed no ear piercing in the photo which the police thought was you, Patrick McDonald. When our doctors checked you out, you had a hole what was a closed ear piercing. I am guessing you swapped wallets round as you two did look nearly the same. I am correct,' he said with the jury looking at the photos.

'No comment.'

'I have no more questions, your honour,' he said, walking back.

The judge looked at his watch with a thinking face on, nodding to the court clerk. Standing up, he said, 'Can we call the last person, DC Walker, to the stand.'

Within a few minutes, DC Walker walked to the stand, placing his hand on the bible and reading his oath.

The defendant lawyer walked over to him, smiling. 'DC

Walker. Can you explain why you let two boys help out with the police with no experience?'

'Simple. At a concerning time during the investigation, we were running low on sightseeing of Gary and Donald at the time, and Nick and his friend offered to help. Using them was good as they could blend in with the public. They offered to help with advice from me and DC Hill.'

'Did you do checks on them before you let them go in the field?' the lawyer asked, walking around the floor.

'No, we didn't do any checks. Time was not on our side after we received a letter saying they were going to kill Ellie West.'

'So, you didn't do any checks, letting a man use a gun who you didn't know. Is this correct, DC Walker?' the lawyer asked, staring at him.

'No, we didn't do checks before they went to Scotland. Damon and Nick do not have any criminal records. We did the checks after the case.'

'Can you explain what happened on the night PC Moon and Nick West died?'

'Around four, I received a phone call from Damon saying Gary had shot PC Moon. We received phone calls from the golf club hearing a gunshot. I told Damon to go in the house and report to me, every time Damon rang me, he was hiding in the cellar. Around five minutes before we raided the golf house, Damon spoke to me saying Nick had kicked the gun into the cellar where Donald McDonald fell to his death. I told him to use the gun only to protect himself or Nick. I gave him permission on my power. As the result, Damon protected himself and Nick.'

Silence for a few minutes with the lawyer walking around.

'Did you see Gary shoot PC Moon?'

'No, I didn't see him, it was Damon who told me.'

'Did you see Gary stab Nick West?'

'No, I didn't see it.'

'With Damon's fingerprints on the knife and gun, could Damon have killed PC Moon and Nick West.'

'Yes, but trust is what I have with Damon. Damon was helping out the police.'

'Trust is nothing, DC Walker. We have two people with fingerprints on the weapons and the only other witness to all this is Nick West. Unfortunately, he died at the hospital.'

'I have no questions, your honour.'

DC Walker left the stand, passing Gary and Patrick leaving through the door.

'We are ahead of schedule for today, resume at two,' the judge said with the court room standing up.

Sitting in the cafeteria, James was sitting next to DC Walker with Sarah outside on the phone. Knowing in a few hours or days, the jury was going to vote on whether Gary and Patrick are guilty or not guilty. Watching outside the window, James saw the press with their cameras relaxing around their necks. 'James, you okay there? You've been staring out of the window for long time.' James turned his head.

'I am fine, DC Walker. I've got a sense that this is nearly over and Nick will be happy. We can move on from this and carry on being normal again. I remember the first time feeling like this. We thought we'd never see Gary again. I am hoping this time it's for good and he will leave my family alone.'

'If Gary is found guilty, he will be in prison for life. Gary has many charges on him, he should be facing over fifty years making him ninety when he is released from prison. I always have faith in the system,' he said, pushing his cup to the side.

'I am going to head back. We've got the closing speech coming next and I want to talk to the lawyer,' he said, walking out of the cafeteria.

James finished off his coffee, having one last look at the press then leaving to find Sarah.

The court was silent with James sitting next to Sarah, DC Walker and DC Hill behind them. Damon was next to James when the guard brought up Gary and Patrick. The defendant lawyer walked in, getting behind his desk then standing up as the judge sat in his chair. The court clerk stood up. 'Can the prosecution do their closing statement,' he said, sitting down when the lawyer walked to the middle of the room facing the jury.

'Gary and Patrick McDonald are charge with three counts of murder, the kidnap of Ellie West, keeping hostages with weapons, attempted rape of Ellie West. We have used evidence to show you what they did and how. We have shown you evidence that Gary McDonald had weapons from the start, meaning the cabin then to the golf house. Their fingerprints are on the gun and knife used to kill PC Harry Moon and Nick West. Damon's prints may be on the weapons but with a reason. Damon touched the knife to make sure Gary McDonald could not stab Nick for a third time, with no experience at a crime scene. The gun was used in the last five minutes before to protect him and Nick West. The details Ellie West gave on the attempted rape was clear by her, both tried to rape her with Gary and Patrick exposing themselves to a fifteen-year-old girl. Ellie mentioned what underwear they

263

were using. Ellie was brave to stand in front of them and tell the details, knowing she was scared. Remember to look at the fine details of the murder of John Tate. Finley Holland was shot by the shop keeper keeping Patrick alive when shooting him. Only one of them had the earring. Patrick's DNA was found in the car and the van when Ellie was kidnapped, what more proof do you need? Both of them kept hostages under their will and refused to let them go, holding weapons to them. Both of them are guilty to all charges against them,' he said, walking back to his seat.

James looked at Sarah, holding her hand. 'Going to be all right.'

'Can the defendant stand up with their closing speech.' The court clerk sat back down.

Clearing his throat when looking at the jury, the lawyer said, 'Gary and Patrick should be cleared of all charges against them. The police might have evidence on Gary killing PC Ben Moon and Nick West but there were two sets of fingerprints; your job is to think did Damon have a role in the killing. The only witness to these killings is Damon. The guys told the police where the box was, but did they look? They only touched the weapons when getting into the golf house. Remember only one gun was used in the shooting. The gun Patrick touched was not used in the process. The police decided to ignore them and charge them. I call that lack of evidence. My clients didn't touch Ellie West, there is no proof they did anything to her. Showing underwear which Ellie knew is no evidence. Where were the guys supposed to get changed? I don't believe they kept them hostage during the process, lacking in evidence again. I have spoken to Patrick McDonald which he changes one of his charges against him. Patrick

McDonald has pleaded guilty to kidnapping Ellie West. My clients are not guilty on rest of the charges, it's now your job to work out where the police went wrong and let my clients walk free,' he finished, walking back to his desk.

The court room sat in silence waiting for the judge to talk. 'This court room has seen all the evidence given, witnesses and one plead turn to guilty. The jury will decide now if Gary McDonald and Patrick McDonald are guilty or not guilty on their charges. You will be given notice when the jury have come back with the verdict.'

The court clerk stood up, said 'All rise' then all were standing up.

The judge left the court with the two guards walking Gary and Patrick down the dock with Sarah looking at them. 'Let's go back to the hotel, Sarah, and have drink,' James said, holding her hand with Damon, DC Walker and DC Hill following them to the exit.

5th July 2019

Sitting on the floor, around the corner from the press waiting outside as the verdict was reached. James sat next to Sarah cuddling her. 'It's all done now. We can't do anything else, Sarah.' They were crying on the floor.

Standing up when pulling his wife up, he said, 'We need to stand behind DC Walker as he talks to the press about the outcome.' He kept cuddling his wife.

'I know, James. I am shocked by what happened in there. Never in my life was I expecting that,' she said, wiping her tears with a tissue.

They were walking around the corner when the defendant

lawyer walked past them, smiling. 'What a cocky lawyer he is. No wonder why he earns too much money,' James said, looking at him leaving the court.

'Duncan is the best lawyer in Scotland but his cases are always the defendant. Are you ready to stand with me to tell the press what happen today?'

The both nodded when the guard opened the door for them with the press taking pictures with DC Walker standing in front of his microphone, James and Sarah stood behind him. 'After three days in court with witnesses, evidence and myself giving evidence. The jury took two days to decide whether Gary McDonald and Patrick McDonald are guilty or not guilty. Today at twelve, the judge called us all back. Gary McDonald was found guilty of the murder of Nick West and murder of PC Ben Moon, kidnapping Ellie West, and keeping hostages of Nick, Sarah and Ellie West. Gary was also found guilty of attempted rape of Ellie West and possession of a gun and a knife. Patrick McDonald changed one of his charges to guilty of kidnapping Ellie West two days ago. Patrick McDonald was found guilty by the jury of keeping hostages of Nick, Sarah and Ellie West, attempted kidnap of Katie Tuner, attempted rape of Ellie West, possession of a gun and a knife. The last charge was murder of John Tate, for which the jury found him guilty. The family has been given justice and the two men are on the way back to prison. Gary McDonald has been given life in prison and will die in prison. Patrick will serve fifty years for all his charges, with no parole. Both men have received maximum prison sentences due to the massive crimes they both committed. On the other members connected to the case, Julie King was sentenced to ten years in prison for involvement in the kidnapping, Julie got maximum due to two murders being committed by Gary McDonald. Billy King was sentenced to fifteen years for GBH of Irene West and kidnapping Ellie West. I can now go further into the case and mention the other names connected to this case. James Smith was sentenced to sixteen years behind bars for keeping information on the kidnappers, holding a weapon to Nick West and Damon Goldfield in Scotland. His last charge was possession and dealing drugs on Bedmoor estate. David Gilford was sentenced to seven years for possession and dealing drugs; there was little proof he knew about the kidnapping. Frank Gold, Dave Yates and Henry Wilson were sentenced to five years for holding a knife to Nick West and Damon Goldfield on Bedmoor estate. This has been a long case which nine people were involved in and all have been caught. We lost a few good people in the process: PC Ben Moon. He didn't know what was going on when Gary shot him dead. PC Moon was a good police officer, family man and didn't deserve to die. His memories will go on forever at the police station. Second was Nick West. Nick was a hero to his family, his love for his family and wanted to help out. Nick was good finding out information for us leading them to the golf house where he lost his life to Gary McDonald. Memories will be there forever, what he did to save his family. Now is the time to let the West family move on from all this. Justice is served and the case is closed.'

Final chapter

20th December 2019

Five days to Christmas with the chilly winds setting in with the rain coming down, holding her passport and boarding pass. Walking into the airport around eight in the morning, with James holding her hands. The airport was busy with people walking around to check in or going through security. Sarah went to the departures board, checking her flight. 'It's been delayed by an hour, thought so with the weather today. Can't imagine the weather being better in Scotland,' she said when walking over to check in.

'The line is short so better line up. We can have a coffee before you leave. There is still time for me to come with you, Sarah,' he said, looking at her.

'No, I need to do this alone, James. I have put this off for a long time now. The man is dying now, he can't hurt me any more,' she insisted, passing her passport and boarding pass to the lady.

The lady scanned her passport, with a new boarding pass. Walking back to the main entrance finding a coffee shop. 'Perfect, you get the coffees while I find the seats.' James was getting the coffees.

Finding seats when looking around the shop, couples with suitcases laughing away. Children playing in the soft play area with their parents watching them. Seeing young couples cuddling and kissing, thoughts of Nick went through her mind. Nick wanted a Christmas holiday, skiing in the alps or going to Australia for a hot Christmas. Two cups were placed on the table when James sat down, kissing Sarah on the lips. 'I am worried about you seeing your dad. The last person to see him was Nick. He was rude to him. Remember, he threw a cup which missed his head,' James said, picking up his coffee.

'James, the man has no one left. My brother is in jail for life, his grandson in jail. Brother died so I know I'll be safe. After today, it will be the last time I see him. My father will have no one left. I want to find out a few questions about what he did and why he did it,' she said, staring James in the face.

'I know you do. I understand why you need to talk to him for the last time. How long did the doctors give him?'

Taking a gulp of her coffee, she said, 'They gave him six months. Lonely violent man is dying and I am not one bit sad. I need to know why he wanted one of my kids dead, why he treated me badly and why he is miserable. It's been twenty-one years since I left, all the feelings have gone now.' She held James' hand.

'You might change your feelings about him when you see him, that is what I am worried about. You know how he can twist his words,' he said, looking worried.

'I promised you, nothing can change the way I feel. My father was a part of the kidnapping, one of my children he wanted dead, Nick would never forgive me if I did that. I want him to feel bad about what's he done to me, getting one of his grandchildren killed.'

Sarah sat in silence looking at James, staring at the young couple again. 'This is our first Christmas without him. It hurts.

Only one thing is keeping me smiling, our first grandchild. The smile while holding her, it's like looking at Nick. That is what I am looking forward to, with Nick watching us with his child.' She wiped her eyes with a tissue.

'I know, Sarah, she is so beautiful. She will be five weeks today. I remember bringing Nick home for the first time. Not knowing what to do, worried each time Nick made a weird noise. I am happy Katie kept the baby. Katie's has got so much support from both families.' James was getting a bit emotional.

'Like your mother said, when one dies another is born in the family. What are you plans when you leave here?' she asked, finishing off her coffee.

'The plan is leave here soon, get the train to Kings Cross station where I am meeting the rest of the family. The train leaves at nine thirty so I'll arrive at Leeds around twelve or one. Colin is getting someone to pick us up. Spend two weeks with our little granddaughter. What about you?' he asked, smiling at her.

'I should arrive in Scotland by half nine, meeting DC Hill who is driving me to the care home. See my mother's grave with some flowers, meeting Lucy's mum hoping to leave at one or two to catch the train to Leeds. Nice easy day travelling around,' she said, smiling at him.

'Will DC Hill be with you when seen your father?'

'Yes, only at the care home for my protection against him. My father will be shocked to see me, something which he is not thinking would happen. Did Damon message you last night about his new job?' she asked, with James finishing off his coffee.

'No, did he get the job after the training?'

'Yes, Damon is now PC Goldfield. It did help with DC

270

Walker helping him get through it. I am so proud of him. Damon wants to get trouble off the streets and make Nick proud,' she said, wiping her tears again.

'I am more than proud of what Damon did. One day he will make DC or DI. I am going to make a move. I'll meet you in Leeds. Ring me after you meet your father.'

They both walked to the exit, kissing each other with Sarah walking to security waving at James.

Arriving at the care home with DC Hill, looking all modern when waiting to be buzzed in. Sarah felt nervous knowing her father was in the building, seeing a nurse open the door. Opening the door and letting them in, following her in the building. 'I am sorry to hear about your son. What Gary did was a terrible thing. How've you been doing?' she asked, walking along the corridor.

'It's been a tough year without him, with Christmas coming up it's just got a lot harder. On the brighter side, I get to spend it with his daughter. My first granddaughter,' Sarah said, smiling.

Stopping outside the staff room when taking a seat, the nurse said, 'That is lovely to hear. John might cheer up knowing he is a great grandad, if you're going to tell him.' She was sitting next to her.

'Sorry. I didn't get your name. John is not a great granddad. He is just a man who got my mother pregnant. I am here to get some answers.'

'My name is nurse Hilda. I am sorry if I got it wrong. I thought you were here to give him good news, please forgive me,' Hilda said, holding her hands.

'Don't worry about it, is there anything I need to know

271

before I go in and see him?'

Nurse Hilda took a few minutes before speaking. 'Since finding out John has six months left, his moods are horrible. We took away anything he can throw at us. Just don't stand near him, only advice I can give you,' she said, sounding worrying.

'Sarah, do you want to record anything your father says? We can nail him and make him the tenth person to go down, all you need to do is place this in your pocket.' DC Hill passed her a voice recorder.

Sarah passed it back to her. 'No. Even if John admits to helping out on the case, my father has his life sentence already. I want him living with his pain till he dies. I am ready to see him,' she said, looking at them both.

'John is down the corridor, second door to the left. I have advised DC Hill to sit outside just in case and for your safety. I hope you get what you are looking for.'

Sarah started walking down the corridor when reaching his door, standing there not moving. Feeling nervous about meeting him, legs not moving when opening the door to find an old man sitting in his chair. Walking in the room, leaving the door open when staring at her father. Both of them were staring at each other with John giving her dirty looks. 'Oh, look who it is, Sarah McDonald. My long-lost daughter, do you know how long it been?' he said, staring at her.

Taking a seat when talking back, she said, 'I am Sarah West, not McDonald. I am not connected to that name for over twenty years. I do not murder or rape people.' She was talking straight into his eyes.

'You will always be a McDonald. West is your married name. You were my little girl, my little angle and then you were gone. It hit me hard knowing you were leaving with that stupid English man,' he said, changing his tone of voice.

'Did you expect me to stay with you till I got old? I wanted a new life away from the estate. If Gary and Donald hadn't committed those crimes, I would have visited you back in Scotland. Unfortunately, they did. I am happy I got away from that crime land.'

'Crime land! How do you think I paid for clothes, food, all your fancy toys? You were the one who grassed on your own family and got them sent down. I was alone. My son in prison with my brother, granddaughter killed by a car then my daughter walked out on the family when I needed you the most. You ruined this family,' he said, moving around in his chair with Sarah watching him.

'Best choice in my life, until you decided to get one of my children killed by Gary,' she replied, getting angry.

'I was wondering when you were going to mention this. That's why you're here. Not to see me but to get answers. You've got a recording thing like that boy did.' He was moaning when moving in his chair.

'That boy was my son, your grandson which you arranged. I don't have a recording device. You'll be dead in five months. This is your sentence, Father. I want you to feel guilty for getting your grandson killed. Did you arrange all this with my brother and his wife?'

Walking over to him standing next to his face, she asked, 'Did you get my son killed by Gary, my evil big brother?' She stood back and sat down.

'Yes, I did, the day you walked out on me. I planned this with Julie to get revenge on you and your family. I was alone, Sarah. Imagine, all my family gone. I have spent twenty years alone and now you turn up, too late, Sarah. Your mother would be turning in her grave,' he said, spitting on the floor.

She pushed her chair closer to her father. 'My mother never loved you, she was trapped by you. Mother only stayed because of us kids. The way you treated us and turning Gary into a gangster. I got out and Mother would have been proud. Mother would be turning in her grave knowing what you did to her grandson,' she said, standing up.

'Don't speak bad about Mary. I loved her and cared so much about her. When Mary died, I was lost, a little out of control and didn't take care of you. You look so much like her so I was finding it hard looking after you. Can you forgive me?'

'No, you can rot in hell. I came here today to get the truth and I've got it now. I'm not going to the police but I want you to feel guilty for what you did to me. We have no relationship as father and daughter,' she said, walking out of the door.

'Stop, come here, Sarah.' She stopped at the door.

Turning around staring at him, walking back to him face to face.

'I am sorry, Sarah. It was a mistake, what I did. Will you forgive me?'

Hugging her father then standing back up, she said, 'I will never forgive you. You got my son killed. His girlfriend gave birth alone without him. Nick will never see his child grow up or know what it feels like to have his daughter around. Have a happy, few months, Father, before you die.'

Walking out of the room, staring back one last time knowing this would be the last time. Feeling no emotion inside her about not seen her father ever again. The pressure of seeing her father again paid off. Nothing changed from leaving

Scotland the first time to now.

Sitting in the car park of the graveyard staring at the gravestones in front of Sarah, picking up her coffee then drinking it. Sitting on the passenger seat were two sets of flowers. She was feeling emotional about walking in the graveyard. Her mother's and best friend Lucy's gravestones were in there. Then there was a knock on her window. An older lady was waving at her. The lady was in her late sixties wearing a long red jacket with gloves and hat. Opening the car door when hugging the lady, hugging in silence then stopped. 'You have grown into a wonderful lady. Leaving here was the best decision you made. I am sorry to hear about your son, but good news on your first granddaughter. Only if Nick was here to see her.' She touched Sarah's necklace.

'You still have Lucy's necklace, she would love that,' she said, crying into her shoulders.

'It's okay, Hazel. Lucy is always on my mind. You must miss her so much. I know how it feels to lose a child. It's the worst experience in the word. How are your other two kids?' she asked, picking up the flowers from the car and walking into the graveyard.

'They are doing good. Both have got families and live near me in Inverness. I've got six grandchildren so keeping busy all the time. You have only started, you've got the other three to go yet. You might end up with eight to ten grandchildren!' They were laughing together.

'I am happy with the one at the moment, she is a little cutie and perfect,' Sarah said, showing Hazel a photo.

'She is so cute, so much like Nick. How many times have you seen her?'

'This will be the third time I've seen her. Each time I see her she changes so much. James and the family are with her now, just had a few things to close in Scotland for the last time,' she said, smiling.

Walking to the corner and sitting on the bench. 'May I ask how you got on with your father today?'

'I got what I wanted from him. My father set up the whole kidnap. He is the reason why Nick is dead along with Gary,' she said, looking ahead at the gravestones.

'Nothing surprises me with John. Gary attacked my daughter, ex-husband and now your son. You must feel devastated about this. Are you going to the police?'

'No, no point really. My father has less than six months to live so to me that is his sentence with no family visiting. I can't remember where Lucy's gravestone is, left or right?' Looking around.

'Left here then second row back, should we go. When we get there, I'll give you some time with her,' she said, getting up from the bench and walking over.

'You've not changed one bit, strong and brave. Even doing it a second time in court with Gary, I can't believe he tried to blame it on the young lad. Here we are.' They saw Lucy Swell on a gravestone.

'The main thing is, Gary was found guilty and sentenced to life in prison.' Sarah walked forward to Lucy's gravestone.

Laying some flowers on the gravestone looking clean and white, removing the old flowers when touching Lucy's name with her hands. 'I am sorry it's been over twenty years since I've seen your grave. I don't have a reason to give. If you're watching me, you must have seen Gary attacking my family. Done it again after raping you, that man will never change. It's

276

nice coming back while it's safe again. Your mum was telling me you would have been an auntie to six kids. You would have loved that. I've got your necklace on today. I am passing it down today, I am going to give it to my granddaughter. I would like you to watch over her with Nick. Love you, Lucy,' she finished, getting up from her gravestone.

'I am going to see my mother's grave. I'll meet you after for a coffee,' Sarah said, smiling at her.

'Yes, I would like that. I have a bucket of water and sponge for you. Last time I cleaned it for you was last year,' Hazel said, hugging Sarah.

'Thank you.' Sarah walked over to the next plot of gravestones.

Walking through the gravestones with some of them broken, dirty and unable to read them when arriving at her mother's. The white marble was greyish when sitting next to it, placing the sponge in the water and washing down the gravestone. Seeing her mother's name saying Mary Violet McDonald. The numbers showing when her mother died, ninth of January 1985. Brushing the leaves to one side with the roots, placing the fresh flowers in the pot. 'Hi, Mother, been too long since I've seen you. I am happy to see Hazel has been cleaning your grave for me. I take it you know your husband is dying. I promise you I won't put my father's ashes here for you. I know where I am putting them, straight into the river. I hope you're looking after your grandson up there and not causing trouble. It's weird, this, I am looking after my granddaughter while you look after your grandson. I miss you. You were taken from me so little, I needed you and maybe all this wouldn't have happened if you were alive. My son would be alive now spending time with his daughter. I hope you're proud of me and what I have achieved since leaving Scotland. James is so nice, you would have loved him. James is the most caring bloke. He loves his kids so much and would do anything for me. If you're watching anything, you would have seen Gary be worse than before. You controlled him and Father. I love you, Mother, and miss you so much,' Sarah said, learning over the gravestone crying.

Arriving at Leeds station in less than five minutes, staring out of the window thinking how nice it was seeing Lucy's and her mother's graves. Sarah spent a few hours drinking with Hazel before leaving Scotland for the last time, feeling great but wishing her mother's grave was in London so she could visit her. Putting her photos away into her bag as the train was slowing down, in less than half an hour Sarah was getting cuddles from her granddaughter. Finishing off her takeaway coffee when placing it in the bin, then standing near the door. Few people standing behind her when the doors opened to the station. Walking through the station with a bitter cold wind hitting her, her mind was thinking not long till her cuddles. Putting her ticket in the barrier, walking through into the main station and looking for the exit. Lots of people walking around when seeing the exit sign, the bitter cold hit her again when she saw a taxi free. 'You are not getting a taxi, Sarah.'

Turning around to find Katie looking at her, smiling and a little emotional hugging Katie. 'You didn't need to do this. I am able to get a taxi to your dad's house.'

'Don't be silly, I can't let you do that. Get in the car,' she said as they both got in.

Katie drove out of the station and was driving out of the High Street. Driving along the country roads when Sarah turned down the radio. 'How have you been? I hope the kids have been good while I was in Scotland.'

'I have been good, university being good up here with me having a baby so able to complete my second year. I was glad I moved back to Leeds, but feel guilty about you not seeing your grandchild much. How was Scotland and seeing your father?' Katie asked, slowing down the car.

'Scotland was good, I got to see my friend's grave and my mother's. My father is my father, nothing has changed in him. I will explain more later with the family about what he said, just say I got what I wanted. Don't feel guilty for moving back in with your parents, Katie, me and James work a lot. Your parents can help you more. You go to university and get a good job. We need to show our kids what we need to do to get a job. I like travelling to Leeds to see my granddaughter. Also, between me and you, there is something I need to tell you all later,' Sarah said, smiling at Katie.

'I know but this guilty pain will always be here. Mickey is happy playing with Emily again. Jade is playing in the games room with Judy. Ellie is quiet in her room. Not sure what to say to her,' she said, looking concerned.

'I am worried about Ellie. Since she's been home from the kidnapping, I've found her drinking in her room. I had to stop her. We're getting help for her after Christmas. Such a nice area you live in.' There were big houses around them.

'We are here now,' Katie said, stopping at the gates.

The gates opened when Katie drove onto her drive behind her dad's car. Stepping out of the car when the front door opened. James walked out holding his granddaughter. Sarah ran towards him touching her cheek. 'I missed you so much, my little girl. Come and give your nan a cuddle.'

'I have unpacked our things already, so we can relax tonight.'

James passed the little baby to Sarah when walking inside, to the living room. 'You are such a little angel, Nicola West-Turner. I missed you so much,' she said, kissing Nicola on the head.

Colin, Judy and Jade walked into the living room with Jade giving her mother a cuddle. 'Jade, can you get everyone in here, please.' Jade left the room.

'I am sorry, James, I've been waiting all day to say this,' Sarah said with James laughing.

'That is fine. Colin has ordered us all a takeaway. You want to cry holding Nicola, don't you?' cuddling Sarah.

'I miss this little girl so much, I always get emotional holding her. I will explain later what happened with my father,' Sarah said, kissing baby Nicola again.

Walking in the room was Jade, Ellie, Mickey and Emily. Sitting on the sofa then standing up in front of everyone. 'Over the last few weeks, me and James have been thinking about the future. Family means everything to me and with the new baby here, I want to spend more time with her. Me and James have decided to sell the London home to buy round here. James' mother will be moving with us and moving in. James will be transferring to the Leeds office and I will be a home wife. Are you okay with this, Katie?'

'I am more than happy to have your help, Sarah. Nicola would love to have her nan move to Leeds,' she said, hugging Sarah.

'Time to get the champagne and celebrate.' Colin left the room.

'I am happy about this. I will miss my friends but I know

280

this means a lot to you.'

'Thank you, Jade. We will keep to one promise. We will need to visit London to place flowers on Nick's gravestone,' she said, putting the baby in the basket.

Colin returned to the room with three bottles and glasses, pouring the champagne out then handing them out. 'To Sarah and James moving to Leeds, our big happy family,' he toasted, with the family cheering and smiling.